SAFE WORDS

A DEVIATIONS NOVEL

CHRIS OWEN
JODI PAYNE

Safe Words: A Deviations Novel
Copyright © 2010, 2016 and 2019 Chris Owen and Jodi Payne

Garrett Leigh at blackjazzdesign.com
Cover content is for illustrative purposes only and any person depicted on the cover is a model.

First Edition, published 2007 by Torquere Press

Second Edition, published October 2016 Pretty Muses Publishing

Third Edition, published December 2019 by Tygerseye Publishing, LLC.

ISBN: 978-1-951011-26-0

1

Tobias leaned in the doorway, one shoulder against the jamb and his arms folded over his chest, watching silently. He was wearing riding clothes, intending to go for a ride on his horse, but he hadn't yet made it down the stairs to the lower level of the farmhouse.

Instead, while dressing, he'd heard the clink of free weights coming from the newly created workout room, and, a little too like Pavlov's dog for comfort, he'd gone there instead.

Tobias had a weakness for watching Noah exercise. Noah had kept himself in insanely good shape after leaving the police force, maybe even better than he had done while working for the law. He tended to do a lot of work without his shirt on since his change of employment, and while he wasn't ripped and cut, he was certainly firm and tight. Tobias rarely missed a chance to look his fill.

"You're in here early," Tobias said, watching Noah's arms curl so his biceps flexed.

Noah glanced up at Tobias briefly, then back at his biceps. "Nine, ten," he counted out loud. "Good morning.

Thirteen..." He grunted his way through fourteen and fifteen, his teeth clenched and his brow furrowed.

Tobias found he had more than a passing appreciation for Noah's intensity, and he smiled to himself as he felt desire lick up his spine. It never failed -- Noah and weights, that was all it took. Well, Noah and just about anything, but the weights were a sure thing.

"I can't sleep alone," Noah explained, still panting. "In that great big bed." He gave Tobias a suggestive wink as he set the dumbbells back in their rack. "Plus, I'm heading into town today." He patted his face with a towel and smiled mischievously.

"I know." Tobias tried not to sigh. Usually, he had no issue at all with Noah having a day off from his duties as Tobias' submissive. Usually, Noah wasn't all sweaty and glossy from working out on his day off. "Do you and Phan have plans?"

Phantom, Tobias could hear, was in the kitchen making breakfast. It was his day off as well, but Phan didn't seem to think that Tobias was capable of making his own breakfast. Though why toast needed the noisy rattle of a frying pan on a gas range, Tobias didn't know.

"We do." Noah approached Tobias slowly. "Breakfast," he said, just as something clattered in the kitchen, "which you've no doubt noticed, and then shopping and a downtown, greasy dinner. This would be why I need the extra workout." He leaned close and kissed Tobias lightly on the lips. "Are you going to miss us?"

"I always miss you. Well, usually. There are times I'd happily send Phan to town just so he'd stop pinging around the house and making it hard for me to get paperwork done." Tobias slipped his arms around Noah and kissed him again. "But I suppose he does have a valid point that

I'm supposed to do that sort of thing in my office and not here."

"Well, you did insist that Bradford give you that swanky office at the club and a very sturdy desk to keep all that paperwork organized. I have to admit I don't think of the farm as work, either. I tend to leave that mentality at the club. But I'm just a sub; who am I to tell my Master where to do his work, right?"

Tobias snorted. "You do it all the time."

Noah grinned. "But I pay the price."

"One of these days, I'll stop letting you get whatever you want." Tobias barely kept himself from laughing. Noah teased, but he was never actually bad; if there was something to discuss, they handled things far better that way than with mental tug of war. They both liked the teasing, however, and Tobias would have been bored with compliant and malleable submissives.

Even if having two of them was a bit of a handful at times.

Noah grinned again and stepped backward, throwing the towel over his shoulder and reaching for his bottle of water. He gestured at Tobias. "You have a date with your mare? Or are you just working the handsome urban cowboy vibe?"

"I'm going for a ride, yes." Tobias nodded and glanced around the room. "Will you be back tonight or in the morning?"

"Depends on where you want us tomorrow. If we're at the club tomorrow, we'll crash at the townhouse. No point in taking the hour drive out here just to turn around in the morning, you know?"

"Of course." Tobias stepped back out of the doorway and looked down the stairs. "Phantom?"

"Sir?" The clatter grew, followed by muttering, before Phan could be heard jogging down the hall to the bottom of the staircase. "Good morning, sir." He was dressed in jeans. That was it, just jeans, and his hair was a riot of directional choices.

Tobias smiled and shook his head. "Good morning, Phan. Do you remember off the top of your head if I have an early appointment at the club tomorrow?"

"Not until ten," Phan said promptly. He tried to flatten his hair with one hand but failed miserably. "Is Noah dressed yet?"

"Sadly, yes." Tobias looked back at Noah in time to see his smirk. "All right, boys. Stay at the townhouse tonight, and meet me at work. If you run into trouble, just call."

Noah nodded. "Join us tonight if you want to." Noah, unlike Phan, wasn't given to formality on his days off; he rarely used "sir" or "Master" when he was on his own time. That was left over from an arrangement Tobias and Noah had made long ago, when they'd realized what had developed between them was complicated and more than the black and white Dom/sub relationship they thought that they'd been looking for.

Noah stepped around Tobias and leaned over the railing. "Do you need rescue, gorgeous, or can I go shower?"

Tobias snorted as he watched Phan preen at the compliment.

"I think I managed to beat the eggs into shape," Phan said, looking back toward the kitchen. "But hurry, okay? I'll have it on the table in a few minutes."

"For you, I'll hurry." Noah looked back at Tobias and lowered his voice. "Speaking of pinging, is it me or does he seem a little off to you this morning? You think you should check on what our little Julia Child is up to down there?

He's usually pretty competent in the kitchen, you know?" Noah kissed Tobias again. "See you tonight, I hope."

Tobias frowned slightly and caught Noah gently by the wrist before he could escape. "Hang on, sweetheart." He waited until it was clear that Phan was back at work in the kitchen, the sound of running water mingling with the clatter of dishes. "Has he said anything to you? I can put off my ride if you think I should talk to him. You know how he gets."

Phan's desire to please Tobias had led him to downplay issues more than once. There had been several occasions that had made Tobias glad that his submissives loved each other and could talk openly and freely together. Tobias knew that Phan had an outlet, and Noah was very good at figuring out which issues should be brought to Tobias' attention and which could be dealt with on their own.

Noah looked thoughtful and shook his head. "He hasn't said anything, but I've been getting that ungrounded, scattered thing from him all morning. Like something is on his mind. I mean, don't get me wrong, I like Phan without a shirt, but he's way too proud of his hair to forget to comb it. And that's Mrs. M's kitchen; he knows his way around it better than any of us." Noah sighed. "If you have time to talk, I can find something to do with myself for a while. If you don't get anywhere, I can see what I can get out of him today."

Tobias thought for a moment before shaking his head. "No. I think I'll leave it for now. It's his day off, and he might need to be away from here for a while to get his thoughts in order. Will you do me a favor, though, and make sure he gets a bit of exercise today and something vaguely healthy to eat?"

Noah grinned. "A nice salad with chicken for lunch and

I'll run him ragged, I promise. And if anything comes up, I'll make sure you know about it, okay? I'm sorry I worried you. You should enjoy your day off, too." Noah gave Tobias' hand a squeeze. "Now, go eat your breakfast."

"Hey, who's the boss here?" Tobias pulled Noah to him and kissed him once more, deeply this time. "Be good today. I'll probably see you tonight, late."

Noah tossed his head in one of the best Phan imitations that Tobias had ever seen. "Good is so overrated," Noah said, and disappeared into the bedroom.

"I can't really disagree with that," Tobias said softly. He smiled as he went down the stairs, mostly content with his lot in life. He wasn't going to get to enjoy Noah in the afterglow of his workout, it was true, but he would see both Noah and Phantom that night, after they spent the day relaxing and talking and maybe even plotting.

Sometimes Tobias wondered if perhaps they should spend more of their days off apart, but as it was their time to do with as they wished, he never really pushed for it. If they were both happy, then Tobias was happy.

Phantom, however, didn't seem very happy. By the look of the kitchen, Tobias estimated that Phan had been unhappy for at least a few crucial moments that involved batter, a wooden spoon, and what appeared to be the waffle iron. It was hard to tell with all the batter smeared around it.

"Phan?" Tobias leaned on the counter and watched as Phan kept wiping the mess up, not lifting his face.

"Yes, sir." His voice was low.

"Are you all right?" Tobias kept his own voice down as well and tried not to sound anything more than concerned. "Are you upset with me?"

Phantom's head came up so fast that Tobias almost heard the snap. "No! I'm sorry, I didn't mean to make this mess. I was pouring batter and the edge of the bowl slipped and it fell and--"

"It's okay." Tobias reached for him even as he interrupted the flow of words. "It is. I promise. It's okay."

Phan sighed and went to him when Tobias tugged, until he was nestled into Tobias' arms, his head in the crook of Tobias' shoulder. "I'm okay," he said softly. "I am. A little scattered."

"Do you want to talk about it?" Tobias rubbed his hand down Phan's bare back. At least he wasn't losing weight. Phan was slender, but his bones weren't sticking out anymore, not like they had before Phan had come back to live with them.

"Not right now, sir." Phan turned his face up and kissed Tobias quickly. "Maybe later. Sit. Your breakfast will get cold."

Tobias rolled his eyes. Really, he had to get his boys to stop ordering him around, day off or not. Maybe he'd mention it when it wasn't a Tuesday.

2

Noah hurried as promised and made it downstairs in time to give Tobias one more kiss before Tobias headed off to the stable and the only female on the farm, Tobias' favorite mare, Dusky Dianna. Noah enjoyed every bite of Phan's hot breakfast and was grateful for it, being hungry after his workout. After insisting that he do the cleaning up, he sent Phan off to find a shirt and to do something about that hair. He was in his day-off best, a soft, faded T-shirt and a pair of jeans, and was ready to explore the city a little.

He loved being a full-time submissive, but he appreciated his days off, too. Noah didn't get as much time out of the sub role as he used to since he left his job on the police force. He had his volunteer job to distract him from the constant work at the club, but there were days that he missed his badge, missed the intrinsic respect he received while in uniform. Still, the trade off had been worth it; he was more relaxed, happier, and more himself than he had ever been.

While waiting for Phan on the porch with a small duffel

over one shoulder, Noah chatted with Jorge, Tobias' limo driver. In his bag were gym clothes and a basketball, and Noah had instructed Phan to pack the same, only a little concerned about what Phan would come up with.

"Do I pass, kitten?" Phan came out the door with his own bag, dressed in ragged, cut-off jeans that stopped just over his knees and a T-shirt that had seen better service a decade or more ago.

Noah glared for a moment, but didn't say anything. "Kitten" was a pet name he could live with in the privacy of their own home, but he and Phan had had the not-in-public discussion at least three times. Granted, Jorge wasn't really "public," but he was close enough.

"You look perfect. Possibly even a little butch. Although, no, not with that hair." Noah winked, took Phan's bag from him, and headed for the car. Jorge tossed Noah the keys to the trunk and hurried to open a door for Phan. Noah smiled. Nearly everyone fell over themselves to offer Phan the little favors that most people reserved for their dates; he was just too petite and too pretty to be treated like one of the guys. Even Jorge wasn't immune to Phan's charms. "I love what those shorts do for your ass," Noah commented as Phan ducked to climb into the back seat.

"You just love my ass."

"Mmm. Too true."

Phan beamed at him and scooted way over before patting the seat next to him. "Come cuddle me and tell me breakfast wasn't an utter disaster."

Noah snorted and slid into the car. "It was delicious."

Jorge closed the car door and got behind the wheel. "The townhouse?"

Noah looked at Phan. "Sure. We'll start there, ditch our bags." Noah took Phan's hand and gave it a tug, and Phan snuggled into his side as the limo started down the driveway. "Breakfast was only a disaster in the making. The final product was great. I'm still stuffed."

"Good. I like you stuffed. That means I can keep up with you on the basketball court." Phan laughed softly and wiggled even closer. "Did you have a good workout?"

"It was cut a little short; Tobias was lingering in the doorway, and I kind of found it hard to concentrate." Tobias often stopped by while Noah was working out to offer encouragement or just ask how it was going, but there was something different about this morning. Noah sensed what Tobias wanted, saw it in his eyes, and it wasn't that Noah didn't like the idea of being bent over the incline bench or pressed up against the mirrored wall, but something about the timing felt off. He wouldn't be at all surprised if Tobias showed up late that night with flowers: their long-established code for when Tobias needed his lover -- or someone even stronger -- instead of his sub.

Noah blinked, realizing he'd disappeared on Phan for a moment there. "Sorry. I guess we're all a little off today. The workout was good. Penance for the sausage you fed me at breakfast." Noah shifted, changing the subject deliberately. "So what's up with you? You're obviously distracted; usually kitchen explosions like that are my doing, not yours. Got something on your mind?"

"No. Yes." Phan shook his head and waved a hand. He didn't look annoyed, but he wasn't his usual self at all, either. "Let me think about that." He blew out a breath and smiled at Noah, clearly trying to put a better face on. "How do you think things went last weekend? I'm not sure having that many new faces at the farm all at once is a good idea."

Noah nodded thoughtfully, unsure whether Phan's statement was a way of getting at what was bothering him or just a complete change of subject. It felt odd to have a host of near strangers in their space -- in their Master's space -- all weekend, that was true. It was always a little strange to have new people at the farm. But at the same time, it was fun to show it off a little, give Tobias' trainees and their subs a taste of what made them all so proud.

"I know what you mean, Phan," Noah said slowly. "I think things went very well. Tobias seemed pleased with them as a group even if he had a few minor issues individually. But I almost felt like I should be running around telling people not to touch things or something." Noah grinned. "I think I'm glad it's not every weekend."

"That would be far, far too much," Phan agreed with a nod. "I like the training weekends, don't get me wrong. But I think I like it better when it's only two or three Doms and their subs. This was a bit overwhelming. Do you think I should tell Sir that?" He seemed honestly curious about Noah's opinion on the matter, looking at him with serious eyes and a furrowed brow.

"Yeah," Noah said quickly. "Absolutely, you should tell him. Your feelings on all of this are as important as anyone's. If I've learned anything from negotiating with Tobias, it's that when things aren't working, it's better to speak up right away than let it sit. He has more respect for that than if you let things get worse over time. It's probably even more important when things are new, while we're still experimenting, to talk about what works and what doesn't, and why."

Noah snorted and relaxed back into his seat, mentally rolling his eyes at himself for what he knew sounded like a lecture. He had strong feelings about truth and communication and tended to get a little frustrated with Phan sometimes when Phan didn't just speak up. Phan was still trying to overcome his past and his habit of putting himself last in everything. It was a habit that was partly self-defense and partly a damaged and skewed outlook on life. Noah was compassionate, he tried hard to be patient, but it was a completely different headspace. Noah always insisted on holding onto his own sense of pride and his individuality. Phan seemed happy to give those things up.

"So, yeah." Noah cleared his throat and tried to sound more casual and less preachy. "You should probably say something."

Phan rolled his eyes. "You're very cute when you're trying not to be bossy." He poked Noah in the side. "I know. I do. But what I mean is, don't you think Sir should bring it up first? It's his job, after all. We're the support crew. If he wants to run the training weekends that way, he should. Even if we do feel a bit like our home is... uh, overrun."

In fact, they hadn't really talked about the weekend at all. It was a new thing, having so many people out instead of just a few, and Tobias hadn't asked his subs yet how they felt about it. Noah assumed it was coming, since Tobias had a tendency to time things in ways that suited his plans, but the lack of debriefing obviously was bothering Phan, and the more Noah thought about it, the more he could understand why.

"You're right, Phan, it is his show, and now that you mention it, I am also a little surprised that he hasn't gotten our views on it yet. But he should, and I think he will. It's his job to balance things, after all. He can judge for himself how successful the weekend was from a training standpoint, and it looked to me like he was pretty pleased, but he knows he can't read our minds."

Noah shifted slightly and kissed Phan's temple. "In any event, you know he'll listen to whatever you want to say,

Phan. If I were you, I'd try to relax today, and we can bring it up tomorrow if he doesn't bring it up first, okay? There isn't much we can do about it right now except... go shopping!"

As he expected, the promise of a good shopping spree brought Phan around. Quickly. If they hadn't been in the back of the car, Noah would have expected to have Phan in his lap.

"What are we shopping for?" Phan asked, wiggling a little. "Can we get fun things? Do we need fun things? Or are you going to make me try on clothes again? Which, you know, can be fun if it's the right store."

Noah chuckled. "Bradford requested," he winked at Phan because nothing from Bradford was ever really a request, "that I buy a couple of suits for the nights I'm working security at the club. I guess the whole sub look doesn't really fly when I'm trying to cut off someone at the bar or check on Doms in the private rooms."

Phan's eyes went flatteringly wide. "I get to help you try on suits? Oh, yes. This is a good day." His grin turned into a smirk. "If you're very lucky, I'll even help you dress."

Noah mentally chastised himself for allowing himself to fantasize about that idea.

There had been a time, not so very long ago in fact, when Noah had believed there was only one way to sub, but there were many kinds of subs, as he had learned in his time with Tobias at the club. Phan, for example, lived in submissive mode day in and day out, every day, and never completely left that mental space even on his days off. Noah, on the other hand, earnestly needed all the things that being a submissive gave him, but he'd discovered that he had a whole range of roles he enjoyed, and sometimes needed to play, as long as it pleased Tobias.

So the idea of Phan on his knees, well, yeah, he could see what Tobias got out of that.

Noah gave Phan a little pinch. "Be good, Phan. Tobias might join us at the townhouse tonight."

"So? I help him dress all the time. I'm good at it." Phan winked and wiggled a bit. "He won't mind, I'm sure."

Phan had an endearing way of deliberately missing the point.

"Okay." Noah cleared his throat. "So, after you dress me in a couple of nice suits and we arrange to have them delivered to the townhouse, we'll go shopping for you. I don't know if you've noticed, but the workouts you've been doing, no matter how much you hate them, are paying off. You've actually got some muscle on those shoulders. I think you should show them off."

Phan looked down at himself, one eyebrow arching up. "Kitten, this isn't muscle. It's the result of your cooking. You don't want to show off what I've got. I'm all... not pointy anymore."

Noah laughed and poked Phan in a few of his not-pointy spots. "Phan, I hate to say this, but the pointy thing was because you were bony. You spent so long being underweight that you have no idea how good you look now. I know Tobias will appreciate something that shows you off a little better."

"If you say so." Phan looked doubtful. "Before or after you make me play basketball? Can we go home to shower? More fun with two than one, and we'll get kicked out of the gym again if we get caught."

Noah shook his head. "Oh, no. We definitely can't get caught doing that again. Tobias was unhappy enough the first time." Bradford had teased Tobias about it, and that probably made it worse. "Townhouse first, like we told Jorge.

Then suits, because if I don't find at least two, Bradford will kill me. Then basketball, then back for a nice shower and some lunch. Then we'll just go out and play, okay? Try on some clothes, stop into the video store, get something evil to snack on, whatever. No pressure to buy anything. Sound good?"

The limo made a wide turn, and Noah knew they'd reached the city limits. "We're almost there."

"Home first is good -- I'm totally not dressed for suit shopping." Phan plucked at his T-shirt and made a face. "Unless we're going to Fallon's. They know me there and will forgive anything but blow jobs in the display racks."

Noah laughed. "What's wrong with what you're wearing? We can't suit shop like this? Money's money, isn't it?"

Phan winked at him. "Image, darling. Image. I have one to maintain, you know. I have to dress to shop."

"Oh, yes, I'd forgotten how vain you are." Only he hadn't, actually. Noah winked and tugged Phan closer. "I happen to really like those shorts." He kissed Phan, more for effect than meaning, making a point of leaving Phan a little breathless.

"And I really like you." Phan looked a little dazed, and a lot happy. "I'll put them on again later if we don't find anything for my new body. Which I still think is a little more than I like. You'll tell me if I get fat, right?"

"Yes, Phan, I'll tell you if your skinny little self gets fat. I promise. But believe me, no one is complaining right now." He leaned over and whispered in Phan's ear. "You're hotter than ever. If you need me to prove that to you, I won't let you get any farther than the foyer." He slid one hand across Phan's thigh.

"Why, Noah. Are you making a pass at me?" Phan grinned and pulled Noah's hand higher. Under the smile and the comeback, though, Noah couldn't miss the way Phan leaned in closer, like he needed to be near and needed to be touched.

Noah took the invitation, pushing his hand against Phan's groin and sliding his fingers low between Phan's thighs. "This isn't a pass, darling, this is a blatant hit. Or, if it helps, you can call it therapy." He wasn't unaffected by the way that Phan's body responded to his touch, and felt the heat rise into his chest. Privately, he tried to will the limo to go faster.

"Better therapy than my usual." Phan's voice was getting a little throaty and his cock was swelling visibly. "Right inside the door, you say?"

Noah nodded slowly. "In the foyer. With our bags around your feet, me kneeling on the tiled floor, and your voice echoing up to the second floor when you come." Damn, that sounded good to Noah, too.

Phan looked out the window. "God, we better get there soon." He rubbed into Noah's hand and didn't seem to mind that poor Jorge was once again getting a show. It was a good thing Tobias paid well, really.

They did get there, though the five minutes they had to wait felt like an eternity, both of them squirming by the time they arrived. They didn't even let Jorge get their bags for them. Noah just tossed Phan the house key and snatched them out of the trunk.

"Open, open, open..." Noah panted impatiently over Phan's shoulder as Phan fumbled with the lock. Phan made a strained sound when the lock finally clicked, and Noah crowded Phan into the door as it swung open. In a rush of movement, Noah tossed their bags toward the foot of the staircase, kicked the door closed, and pushed Phan against a narrow wall next to the coat closet. One hand dove under the waistband of Phan's shorts and the other punched the alarm code into the keypad over Phan's shoulder. It shut off with a loud beep.

"Noah. Please." Phan's fingers plucked at the waistband, around Noah's wrist and forearm. "Hurry." The button popped and Phan's cock pushed forward. "And you. Show me, okay? Suck me and show me."

"Yeah," Noah said, grunting as he hit his knees. He took a second to free his own erection and wrapped his fingers firmly around it. "See that? Aches. God." Noah leaned forward and slowly took Phan into his mouth, his free hand pushing back against Phan's hip so he couldn't thrust.

Phan made a sound that could have been a whimper. "Pretty. So pretty. God, I love watching you touch yourself." He managed to thrust despite Noah's hand and immediately stilled. "Sorry! Shit, suck me. God, yes." In Noah's mouth, Phantom's cock swelled a tiny bit harder.

If he could have, Noah would have laughed at Phan's enthusiasm. As it was, he was concentrating hard on making sure Phan felt appreciated without getting too distracted by how good the friction of his own hand felt, urgently working his shaft. He was going to come any minute, probably before Phan did, and that was almost embarrassing.

He gave Phan's hip a deliberate shove to get his point across. He wasn't about to let Phan fuck his mouth; that was for shower quickies and middle of the night one-offs. This was an ego boost, and Noah wanted Phan to know just how good he tasted, just how much he was wanted.

Phan behaved and held himself still -- mostly -- but the words kept up. The only time Phantom Shaw was actually quiet during sex was either when he'd been ordered to be or when his mouth was full of cock.

That was a pretty image, actually.

"Noah," Phan whispered. "Love your mouth. Love you. Love the way you touch me." He gasped as Noah's tongue rubbed at the spot just under the head, and his legs shook for a moment. "God, yes. More. Please." There was a thump as Phan's head rolled back and hit the wall.

It might be fun, Noah considered, to keep this up until Phan actually grew lightheaded and wilty and he couldn't stand up anymore. But Noah didn't get a chance to seriously think about that. His orgasm, which wasn't far off even before he'd touched himself, moved heavily through his body, first seizing his abdomen and then shooting downward. It was absolutely unstoppable.

Suddenly needing air, Noah pulled off Phan's cock and gasped as he came, painting the tiled floor of the foyer in streaks of milky liquid.

"Wow."

"Jesus Christ, Phan," he managed to mutter. He took two deep breaths, both of which were ragged and choppy, before he leaned forward again and took Phan back, opening his throat wide and letting Phan's cock slide deep inside.

"Whoa!" Phan's hand landed heavily on Noah's shoulder, his fingers digging in. "I can smell you," he said roughly. "Come on, kitten. That's it. You're the sexiest thing ever, and I love the way you touch me."

Noah pinned Phan with both hands and worked Phan's cock with a practiced tongue in the ways he knew from experience drove Phan wild. Little tricks like pulling away and letting the cool air in for a moment before swallowing him deep again, or digging his thumbs into the hollows under Phan's hip bones.

Phan was more than a lover; he was Noah's closest friend, and Noah wanted it to be good, wanted Phan to feel how much Noah cared about him with every muscle in his body.

Phan's legs started to shake right about the time that the words dried up and Phan's hands dug in harder, clinging. With a gasp and a long groan, Phan started to come, his whole body giving a long shudder as he released pulse after pulse into Noah's throat, moaning and whispering Noah's name.

Noah waited for Phan to finish, swallowing everything his lover had to offer and then gently licking and kissing his way up Phan's body until they stood toe to toe. "Hell, yes," he said softly and then kissed Phan gently, curling his arms around Phan's waist.

Phan leaned, holding on. "You didn't have to do that," he whispered. "But I'm awfully glad you did."

Noah gave him a sly look. "Oh, yes, I did. Or, you know, maybe I didn't, but I wanted to. You figure it out." He reached down and fastened his jeans, then took a step back to give Phan room to do the same.

"Wanting to is good enough for me." Phan got himself put away and reached for Noah again, kissing him deeply. "I love you, you know. Enough that I'll even wipe up your junk from the floor."

"What a gentleman. I'll take our bags upstairs." Noah picked up their duffels. "I suppose I need to let you dress me for suit shopping?"

Phan rolled his eyes and smirked. "I want to dress you in the store, kitten. Much more fun that way."

Noah snorted, taking that to mean that it was okay if he wore jeans. It was, apparently, only Phan who had a reputation to uphold. "Come on up when you're done, hon." Noah winked and headed up the stairs.

"So, I can promise you when Sir sees the dark gray one, he'll be all over you. Again. And often." Phan waved a Popsicle at him and grinned a purple grin. "Wanna have me help you change again?"

"No." Noah held up one hand to stop him. "No, I can change by myself, thank you." He disappeared as quickly as possible into the dressing room and closed the door. Gray, black, navy, solids, pinstripes -- he'd tried on so many suits his head was spinning. How Phan kept it all straight, he'd never know.

He hadn't realized all the working out he'd done was actually detrimental when it came to suits. His shoulders were too broad for a standard length. His hips were too narrow for the inseam that worked. Everything was going to have to be altered. And, to make matters worse, he'd never really felt comfortable in a suit to begin with. He looked good in them, he decided, but he'd choose jeans any day.

"Which was the gray one? Was that the one with the nice shoulders?" Noah called out, hoping Phan was at least nearby.

"The one that makes your ass look even more stellar." Phan sounded like he was yelling from right outside the changing room.

"Whatever. And which other one did you like? What about the navy pinstripe? Too much?"

"Depends. Are you joining the mob?" There was a click, and Phan stuck his head in the tiny room. "Did I ever tell you about how I used to break into rooms all the time at college?"

Noah put his hand on Phan's forehead and playfully pushed him out of the changing room. "Which one, then?

The black one? Or was that too stern? Maybe with a funky tie?"

"You're security. No funky ties. I liked the black one, yes, but it might be too much for weekdays. Get the light gray one for summer. Also, I'll have you know that I'm very good at helping people get dressed. It's my special skill. Well, aside from blow jobs."

"So dark gray and light gray?" Noah knew all about how good Phan was at dressing people, but just then he really didn't want hands all over him again. He might humiliate himself, or worse, get them arrested. He ignored Phan and instead pulled on the jacket for the light gray suit and stepped out of the dressing room. "Let's just get this altered and get out of here?"

Phan nodded. "Dark gray, light gray, and we'll get a second opinion about the black. Nothing in blue, not with your coloring -- plus, all the regular security guys wear blue. You're special." Phan leaned close and kissed his cheek.

"Phan?"

"Yes?" Phan grinned at Noah, his teeth all stained purple.

"Go find me a tailor? Now?"

"Kiss me first." The grin didn't even dim, and he was pretty sure Phan didn't mean it, since he was moving away. "Or maybe when I get back with the tailor. You wanted the girl, right? The pretty one?"

"I wouldn't kiss you right now if you were the last purple smile on the planet!" Noah sneered. "Whoever you can find fastest. Because if I don't get out of here soon, I'm going to start drinking."

Phan snorted. "Right. You live with me, and if I didn't drive you to drink, one little shopping trip won't do it." Phan laughed and skipped off to find the tailor. Literally skipping, like he was a young girl.

"Clearly, I need an attitude adjustment," Noah said out loud to no one. "I'll kick his ass at basketball."

Phan came back in a moment or two, not with the pretty girl but with an older man who clearly knew his stuff, as well as whom he was fitting. He didn't come right out and say it, but he did make allusions to being able to move freely while at work, and having clean lines of the suit regardless of what was in the pockets.

Noah glared at Phan and mouthed, "What happened to finding the pretty girl?" But he endured the jokes and the innuendo; anything to get out of the suit and get out of the store.

"All done?" Noah asked as the man took a step back and looked him over.

"Yes," Phan said right away. "We're all done. Time to go. More shopping. Chop chop, come along, darling."

Noah was only vaguely surprised to find himself being pulled from the store, Phan calling back to put it on Tobias' account and to phone when the suits were ready for pick up.

"Jesus, Phan. I wanted to leave, but I hadn't intended on risking my life trying." Noah tugged his arm from Phan's grip.

"I was bored." Phan smiled at him and shrugged. "Sorry. Where now?"

Noah turned to Phan and grinned evilly. "Basketball."

The court was theirs for an hour, and Noah intended to use that time wisely. He dribbled the ball in slow circles around Phan and finally passed it to him. "Catch."

"I hate you." Phan caught the ball and held onto it, glaring.

"A little sweat is good for the soul, Phan." Noah took a few steps away. "We play half court, and the idea is to get the ball through that hoop. If you move, you have to dribble. Got it?"

Phan rolled his eyes. "I know how to bounce a ball and run. You're miles taller than me, though. Can't we play volleyball or something? Badminton?"

"Next time. Today, I feel like kicking your ass. I'll make it up to you in the shower, okay? Go."

"Oh, a promise!" Phan took off, running hard and dribbling like mad.

Noah let him run, watched him throw the ball up in the general vicinity of the basket, and snatched it right out of the air. "Nice try, slick," he said, dribbling it just out of Phan's reach. "I think you're going to sleep well tonight."

"I sleep well every night," Phan said indignantly. "Even the nights we sleep on the floor. Mostly because I'm a good boy, and I go to sleep with the full and complete knowledge that I did my best. Now, if you would be so kind as to just put me out of my misery..." He made a grab for the ball and missed.

"Yes, sir." Noah grinned and started to move.

Apart from the few times that Noah let Phan have the ball out of pity, Phan spent most of the time chasing Noah around the court. Noah relented after about forty minutes when it looked like Phan was having trouble catching his breath, and called the game. "You okay?"

Phan glared at him.

"Well, at least I can say that I kept my promise to Tobias," Noah said, patting Phan on the back. Still catching his breath, he picked up a bottle of water and handed it to Phan.

"What promise?"

"I promised him I'd make sure you got some exercise."

"You couldn't just fuck me a lot?" Phan sighed and drank from the bottle, then gave Noah a long look. "Why did he tell you that? And I suppose I've got to eat, too? God, he always defaults to food and exercise. Never to movies and popcorn and a nap."

"I'm not allowed to fuck you, remember?" Noah gave Phan a stern look, as if either of them would forget one of the few rules Tobias had imposed on them from the very beginning. "And yes, you are supposed to eat. But movies and popcorn sounds like a plan for tonight, don't you think?" Noah gave Phan a quick kiss. "Come on, let's get out of here."

"Can I pick the movie?" Phan perked up immediately, though Noah wasn't sure if it was the thought of the movie or the popcorn that did it. "And we still have shopping, right? I need to make a stop, too. At, uh. That place. You know. Downtown. By the Coffee Bean."

"Yes, you can pick the movie. Showers as promised, and then we have all afternoon to shop, okay?" Noah stopped and looked at Phan. "Wait, the fetish place or that wacko new age place?"

"Uh, neither. But the wacko new age place is fun. I vote we go to all three." Phan grinned at him and pushed the door open. "Maybe we can find some incense that doesn't make Sir sneeze."

"All three it is. And there's ice cream up the block." Noah found them a cab and they crawled in. He wasn't sure how much good the exercise had really done Phan, but he was feeling fine. A nice shower, some food, a morning quickie with Phan... so far, his day off was perfect.

Noah wondered briefly what Tobias was doing with his day off, besides riding. Chances were good he'd be working, even though he shouldn't be. Or making plans with Bradford.

"No horror flicks and nothing mushy," Noah said, knowing he was ruling out two of Phan's favorite genres.

"You're not the boss of me."

"No, but I'm bigger and I'll hog the remote." Noah grinned widely.

Phan grinned back. "I'll eat sugar."

Noah raised an eyebrow. "Oh, yeah? Well, I'll jerk off in front of you and not let you touch."

"Promise?" Phan wiggled. "We can put that on the plans for the day, right after shopping and before the movie. Which is going to be something really, really scary."

Noah sighed and let his head fall back against the seat. "I don't know how I always lose these arguments."

"There, there." Phan petted his knee gently. "It's not so bad. After all, I'll be right there to save you from the monsters and help you clean up after you make a mess. Now. Do you want to have a shower, or do you think we can risk the big tub?"

"Shower. Save the big tub for later, when Tobias gets home. We have a little talking to do, right?" The cab pulled up to the curb, and Noah leaned forward to pay the driver.

"Bah." Phan sighed and climbed out of the cab, but not before Noah heard him say, "Always talking. Not enough dancing, I say. I like dancing. I'm good at dancing."

Noah paid the cab driver and followed Phan into the townhouse, thinking that Phan was actually good at talking, too. It was just that Phan took his time about settling down enough to get to the talking part; sometimes it took their Master to calm him enough. That was generally the case when Phan had a big issue brewing.

"Hon, why don't you -- Phantom!"

"Yes?" Phan looked down at him from halfway up the staircase.

"We generally don't strip in the entryway."

Phan laughed. "We always strip, all over the house. I'm going to shower real fast." He wiggled his ass and took off, leaving his clothes in a heap at the bottom of the stairs.

Noah climbed the stairs, following Phan and picking up Phan's clothing along the way. He dumped all of it into the hamper in the hall and then added his own. The shower was running and Noah chuckled to himself, not at all surprised that Phan was so excited about shopping he'd forgotten he'd been promised some fun. Plenty of time for that later.

Phan liked his showers hot, and the bathroom was already thick with steam. "Room for me?" Noah asked, poking his head into the shower. "Or did you really mean a quick shower?" Noah didn't have strong feelings either way. He and Phan had never been shy about when and what they wanted, and if they didn't get off in the shower, it just meant it would be later in the kitchen, the living room, or wherever the desire took them.

Certainly there would be plenty of energy left for Tobias later. Noah was already looking forward to it.

Phan gave him a sunny grin and wiggled his eyebrows. "Get in here. We can race!"

He meant it, too, Noah knew. Life with Phan was a never-ending series of games. Luckily, most of them were harmless. Noah climbed into the shower. "I'm gonna win." And have fun doing it, which was one of the many bonuses of Phan's games. Sometimes Noah thought himself incredibly lucky, and this was one of those times.

3

Tobias let himself into the townhouse well after dark, out of consideration for the day of the week and what it meant. Back at the beginning, Tuesday had traditionally been the day that Noah had off, his day to relax and simply do as he pleased. When Phantom had become friends with Noah, they'd begun to use Tuesday nights as a time to watch movies and cuddle, so it had been natural to leave Tuesdays as their day off when Phan once more became Tobias' submissive.

The first time Phan had belonged to Tobias, there hadn't been days off. A lot of things had changed in a decade.

The day off was in both submissives' contracts, and it was important. Plus, there was the added benefit that, with both of his boys having a day off, Tobias also got a free day once a week. Usually he spent part of the day on his farm, riding and doing paperwork, but since he'd sold off most of the land to his former land manager, Tobias found that Tuesdays tended to drag a little.

This time he'd taken his ride, raked the stalls, and then headed into the city. He had stopped by the club, but not to work; Bradford could be rather difficult if it looked like Tobias was either overworking or bored. Instead, Tobias had stopped by to have lunch in the dining room since there wasn't a boy to cook for him, then he'd gone to spend an afternoon at the museum, examining a traveling exhibit of Austrian artifacts.

Supper was solo at one of his favorite restaurants, so by the time he got home, he was feeling more than a little lonely and still had some lingering worry about Phantom's erratic behavior of the morning.

Coat neatly hung up, Tobias walked to the living room, making a point not to move softly. He'd done that once before and wound up with his arm twisted up behind his back.

Noah waved but didn't look up, his eyes glued to what appeared to be the end of a horror movie. Phan, who was half in Noah's lap, patted the empty space next to him on the couch.

"I hate these movies," Noah whispered.

Phan chuckled and snuggled closer into Noah. "No, you don't."

"Shut up." Noah picked a bowl up off the coffee table and reached across the couch to Tobias. "Popcorn?

"No, thank you." Tobias hated picking popcorn out of his teeth. He sat, however, and petted Phantom's hip as he leaned over to kiss Noah. "Is this almost over?"

Phan wiggled around and draped his legs over Tobias'. "Shhhh." His eyes went wide and he looked at Tobias, then cringed. "I mean..."

Tobias laughed softly and shushed. It was their day off; he could make allowances. Which was not to say that he wouldn't hesitate to smack Phan's ass if he did the same thing on a Wednesday.

"Yes. Shhhh." Noah waved his hand to quiet Tobias down. Noah, being a bit more self-possessed, had no such qualms about ordering Tobias around.

Moments later, the music ramped up and the screen faded to black. "So, wait, it was her all along? What a bloodthirsty psycho! God, women really are evil." Noah threw up his hands. "I can't believe you make me watch this crap. Ugh."

"You love it," Tobias and Phan said at the same time. Tobias grinned and dug his fingers into Phan's side, wincing as Phan shrieked. "God, Phan. You're shrill."

Noah snorted. "It's a defense mechanism. It drives away predators. Too bad it can't drive away memories of really bad movies."

Tobias laughed and tickled Phan more, moving with him as he flailed on the couch. "I appear to be an immune predator."

"Noah!" Phan yelled, laughing and reaching for Noah's arms. "Save me! Eek!" He thrashed harder, and Tobias had to almost lie on top of him to keep him from tumbling right off the couch.

"Yes, Noah." Tobias grinned. "Save him. It'll be fun."

Noah slipped out from under Phan. "You asked for it." He disappeared from Tobias' view for a moment and strong fingers landed on Tobias' ribs. "Tickle, tickle," Noah teased, digging his fingers into Tobias' sides. "I'd go for your toes, but they've been in your shoes for a while. Yuck."

"Hey!" Tobias held Phan's wrists with one hand and reached back to grab at Noah with the other. "There's nothing yucky about my feet." He laughed as he missed Noah and looked back at Phan. "You've stopped trying to get away."

"I kind of like being smooshed into the couch, sir." Phan

wiggled under him, and Tobias had to agree that Phan really liked it.

He looked back at Noah. "One moment, please."

"Take as many as you like, I don't mind." Noah grinned and went back to trying to tickle him, which of course made Tobias move.

Which made Phan moan.

Which made Noah laugh.

"I think the couch is too small for this," Tobias said dryly. "Did either of you save any energy for me today?"

"Plenty," Noah said, and Tobias felt Noah's hands move from his ribs to parts a bit farther south, where they loosened his belt.

Tobias let Noah do that and dipped his head to kiss Phan for a moment, licking his way into Phan's mouth without any trouble at all. Under him, Phan was still wiggling, but Tobias was fairly sure Phan wasn't trying to get away. When Phan's hands joined in to help Noah's and started on the zipper, Tobias said, "This is still the couch. If we make a mess out here, someone is going to have to clean it up, and it's not going to be me."

Tobias felt a tug on his waistband. "As if there were somewhere in the house that you would actually have to clean up." Noah laughed, getting an arm around Tobias. "Come on. Bed's bigger. Phan, let him go."

Phan twined one hand around Tobias' cock and squeezed. "Remember where I was, okay?"

"Like I'd forget." Tobias kissed Phan again and got off his sub, turning to pull Noah close. Really, there were times he wished he had more hands. He offered his free hand to Phan and pulled, lifting the slight body right off the couch. Phan managed not to fall, though it was a near thing. It was hard to walk with his tongue in Noah's mouth and his legs tangling with Phan's, but months of practice got them all to the bedroom.

Tobias tumbled all of them down and kept Noah against him. "Was he good today?"

"Hmm. Yes, but he kept trying to feel me up." Noah sounded affronted.

Phan snorted in response. "It's called helping you dress, Noah."

"Okay, he helped me dress, taking every opportunity to grope me."

"Typical." And usually a lot of fun. "But what were you dressing for?" Tobias asked, genuinely curious.

"Oh! I bought suits today," Noah said, as if small talk were warranted at that moment. "For Bradford. Phan likes them. Do you think that's a good sign or a bad one?" Noah's fingers opened Tobias' shirt and played against his skin gently. "I worry a little."

Tobias watched as Phan's fingers tangled with Noah's against his chest. He liked the touches, Noah's a gentle caress and Phan's a tease since Phan was actually trying to stop Noah but unavoidably brushed against Tobias to do it.

Noah smiled at Phan. "Just getting a second opinion."

Phan sniffed and looked annoyed at the playful aspersion cast upon his character, but Tobias could both see and feel the way Phan was caressing Noah's fingers. There was a lot of love there, even if they did tend to act like bratty siblings sometimes. They couldn't even manage to work against each other for more than a moment.

"I'm always good. And I'll prove it." Phan sat up and straddled Tobias' thighs. "You two go ahead and talk about me. I'll just do what I do."

"Works for me." Noah stretched out along Tobias' side, propping his head up on one elbow. "Pretty much every time." Tobias felt Noah's lips on his shoulder. "How about you?"

"Uh-huh." Tobias watched Phan peel off his own shirt and nodded. What Phan did certainly worked for Tobias. "Often, even. Did it work for you today, Noah?" He sometimes wondered how much the two of them indulged on their days off. Maybe it was time to tighten the reins when they were working, just for the fun of it.

"Yes and no," Noah lifted his head and looked into Tobias' eyes. "Today I did a little work for him. He needed it."

"Did he?" Tobias kissed Noah and ignored Phan as much as he was able to, considering that Phantom was working at getting both of them undressed while remaining seated on Tobias' legs. "Here, or off when you were buying suits?"

"Ha! Here. I'm not risking the public thing again unless you're with me. If I close my eyes, I can still feel the sting after the locker room incident." Noah leaned over and nibbled Tobias' ear. "He's okay, but he wants to talk," Noah whispered. "You know, later, when you're less... distracted."

Tobias was definitely distracted. It was hard not to be, with Phan's hands on him, his clothing vanishing item by item. He nodded to Noah and kissed him again, but stopped when Noah leaned back. "Hey. I was busy with that."

"Me, too." Phan grinned at him and patted Noah's leg. "Help."

Noah shifted, letting Phan tug his shirt off, then he shifted again and pushed his jeans down over his hips. "Better?" he asked Phan.

"Yes, thank you." Phan said, tugging Noah's jeans off completely. "A little cooperation goes a long way."

"That should be our motto." Noah rolled again, pressing a stiff erection into Tobias' thigh.

Tobias grinned and curled a hand around Noah's ass. "I agree. I like it when you two work together."

"That's right," Noah purred. "You're just hedonistic and like to be worshipped."

Tobias nodded. "Something like that."

"And I'm never sure where to start." Noah, belying the words, didn't seem to have any trouble knowing what to do next. He rolled slightly and kissed Tobias hard, not in a submissive way as Tobias could have expected on any other night, but in the way of a hungry lover. He thrust his tongue into Tobias' mouth and ground his cock against Tobias' hip.

Amused, and more than a little turned on by his pet's show of force, Tobias kissed him back and even let Noah control the kiss for the time being. His concentration was being split between his lovers, not an unusual occurrence and one that none of them really minded. He made sure to have one on one time with each of them, for work and play and loving, but when it was all three of them together on a Tuesday, things sometimes got a little loud.

Phan was being unusually quiet, and Tobias had just started to break his kiss with Noah to find out what was wrong when sudden warmth engulfed his cock and then vanished again. He could feel Noah's hips being shoved away, and then Phan said, "Come on, kitten. Just lift up a bit, that's it," as he coaxed Noah into position.

Tobias felt Noah roll and lift his hips as Phan directed. "This isn't teamwork," Noah explained, his voice hoarse. "I have no idea what he's up to. You taste good, though. Scotch after dinner?" Noah kissed and nibbled at the corners of Tobias' mouth.

"Just one." He couldn't see Phan if he kept on kissing Noah, but he could feel. Phan arranged his legs with Noah's, then settled and curled around them; it was odd and convoluted, but when Tobias ran his fingers through Phan's hair, he heard a happy hum. "I have no idea what he's up to, either," he whispered to Noah. "Oh!"

Phan's tongue started licking Tobias' belly and cock, and warm fingers held him by the root. When Tobias' erection was lined up with Noah's, the shafts pressed together by Phan's hands, Tobias started to see where Phan was going with the gymnastics.

Noah groaned. "Jesus. Phan..." His voice was low and husky, and Tobias felt him arch his hips even more, as if looking for friction. "He's fucking insane."

"He's delightful," Tobias said unevenly as Phan's tongue slid down his cock again and then back up, where he and Noah were held together. "Don't hurt yourself, boy."

"Have a little faith," Phan mumbled, his voice obscured. "And then feel free to brag me up." His tongue lapped over the head of Tobias' erection, and then Phan took both Noah and Tobias into his mouth, just the crowns.

Noah hissed. "Extra credit for creativity," he somehow managed to say despite his obvious inability to get a deep breath. He lowered his head to Tobias' chest and rested his forehead there, his fingers digging into Tobias' sides.

Tobias nodded and closed his eyes. He held Noah close, petting Noah's back absently and counting the beats of Noah's heart as felt through his cock. With his other hand, Tobias carded through Phan's hair and encouraged Phan to go down on them. Phan could do it. "That's it, dear," Tobias whispered. "Perfect."

Phan hummed, and his tongue rubbed. He wasn't really able to lick, what with his mouth stuffed full, but he did what he could. He bobbed his head slowly, taking in more and more each time and jacking them with his hands as well. What he couldn't lick and suck, he teased and petted and stroked until Tobias was shaking from the effort not to thrust.

"Noah," Tobias said, listening to Noah's moans and gasps. "I want you to come after me, okay? A favor. Not an order." But he was so going to make sure this happened on a day when he could order it.

Noah made a sound, possibly trying to answer, but the words didn't come. A moment later, he nodded sharply against Tobias' chest. Tobias could feel the arch in Noah's back and the way Noah's legs were tensing and moving, likely also in an effort not to choke the very well-meaning and undeniably gifted Phan.

Noah made another low sound, and Tobias felt the sting of teeth around his nipple.

"Phantom." Tobias' voice was rough, and so were his fingers as he pulled hard on Phan's hair. "Stay, boy."

He'd broken character, unable to override his nature when pushed to the limit, but it didn't seem to matter. Phan stayed, moaning loudly and wiggling as Tobias started to come. He could feel Noah's efforts not to shoot as well, could hear Noah's desperate gasps each time Tobias' cock pulsed, but at least no one was objecting to Tobias issuing orders.

When come escaped Phan's lips to slide over Tobias' balls, Tobias let go of Phan's hair. "Now, Noah," he whispered, breathless and trembling. "You can come now."

"Thank you." Noah made a desperate sound, then rocked his hips through Phan's fingers and against Tobias' cock a couple of times before he came. He pushed away from Tobias slightly and gulped air, his eyes squeezed closed and his whole body rigid.

It was several moments before Noah relaxed, sinking gently against Tobias' chest. Tobias caught sight of

Noah's fingers reaching for Phan and tangling in his hair.

"Up, dear," Tobias said to Phan, tugging far more gently than he had earlier. He held Noah nestled against him and urged Phantom to join them. "We'll take care of you."

Phan whimpered a bit but crawled up to lean on him, his eyes wide and his lips red and swollen. "Wow," he said, breathlessly, clearly proud of himself. "Neat." He wiped come off his chin and grinned. "Messy."

"If sex isn't messy, you're doing something wrong," Noah offered, reaching a hand across Tobias and stroking strong fingers down Phan's side.

Tobias laughed softly and drew Noah's hand down to Phantom's erection. "Not messy enough, yet." He curled their hands together around Phan's cock and started stroking, setting a quick pace. "When you wish, Phan."

"Oh!" Phan's eyes went wider and his shoulders went back a bit, his whole back arching as he thrust. "Sir! Noah!"

Tobias felt Noah's fingers tighten further around Phan's cock as he stroked. "That's it," Noah encouraged. "Show us the pretty, Phan."

"I am the pretty," Phan said with a gasp. Then he grabbed Noah's shoulder and started to come in ragged, jerky motions. "Oh, man!"

Tobias laughed softly and kept them going through it, only letting Phan go when he fell forward. "You're very pretty," he assured Phan. He kissed both his boys and tucked them in around him. "Both of you. What a nice way to come home."

"He's pretty, I'm handsome," Noah said in weak protest.

"Oh?" Tobias arched his eyebrow. "And what, then, am I?"

"Hot." Noah and Phan answered in unison. They stared at each other for a second and then started to laugh.

"And a little sticky," Noah added.

"Very sticky." Tobias smiled. "I kind of like that part, since the shower is right over there and I can get unsticky fairly fast. Tell me about your day. You shopped?"

Against him, Phan nodded. "Uh-huh. Noah got suits and wouldn't let me feel him up. Then he embarrassed me at the gym for a while."

"I beat his ass at basketball. You did say to get him some exercise."

"It was horrible." Phan looked unimpressed. "But we came home and showered."

"And Phan forgot I'd promised him some fun in the shower."

"I can't believe I did that."

"I know, I thought maybe you were sick." Noah laughed.

Phan stuck his tongue out at Noah. "I was exhausted and not thinking clearly. You reminded me, though, and then there was a shower race."

"Which I won."

"We both won."

Tobias blinked at the back and forth between his boys. He ought to be used to it by now, and he was, mostly, but it still amused him.

"Whatever." Noah grinned. "Oh, and then you actually ate the salad I put in front of you for lunch."

"Of course! You made me run and stuff. I was hungry."

"Good."

Phan snorted. "I'm hungry sometimes."

"Uh-huh. You know what I think? I think you forgot to eat breakfast yourself this morning with all the clanging around you were doing."

Tobias almost missed the tension that ran though Phan's body and vanished with a twitch. Almost.

"I ate," Phan said lightly. He looked at Tobias and added, "Then we went shopping again, for me. We went to the Coffee Bean and hit up the stores around there; you know, the leather shop."

Tobias nodded. "I see. Did you buy clothes, too?"

"Yep. Noah said I have muscles now. I don't know about that, but we did find pants that fit and some shirts. I wanted to go buy you incense, but Noah wouldn't let me."

"It makes people sneeze." Noah rolled his eyes. "Phan's got some nice definition, don't you think so? I was trying to pick out some new tops that would show off his muscles." He reached out and gave one of Phan's biceps a squeeze.

Phan rolled his eyes, the expression nearly identical to Noah's. "Please."

"And then I thought I'd lost him for, like, ten minutes. He ran off and bought something and he wouldn't show me what it was. Bad boy."

"I am not a bad boy." Phan stuck his nose in the air and said nothing further, which wasn't exactly typical.

Tobias nudged him and gave Phan most of his attention. "Phan?" he asked softly. "What did you buy?"

Phan looked distinctly uncomfortable, and if they'd had a more mainstream relationship, Tobias doubted Phan would have met his eye. As Phantom so rarely did that anyway, it was hard to tell, but his shoulders were certainly tight and there was a great deal of reluctance on his face. "It's a surprise, sir," he finally said. "For you both. I'd really rather not say."

"Oh." Startled, Tobias exchanged a look with Noah, who looked just as baffled. "From the clothing store?"

"No, sir." Phan shook his head and pointedly looked away, clear across the room to a wall. "I went next door. It's a gift."

Tobias tried to remember what was next to the shop and failed. There was the fetish place, a bookstore, a new age place... an art supply place, maybe? Something with colors in the front window. "Okay. If it's a gift, it's a gift. I can't think of any occasions coming up, though."

Phan remained resolutely silent on the matter.

Tobias looked at Noah and shrugged. "I think, my lovelies, that it's time to clean up. And then perhaps change the sheets. I have something I'd like to talk to you both about."

Noah rolled onto his back and then stretched out long like a lazy cat, his arms up over his head and his toes spread wide. After a lengthy yawn, he nodded. "Shower. Okay." He sat up. "Phan? Okay with you if I get selfish and greedy and take him with me?" Noah indicated that he meant Tobias with a tilt of his head. "I'll help you with the sheets after."

"You sure will," Phan said as he rolled away from Tobias and wrapped himself around a pillow. "It's a very big bed, and I can't do it alone."

Tobias laughed as he got up and slapped Phan's ass. "That's entirely untrue. You do it all the time, under orders."

"Noah's orders don't count. Slap me again?"

"Only because you're a good boy." Tobias bent and kissed him, then slapped his ass hard enough to sting his own palm. "That's it until morning."

"Thank you, sir!" Phan winced and rubbed the red mark on his butt. "Ow."

"Just the way you like it." Tobias grinned and took Noah's hand. "Shower, sweetheart, before I stick to everything."

Tobias felt Noah's fingers tangle with his as they made their way to the large master bathroom. Tobias had thought of every detail when he renovated the townhouse, including a shower that would suit the needs of at least two with enough luxury to suit himself. Noah started the water and got out a few towels. "After you," he said, smiling and gesturing for Tobias to step in.

"You're not on the job," Tobias said with a soft laugh. Still, he got in the shower and held out his hand. "Come here. I want to hold you for a bit." The water was warm, and it was one of life's little luxuries to stand and hold his lover close to him.

"Mmm." Noah hummed and slipped easily into Tobias' arms. "Missed you today." He ran his fingers up Tobias' back and then let his arms rest around Tobias' waist.

"I missed you, too." It was true. Once upon a time, Tobias would have laughed if he'd been told he'd say such a thing to his sub. Those days were long gone, however, and he'd grown comfortable with the complex relationship he and Noah maintained. Balance had been hard to find, but they seemed to have at least worked out the communication part.

Tobias held Noah to him and touched his skin gently, moving water over him. "You would think that we'd all be eager to spend time apart, since we live and work together. Always near, always knowing everything. But I just feel vaguely wrong when you and Phan are off doing your own thing."

Noah nodded against Tobias' chest. "The sub in me is happy with our customary six days a week. The lover sometimes wants more of... well, this. I think about that more when we're not together, I guess." Noah stepped back and ran his hands over Tobias' chest. "Phan and I had a nice day. Nothing wrong with that. I'm just glad you decided to join us tonight."

"I'll tell you a secret." Tobias kissed Noah's shoulder and more or less just hugged him as the shower rained down on them. "I really, really hate sleeping alone. I like sleeping with you in the bed or on the floor next to me, but the nights we're in separate houses drive me mad. I even like the nights you're both sent to your own rooms here better than being in different houses."

"Then unless you're specifically banished, you should just plan to join us on Tuesday nights. I prefer it, and no matter what Phan says, he doesn't really sleep well when you're not at least in the house somewhere."

Tobias had to laugh at the choice of words. "Banished?"

"Yes. Banished. As in it's our day off, no Doms allowed." Noah grinned, showing off his pearly whites and reached for the loofah. "Back scrub?"

"The banished get back scrubs?" Tobias smiled and kissed Noah softly. "Scrub away. May I ask you if Phantom's mood this morning affected your day off? I should have dealt with it. Sometimes it's not easy to tell with him. You're much more in my face with it when you've got something that needs talking about." He grinned and wondered if he maybe should have phrased that a little more delicately, since Noah was armed with a loofah.

"In your face, huh? That's... flattering." Noah snorted and set to scrubbing Tobias' back with the loofah. "Phan's mood always affects our day off together. Usually in a good way. It wasn't a bad day, we had a good talk on the way in this morning. We didn't resolve anything, really, except that he does need to talk to you, he has a legitimate concern, and I actually agree with most of what he's feeling. Like you said, it's something I would have jumped on by now if it were bothering me, but Phan is a little less confident about coming to you right away. Either he wanted to know how I felt about things before talking to you, or he's concerned that he's going to sound like the squeaky wheel, bringing every little thing to your attention. I wonder if maybe you need to make it clear to him that you want to hear everything, no matter how small he thinks it is, you know?"

Tobias nodded. "You're right, of course." His back tingled and he reached for the shampoo, suddenly wanting to be clean. "Honestly, if you'd met him when I did, you'd be blown away. He's almost a completely different man. In some ways that's very, very good. In other ways... his act, the way he is with everyone but us, how self-assured he can seem... I'd like to give him some of that for real. It was there, once."

"Sometimes it is real for him, Tobias. Give yourself a little credit; I don't think it's always an act." Noah took the shampoo bottle from Tobias and lathered up his own hair. It was still pretty short, but not as short as he'd worn it when he was a cop. After Tobias rinsed off, Noah nudged him out of the way and ducked under the spray. "But he still has a lot of fear, you know?"

"Yeah, he does." Tobias watched Noah wash and smiled. "How did this turn into talk about Phan time? My fault." He leaned close and held Noah's hips as he kissed a path on Noah's jaw. "I love you. Thanks for not banishing me."

Noah nodded. "I love you, too. And you're welcome." He ran his hands down Tobias' arms. "All clean?"

"The outside, anyway." He shut off the water and allowed Noah to hand him a towel. "Bradford told me this afternoon that I have a dirty mind. You can imagine my reaction."

"And your point would be?" Noah deadpanned.

Tobias laughed, hearing his reply and delivery from Noah's mouth. "That's the one. Then I pointed out that he's the one who owns a sex club, not me."

"Ah ha! A. It's not a sex club, it's a BDSM gentleman's club. This is an important distinction, says the ex-cop." Noah laughed. "And B. I beg your pardon, but you do own it.

You're his business partner, and as such you share in the profits as well as the deviance, remember?" Noah headed into the bedroom with his towel wrapped around his waist.

Tobias followed, not bothering with the towel. "I don't own it, I'm merely a very highly placed employee who happens to pay some bills and own outside property and have a say in what happens." And was listed as part owner on many, many legal documents. "Phan, did you fall asleep?"

"Nope!" Phan rolled to his feet and gathered up the sheets, which he'd clearly stripped off while Tobias and Noah showered. "You're a part owner. Noah, can you help me make the bed?"

"See?" Noah said throwing a glance in Tobias' direction. "Nice try, owner." He picked up a clean sheet and shook it out, sending the other side across the bed to Phan.

Tobias rolled his eyes. "Morning will come, you two."

Phan wiggled and winked at Noah, but said nothing as he tucked in his side of the bed.

Noah winked back. "Ah, that's one way to win the argument. Wait it out." He laughed and tossed a couple of pillows to Phan.

Phan's eyes went wide, and he got busy fluffing the hell out of a pillow as Tobias walked toward Noah, one hand lifting a bit. He stopped, though, reasonably sure that even a light spank would turn into a wresting match and more sex; he had things to discuss. "On the bed, you two. Oh, get drinks and such, if you want them. We need to talk about the farm."

Noah glanced up at Phan and gave him a wink, but Tobias couldn't make out the meaning of the look that passed between them. "I'll get us all some tea," Noah said, brushing a hand along Tobias' side on his way out of the room.

Tobias thought about the wink as he watched Phan finish making the bed, dragging blankets and the bedspread into place, then the pillows before he turned down the sheets for Tobias. "You know, sometimes I think I'm missing a good deal of what goes on around here." Tobias climbed into the bed and gathered Phan into his arms as he spoke, keeping his tone teasing. "You and your best friend there have almost a secret language."

Phan curled into his side, still smelling of sex. "We thought about writing it down for you," he said seriously, "but then we realized that all the fun would be lost. Did you have a good day?"

Tobias smiled and kissed his forehead. "I did. I think I'll take Noah out to dinner where I went tonight. You'd be bored to tears and likely start redecorating for them. We should go downtown, you and I."

Phan perked up. "Thai?"

Tobias nodded. "Thai. You know the place, down where you used to live."

"Mmm. Thai. Spicy." Noah walked through the door carrying a tray with three mugs of tea. "God, I love that electric kettle, the water heats up so fast." His towel chose that moment to fall from his hips and hit the floor and Noah blushed. "Oops. Guess I didn't need that anyway, huh?"

"Nope." Tobias and Phan spoke at the same time, then Phan giggled and got up. "Let me help you," he said, taking two of the mugs off the tray.

"Thanks." Noah climbed up on the bed carefully so as not to spill his tea and sat cross-legged alongside Tobias so that he was facing Phan as well.

Phan passed Tobias his mug and then looked up. "What? Why are you both staring at me?"

"Because you're pretty," Tobias said with a grin. He

sipped his tea and studied his mug for a moment, hoping Phan would unruffle his feathers. "And because you have something on your mind." He glanced up at Phan and smiled gently. "It's okay if you don't want to talk about it yet, dear. Just know that I love you, have loved you for years, and I know you. You can't actually hide from me."

Noah nodded but said nothing, though he did brush Phan's leg with his foot in what Tobias took for a show of support.

For a moment Phan seemed to want to deny that he was thinking about anything, but then he rolled his eyes and more or less crumpled. He didn't look precisely dejected, just annoyed that he wasn't good at keeping things from either of them. "I'm still thinking," he admitted. Then he sipped from his mug, hiding behind the rim.

"That's fine, too." Tobias nodded and leaned back on the pillows, careful not to spill his tea or Phan's. "So, the farm. I'm still mulling over the last weekend, and I'd like your thoughts. We had a full bunkhouse, every bed full and each chain with a sub attached. Personally, I think the actual work went well. Having that many Doms in the ring with me kept me busy going from one to the next and helping them. But I'm not so sure about the rest." He frowned to himself. "I don't want to use the farm as a drop-in resource for afternoon classes. I like having pairs of men there for a full weekend as it gives the subs time to really sink into their roles. And I liked having that many people in the ring. But it felt off when we weren't doing actual BDSM workshops. Thoughts?"

He looked down at Phan, sure that he'd have something to say, but Phan was staring hard at Noah.

Tobias nudged him, but Phan shook his head. "I have

thoughts," he said with a short nod. "But I. I mean. Sir, they're all mixed up."

Noah seemed to take that as his cue. "I think Phan and I both found having that many strangers around a little overwhelming." Noah looked thoughtful for a moment, and then looked at Phan. "Right? So many people around in what is usually our space... it was a little uncomfortable."

Tobias tried to see Phan's face, but Phan's look had turned thoughtful and his eyes remained on his tea. "It's different when it's just two or three couples," Phan said slowly. "We're working and all, but it feels like a weekend gathering, like we have friends over. They eat with us, Noah and I cook with the subs, and it's very friendly and warm. I like that, I like having people into our home, living our lifestyle. It means a lot to me that I get to spend time with the subs and they get to know me a bit. Because I am who I am, and it's really important that I have their support when I do the rest of my job."

When Phan looked up, it was to talk to Noah, not Tobias, which was completely natural. The two of them had a long history of sorting out Phan's thoughts, and when Phan was explaining only to Tobias, he often kept his eyes low even when Tobias would prefer he not be submissive. Talking directly to Noah was a sort of proxy that everyone recognized and was comfortable with.

"It's important that they trust me, see," Phan explained. "I'm the guy their Master is practicing the hard stuff on. I'm the one tied to the cross and getting walloped. They need to know that I have no designs on their Master, and that kind of knowing happens best when I spend time with them. So, when there's so many people out there that people are moving through the house in shifts, when it's crowded in the kitchen and when there's a line up for the bathroom, it's not a house party, it's just work. And there shouldn't be work in her home."

Tobias barely kept himself from blinking in surprise. He'd been following along and completely agreeing with Phantom's points, but the last statement brought him up short. "Phan?" Gently, he petted one hand down Phan's back.

Phan sighed deeply and handed Noah his mug, then curled into Tobias' side. "I miss her," he whispered. "And Elizabeth would welcome our friends. But it feels so wrong to have her home full of people we don't even have time to talk to between floggings and lessons and cleaning up all the messes. It's cold and too far removed. I didn't like it. Sir."

"I can tell." Tobias smiled a little bit and held Phantom in a one-armed hug. "Okay, too many people for Phan." He kept petting as he looked at Noah. "Sweetheart? What do you think?"

"I had a different reaction," Noah said slowly. "First of all, and I mean no disrespect to Mrs. M, because you both know I loved her, but I don't think of it as her home, I think of it as ours. Well, yours originally," Noah explained, gesturing to Tobias. "But ours now."

Noah shifted and set Phan's tea down on the side table, and his own beside it. "I actually liked having people around. What bothered me more was that they were strangers to me. It wasn't their numbers, it was their unfamiliar faces. If I'd known them better, and I think I will get to know everyone better the more I work at the club, it would have been much more comfortable."

Noah looked like he was done, but he took a quick breath and went on. "Also, and maybe another discussion entirely, but I think, Phan, that you've earned the respect of those subs simply by being Tobias' sub. By being the one experienced enough for their Masters to work with. I think that respect is due to you, that you should expect it from those subs, and their Doms, too, for that matter, long before anyone lays a hand on you." He shrugged. "I guess that's just my opinion, but... well, you've earned that."

Phan shook his head. "No."

Tobias, his head reeling a bit as he tried to gauge the pace of the conversation and judge what to tackle first, looked at Phan. "No? 'No' what?"

"No, I'm not talking about them respecting me. I don't give a fuck if they respect me or not; I know my place. But I do care about them feeling secure and safe when they are at the farm, and within an entirely new experience. I've been on their side often enough. A Master's word is one thing, often everything, but there are real people in there, and they appreciate it when the one taking their place at the cross has shown them the honor of being kind. It's not about respect at all; it's about kindness and being approachable. I'm also the guy they turn to for advice, remember."

"Hmm." Noah raised an eyebrow, looking back at Phan. "Wow, good point. I hadn't thought of that at all." When Noah turned to look at Tobias, he shrugged. "I don't know. I think, given Phan's position in all of this -- the fact that he is stepping into another sub's place for these demonstrations -- he's really the one we need to listen to here. I like to be friendly with the subs, too, but I'm not at all in the same situation he is. In the end, it always comes down to you and me. Not me and someone else's Dom."

"Sure." Tobias nodded and petted Phan as he thought. He finished drinking his tea and put his mug aside, then made Phan turn enough to look at him. "You look upset."

Phan actually looked pretty miserable. "I don't like disagreeing with Noah. I don't like it when I feel out of sync with what you two are doing or feeling. I mean, like I said, I like having people at the farm. I just like a chance to know them better, like Noah. But I also don't like her -- our -- home feeling like a hotel."

With a sigh, Tobias held Phan a bit closer. "There are a lot of things in there for me to think about, and I promise I will. I'll probably talk to you both about this again, too -- it's only a month until the next weekend retreat, and only a week until the date is open for applications. But I'm more worried about the look on your face right now and what you said about disagreeing with Noah. You're not really disagreeing, you know. And even if you were, that's okay. You're people with opinions. It's unnatural to share every opinion with someone, no matter how close you are."

"Phan, hon, we're not arguing here." Noah leaned a little closer to them both. "I think you're absolutely right. You and I are just approaching this from completely different perspectives, and I didn't understand the situation from your point of view until now. We don't have the same responsibilities during the weekend workshops; they affect us each differently. And we're talking so we make sure we don't stay out of sync, right?"

Phan nodded, and Tobias nudged him a bit, knowing he would go to Noah. Sure enough, given a little encouragement, Phan crawled almost into Noah's lap.

"Come on, boys." Tobias slid down in the bed and made room next to himself. "Phan in the middle tonight, I think. Well, at least to start." He couldn't remember a night when all three of them had shared the bed where he didn't wake up in the middle.

He rather liked that, but he wasn't about to tell them.

Noah and Phan sank into the pillows easily, fitting comfortably together without effort. "This was a good day, Phan. Promise." Noah kissed Phan on the forehead. As

Tobias watched them together, he could almost see Noah slowly shifting headspace as he settled down, preparing himself mentally for the next day, things Noah did regularly that seemed so easy, but that Tobias knew took practice. "Night, sir."

Tobias smiled. "Good night, pet. Good night, boy."

"Good night, sir." Phan wiggled a bit and snuggled into both of them, his eyes closed. "Good night, kitten."

Before they could go through another round of good nights that would remind Tobias of Walton Mountain, he leaned over and shut off the light. In the dark, they might not see him thinking.

It was a good thing they were going to be working at the club in the morning. Tobias knew he had another voice to listen to there, within the walls of private offices.

4

Tobias loved ritual. He adored it. He knew that there was always a place for mixing things up, for being spontaneous and doing things in whatever way fit a situation, but in his heart he found immense comfort in ritual.

Like his morning routine. Like being called "sir" or "Master." Like knowing precisely who was doing what and why.

Like giving out morning discipline for the day and starting Wednesdays off on the right foot.

Both Noah and Phan had slipped into their proper roles when day broke, and after his morning blow job, his cup of coffee, a nice shower, and having Phan dress him, Tobias reddened both their asses and told them what they'd be wearing for the day.

Tobias liked Tuesdays well enough, but he really loved Wednesday mornings.

By the time the three of them arrived at the club, himself in a suit, Phan in leather, and Noah in business casual since his actual shift didn't start until later in the day, Tobias was downright cheerful.

"Right to the office, boys," he said, nodding good morning to Brian, who was setting tables in the dining room. Though the club didn't officially open until afternoon, members occasionally came for breakfast. Arrangements could be made for almost anything at the club. "And then we'll see if Nikki needs any help or if there are things Bradford needs done. I have paperwork before my ten o'clock member interview, and I'll need Phan for that."

He led them into his large office and rapped on the wall he shared with Bradford. It annoyed the hell out of his business partner -- it wasn't exactly dignified -- and Tobias did it as often as he dared. "Noah, did you say you had things you wanted to check out in the security office? Equipment upgrades or something?" Tobias pointed to the floor, and both of his boys sank to their knees.

"Yes, sir," Noah nodded, head up but eyes low. "Master Bradford told me that the playroom surveillance system on the third floor wasn't upgraded when the rest of the building was, and requested that I have a look and make a recommendation."

Tobias' phone rang. He didn't need to look at the ID to know who it was.

"All right," he said, leaning over for the receiver and picking it up. "Stay. Good morning, Bradford. Have you had breakfast yet?"

Bradford snorted. "I love it when the plaster comes raining down off my walls," he answered, sounding grumpy. "Why are you always so damn cheerful on Wednesday mornings?"

"Because all is right in my world." Tobias smiled and petted Noah's head. "When do you want Noah to look over the third floor? And shall we have coffee?"

"Ah. I'd like to do the upgrade next week, so if you can give him the time to look it over today or tomorrow, that would be ideal." Bradford sounded a great deal less grumpy now that he was discussing his club. "And coffee was my next order of business. I'll have Nikki bring us a pot. Your office or mine?"

"Mine, I think." Tobias ran his fingers through Noah's hair and wished it was another inch longer. "I haven't been here since Thursday; it would be a shame to run out right away."

"Good. I could use a change of scenery," Bradford joked. "Be there in a few." The line went dead as Bradford hung up the phone.

Tobias set his receiver down and let go of Noah. "Phan, when Nikki comes, I want you to help him with the coffee. Noah, can you make sure the file I need at ten isn't lost on my desk, please? I'll get to the rest of that stuff later, but I need that one on top." He crossed to where two easy chairs were positioned with a table between them and sat down to wait.

Without being told, Phan went to open the office door and knelt again, waiting for Nikki, and Tobias took a moment to watch him. Phan always looked so easy in his skin when he was kneeling, like there was nowhere on earth he'd rather be.

Noah went to Tobias' desk and searched through the stack of files Tobias had left there last week. "I'll dig it up, sir."

"Thank you, pet." Tobias transferred his gaze to Noah

and watched him for a moment as well, smiling when he realized he just wanted to look at Noah's ass.

Nikki came through the door moments later, dressed much like Phan in leather shorts and a leather vest. Spotting Phan waiting, he stopped in the doorway. "Good morning, Master Tobias," he said cheerfully. He looked down at Phan. "Morning, Phantom."

"Good morning, Nikki." Tobias sat up a little straighter, eagerly anticipating his second cup of coffee for the morning.

Phan rolled up to his feet and kissed Nikki on the cheek. "Morning," he said, just as cheerfully. "I'm going to help serve."

"Thank you." Nikki nodded and moved to the table. He held the tray to let Phan remove the masculine, yet graceful coffee cups and matching pot from the tray.

Bradford arrived with his organizer and pen in hand, along with a couple of manila folders and a small plate of breakfast treats. "Brian handed me these as I passed him in the hall. Apparently Chef has acquired new baking skills." He set them down on the table. "I remain skeptical, but you never know."

He glanced briefly in Phan's direction while Phan poured his coffee, and sat in the opposite chair. "Thank you, Phan." After another, longer look, he smiled and winked at Tobias. "On second thought, Tobias, I see exactly where your morning cheer comes from."

Noah coughed over at Tobias' desk.

Tobias glanced over and raised an eyebrow. "Something to say? Thank you, Phan. Sugar, please."

Noah swallowed. "I found your file, sir." He held it up and then set it down on top of the stack so that Tobias could see where he put it. Somehow he managed not to look the least bit guilty as he moved out from behind the desk and went to his knees beside Tobias' chair.

Tobias rested a hand on Noah's shoulder and accepted the mug that Phan handed him. "I think Noah would like to spend some time with the housekeeping staff today, too." He smiled at Bradford and winked. "Really learn the ins and outs of setting up the rooms and keeping them clean."

"I'll be sure to find something appropriate to occupy his time," Bradford said easily, without sparing Noah a second glance. Noah, for his part, was appropriately quiet as well. "I've received several phone calls about the weekend at your farm, Tobias." Bradford sipped his coffee. "The feedback has been, not surprisingly, very positive."

"Mmm." Tobias wasn't surprised, either. He sat back and sipped his coffee, his boys kneeling next to him and being the quiet statues they were trained to be. "In some ways the weekend was all that I thought it could be. In others, I've discovered issues I need to find a way to accommodate so things may continue to be successful without undue... " He thought for a moment, looking for the correct word. "Without causing unneeded stress or creating a different set of problems."

Bradford nodded slowly, watching Tobias long after he'd finished speaking. "I see," he said carefully. "And these issues are related to the visitors or... are they domestic?"

"It's all one and the same in my life," Tobias said dryly, but he slid a significant look toward Phantom. "In this particular case, however, there may have been too many bodies for anything other than the actual lesson times."

Bradford nodded, now apparently aware that Phan was having particular trouble. "You might have to spell it out for me, Tobias, but I think you're saying that the number of men you had was manageable when you were working but overwhelming when the sessions had concluded? What specifically was the frustration? Just too many people? Not enough down time?"

"Too many people at meal times, not enough time to get to know anyone." Tobias glanced down. "Phantom has a very unique role within the club in general and at the farm in particular. It's important that he develop at least a passing familiarity with the players."

"So what you need is some help," Bradford suggested. "To give your boys some time to get to know people. Staff."

"That would entirely depend upon what the staff is to do. Phan and Noah spend time with the subs while they're doing chores; staff might actually be counter-productive."

"Ah. Yes, I see. Well, I had thought to offer you a couple of our staff subs on those weekends, but it sounds like what your boys might need is more time, not necessarily more help. How do you structure your sessions? Are there sessions that could be conducted without the subs present? Things that could be done in workshop style or just sitting around talking? Maybe you could structure things in a way that would give the subs blocks of time on their own? Would that help accomplish what you're talking about?"

Tobias felt his brow furrow as he thought and made himself stop frowning. He wasn't ready to have lines gouged into his forehead from thinking. "Well. This past weekend, there was a lot of one on one instruction in the ring, but that's needed, and the subs -- at the very least, Phan and Noah as examples and models -- need to be there for that. But I suppose I could structure time for the discussions that naturally crop up. Noah, do you find that you're kneeling a lot and waiting for us tops to just finish up our fascinating sidebars and get on with things?"

"I... um." Noah seemed to take a moment to think about his answer. "To be honest, sir, it's my pleasure to kneel by your side. I spend the time thinking about how I'm serving you, not worrying about whatever is supposed to come next; that's up to you. It was an intense weekend, and I spent a lot of time in subspace, so... I don't know, I guess I didn't notice?" Noah sighed and shook his head. "I'm sorry. I don't think I can answer that question, sir."

"That's okay." Tobias nodded and rested a hand on Noah's shoulder. "You did answer it, thank you." He looked back at Bradford. "Phantom tells me that he needs to have a relationship with the subs, and that it bothers him when our home feels like an inn. He doesn't like having dinner in shifts, and when there are that many people in the house, it feels less like we have company and more like..." He trailed off and glanced at Phan. "Like what, boy?"

Phan held his position and didn't slump at all, but he was clearly reluctant to say anything. "It feels like a boarding house, sir. Impersonal and rushed and stressful."

Tobias looked at Bradford. "Which isn't exactly the best way to have things. So, I weigh the needs of my sub against the success of the weekend."

"Hmm." Bradford looked thoughtful and sipped his coffee. "Adding a day would make things less rushed," Bradford suggested. "Making it a three-day workshop, instead of two? But that's assuming you stay committed to having so many Doms out at the farm at once. How tired were you after the weekend? Were you still on top of your game by Sunday night? Can you handle that many Doms at once?"

"I can. Easily. I thought the actual work went very--" He broke off as Phan patted at his foot. "Phan?"

"Please, sir." Phan's face was drawn. "I don't mean to be disrespectful. An added day would be worse. It would be another day of people trooping in and out of the house, an extra day of too many people in the kitchen, another three meals of people touching her things and in our space and just there. Too many people. It's not time, it's bodies!"

"Whoa." Tobias reached down and lifted Phan bodily into his lap. "Calm, boy. Breathe. I've got you."

"I only meant it might slow things down and make them less... what was the word you used? Rushed. Stressful," Bradford suggested, his eyes on Phan. He sipped his coffee again. "I'm concerned that this may be a sticking point, Tobias, but... if I may?" He glanced up at Tobias clearly asking permission to speak directly to Phan.

Tobias nodded slowly.

"Phan, if the numbers were non-negotiable -- and I'm not suggesting that they are, but suppose they were -- is there anything that could possibly make the weekend more manageable for you? Perhaps fewer responsibilities? More one on one with your Master?" He raised an eyebrow. "Perhaps not participating at all? Answer frankly, boy, you've my permission to speak your mind."

Phan shook his head and curled into Tobias. "I just want the house to be treated like a home and not a pit stop. Too many people and it feels like a hotel."

Tobias slid his hand down Phan's back and absently traced one of his scars. "What if the bunkhouse or barracks or whatever you want to call it had a kitchen and a common room? Would that work?"

"That's something I hadn't thought of, moving some of the chaos out of your home," Bradford sounded thoughtful.

Noah straightened up a bit beside Tobias, and Tobias dropped a hand to his shoulder. "Pet?"

"I can't speak for Phan, sir, but I think I would actually prefer that myself."

Bradford made an approving sound. "Phan?"

Phan's head lifted a bit. "We could do that?"

"Sure. It's only money." Tobias rolled his eyes. "Of course we can do it. We can almost always find a way to make things work; you know that. You're a testament to that."

"I'm sure we can find some room in the budget for improvements to the sleeping quarters," Bradford offered. "It's certainly preferable to cancelling the group sessions altogether, which was where I was afraid we might be headed."

Phan shook his head quickly. "No, sir, Master Bradford. I like it when there's two or three couples; it's fun. But four or five was just too much. I'm sorry."

Tobias petted Phan once more and urged him to go back to his usual place. "You don't need to be sorry, Phan. All you need to do, ever, is tell me how you feel. We can work it out from there. However, you and I are going to have to work through some things, I think. You're missing Mrs. Miller a lot these days."

Phan nodded miserably and sighed. "Yes, sir."

"It's okay, Phan," Noah said softly as Phan knelt beside him again.

"The offer for extra staff remains open should you decide you need it," Bradford offered, picking up one of the pastries he'd brought with him. He inspected it dubiously.

Tobias held out his coffee mug to Noah and thought about staff. "I'm not sure what I'd have them do, really. The subs do the work and care for their Doms. I suppose I could use someone in the day or so before the weekends to do

60 | CHRIS OWEN & JODI PAYNE

things like getting the food delivered and make up the beds and such. If we're going to have a dozen people, that's a bit much for Phan and Noah to manage on top of our work here in town."

Bradford finished chewing before he spoke. "Well, you think about it and we'll set up whatever you need. Certainly we can cut down on the numbers until we get the barracks operating independently. Hey, these aren't half bad."

"Who made them?" Tobias took his newly filled mug from Noah and sipped. "And did Brian get his session with that new fellow yet? Phan, what was his name again?"

"Hayden, sir."

"Right, Hayden. Loves to spank, so I thought he'd be perfect for Brian in terms of fun. I'm not sure if they're a good match long term or not."

"Brian's begged him for another session at least three times that I know of," Bradford said, grinning widely. "If Hayden can handle Brian's energy level, I think they might well be in for a long relationship. We'll see. As for the pastries, Chef made them. Thomas. Try the little muffins."

"How long has Brian been working here?" Tobias tried to remember a time without Brian and failed, though he knew there had to be one -- Brian was a lot younger than Tobias.

"Brian started here shortly after I took over the business. He was barely eighteen then if you'll remember, and out on the street. He was much too sweet for that kind of work."

"He's never had a consistent Dom, has he?" Tobias frowned. "Noah, please get me Hayden's folder. I'm going to meddle, I think."

Noah moved quickly and searched through the folders in Tobias' large cabinet against the wall.

"He never has," Bradford said, nodding slowly. "I have no doubt that he'd like one in an ideal world, but you know how he is. He overcompensates, he tries too hard to impress, he's got issues with commitment and abandonment."

"The file, sir." Noah knelt by Tobias' side and held up the folder.

"Thank you." Tobias started reading, flipping through the application form and his own notes from their interviews. "Oh, right, I remember now. Mild, patient. Phan thought he was far stronger as a domestic dominant than a SM player." He nodded. "I think I'll invite him to have a drink with me one evening if I see him in the bar. If I call him in, he might think something's wrong."

"Oh, and 'Care to have a drink with me?' isn't at all ominous." Bradford laughed. "You're known for keeping to yourself, Tobias. Any social interaction with you is meaningful around here."

"Oh." Tobias thought about that for a moment. "Really?"

Phan giggled.

"Oh, it's a sad day when one's subs are more observant than one's self." Bradford grinned at Tobias as Nikki refilled his coffee cup. "Tobias, do you not recall the stir you made when you walked in here on your forty-first birthday? Granted, you've been a bit more visible around here since then, but the fact remains that you are *the* Tobias Vincent, and your reputation precedes you. Moreover, your boys are practically celebrities."

That got a snort out of Noah.

"Phan is," Tobias agreed with a roll of his eyes. "But mostly because he doesn't like to wear clothes and does like to lick my boots in public." Actually, it was probably more because of the sheer amount of pain Phantom could take, but Tobias didn't like to dwell on that.

"True enough. Though I wouldn't underestimate your Noah's reputation, either. In any case, you meddle in whatever way suits you, and the rest of us will sit back and watch with great interest. And when you're done with that," Bradford slid a file out from under his day planner and handed it to Tobias, "that is the security information I have on file for Noah to look over at your convenience, and this," Bradford handed Tobias another file, "is the draft of our new calendar. Party and theme weekend dates, new room reservation policies, and our new schedule of membership dues and special event fees. I thought you might like to look it over before I put it in final form and mail it out."

Tobias looked at the pile of paper in his hand. "Well. Suddenly I have at least an hour at my desk. Noah, you can go and see housekeeping now, and after lunch you can start on the security work for Master Bradford. Tell housekeeping that you're to change beds and do whatever they set for you. They can report errors to me. Phantom, you can help me at my desk. Naked."

"Yes, sir." Noah's feet looked a little leaden as he walked, but he left the room as ordered, and Tobias had no doubt he would do exactly as he was told.

Bradford stood and gave Nikki a wave. "Come along, boy. Looks like Tobias is going to actually use that antique desk, and I wouldn't want to discourage him."

"Should I put your name on the list for one of my technique weekends, Bradford?" Tobias smiled as he watched Phan strip down to nothing but a leather cock ring.

"No, thank you, I might be bored." Bradford winked at Tobias and then looked Phan over with a critical eye. "Come along, Nikki, suddenly I have plans for you." Bradford turned and left the room.

"Do you think I'd bore him, boy?"

"No, sir." Phan knelt by the desk, his face serene and his cock filling. "Absolutely not, sir."

"That's what I thought." Tobias took his coffee and the files to the leather chair and began to go through the list of dates from Bradford, putting things on his personal calendar and flagging events to cross reference with his own schedule at the farm. Every once in a while, he'd pet Phan or tug his hair, just because he could.

Tobias absolutely adored his job.

5

It was mid-afternoon when Tobias decided to take a break. He'd had two meetings, kept an eye on Phantom, done a pile of paperwork, stayed at his desk until Phan's eyes had gone glassy from boredom, and then he'd woken Phan up with a few stripes on his ass just because Tobias could do that. He liked it when Phan had lines on his butt.

Tobias had taken lunch in his office with both Noah and Phan, and then Noah had gone to change into his dressier clothes; when he was working on security, both Bradford and Tobias liked Noah to have a certain aura of subtle authority. He was still a submissive, but he was Tobias' sub -- no one else had any right to be anything but respectful of Noah. Therefore, he wore a suit or, at the very least, proper trousers and a button-down shirt.

They were still working on the suits; Noah had resisted for a long time, but Tobias was eagerly awaiting the new acquisitions from the tailor's.

"I think we should go see how things are working out on the third floor," Tobias said to Phan. Without waiting for a reply, though he did hear the quiet "Yes, sir," Tobias left his office and started up the stairs with Phan at his heel. He hadn't told Phan to dress, he realized belatedly.

Phan didn't seem to care.

Still, Bradford might care that Tobias was parading naked subs around, so Tobias quickened his pace as they went up the steps. This, however, merely made Phan's cock bob and sway and draw more attention to itself.

"Oh, dear." Tobias stopped at the second floor landing and looked at it. "We seem to have a problem."

Phan grinned impishly.

"I'll tape it down when we get upstairs, shall I?"

Phan winced. Tape wasn't a lot of fun when it was coming off. "Yes, sir."

Tobias rolled his eyes. "Stay here." He went into the nearest open room and walked to a cabinet. Every playroom was well stocked, and this one was no different. He got a spool of red bondage tape and returned to Phan in the hallway. "With this, boy. I wouldn't damage you, you know that."

Phan still didn't look overly delighted as Tobias taped Phan's erection to his thigh.

"There. Much better." Tobias gave Phan a pat on the head and sent Phan to put the tape away, then led him up to the third floor. "Let's see if we can find Noah without looking in every room or calling him."

Phan nodded and looked thoughtfully at the doors, some open and some closed. "He's probably in one of the closed ones, sir. If he's running tests on the current equipment to see what needs to be updated, I mean."

Tobias agreed. "Okay. Pick one."

After considering the choices, Phan pointed to a door on the left, and Tobias went and knocked lightly.

"Um... just a minute," Noah's voice called through the door. There was a scraping noise and the sound of something metallic clattering to the floor. Moments later, Noah unlocked and opened the door. He looked artfully disheveled, had a smudge of something on his chin, and held a wrench in one hand. "Sorry, I was up on the ladder and... oh. I beg your pardon, sir." Noah lowered his eyes instantly and slipped to the floor on his knees.

Tobias stroked Noah's hair lightly. "Good boy." He walked past Noah into the room and pointed to the refrigerator. "Phantom, see if it's being kept stocked even though the room is off the roster while Noah does his upgrades."

Phan scurried off to the fridge and Tobias looked around for a moment, then simply admired Noah on his knees. "Are you working hard?"

"Yes, sir," Noah answered, eyes dutifully on the floor. "I've found the issue, and it looks like it should be an easy install once we order the new equipment. This camera just needed a temporary repair."

"Is it offline now?" Tobias looked around the room again, taking in the bed, the open toy chest, and the chains on the wall.

"There's water, sir," Phan said, zipping into place next to Noah and going to his knees as well. "But no grapes."

"Don't interrupt, boy. I asked Noah a question."

Phan's face fell, and he stared hard at the floor.

"Yes, sir. I've just finished the repair. I'll have to call downstairs to security and have them turn it back on."

"Who's in charge down there this afternoon?" He wandered over to the toys and picked up a flogger at random. "Pat?"

"No, sir. Pat is on evenings -- day shift is Shiloh."

Tobias nodded and dragged the tails of the flogger through his hand. "Very well." He crossed to the in-house phone and called security.

"Good afternoon, sir, this is Shiloh. How can I help you?"

"Hello, Shiloh, it's Tobias. I just wanted to let you know that I'll be using the room Noah was working in. There's no video feed, and I expect there will be yelling. If you wish, you may station someone outside the door."

There was a short pause. "Do you wish that, sir?"

Tobias grinned. "No. But if Bradford insists, I won't make anyone's life hard. Clear it with him, if you'd like." Then he hung up and looked at his boys. "Strip, Noah."

Phan blinked. "'Strip, Noah,' or 'strip Noah?'"

With a snort, Tobias pointed to the corner. "Guess. You can go over there and wait your turn. Does your tape need to be adjusted?"

"I don't think so, sir." Phan looked at his trapped cock without enthusiasm. "It seems to be doing what you wanted."

"Aching?"

"Yes, sir."

"Perfect. Noah?"

"Yes, sir." Noah had hesitated, apparently waiting for Tobias to get Phan sorted out. He stood this time and began to remove his clothes, carefully hanging them over the rungs of the ladder, presumably so he could still look presentable when Tobias was finished with him. Once naked, he remained standing and presented neatly for Tobias, chin up, but eyes low.

Tobias eyed him critically. "I want to play, pet. What shall we do?"

Phan looked like he had suggestions, but Tobias ignored him, alone in his corner.

Noah's gaze seemed to turn inward for a moment as he thought about Tobias' request. "Well, sir," Noah said quietly. "The chains in here are heavy and they make great sounds... the ladder is sturdy... um. Play, as in play? Or play as in role play? Or just play at seeing how long Phan can sit still?" Noah grinned a little at his last statement.

"Play as in your skin is too free of marks, I'm horny, and I can do as I please." Tobias grinned right back at him. "So I suggest you get in the mood really, really fast."

"Yes, sir!" Noah barked in answer, somewhat reminiscent of his patrolling days. He even widened his stance a bit and straightened his shoulders more. "Please, sir."

"On your knees." Tobias walked behind Noah and helped by shoving Noah off balance as soon as Noah started to comply. "Sloppy," he said mildly, whipping Noah's back. The skin across the center of Noah's back went white for a moment and then blushed up a warm pink. "Don't you think, Phan?"

Phan was watching with wide, envious eyes. "I think whatever Sir wants me to think."

Tobias laughed. "Sir thinks you're too hopeful. Noah, are you getting hard for me yet?"

"Yes, sir!" Noah responded in a rush, scrambling a bit to get his knees under him and straighten up. "Yours, sir."

"Oh, absolutely. I never doubt that." Tobias examined his back and put a guiding hand on Noah's shoulder. "Hands and knees, pet. Tell me if the floor is too hard."

"Floor's fine, sir." Noah shifted forward, placing his hands flat and shoulder width apart. "Thank you, sir." With the exception of one room, all of Bradford's playroom floors were rubberized, mostly for easy clean-up, but it had the added effect of being easier on the knees than hardwood.

Tobias caught Noah peering down the length of his own

body toward his erection, which angled stiffly away from his abdomen. "It is a lovely thing," Tobias said calmly. "But it's mine. Eyes on the floor. Phan, put a ring on Noah and then go back to your corner." He started to unbutton his own shirt.

"Yes, sir!" Phan dashed to the chest and found a wide leather cock ring, then hurried to Noah. "You're so lucky," he said as he wrapped it around Noah's erection.

"I am." Noah's words were followed by a soft grunt as Phan positioned the ring. "Don't have so much fun with that."

"But I like it." Phan kissed Noah's cheek and retreated to his corner, where he seemed to have trouble finding a position that didn't make him want to wiggle. Or maybe Phan was just feeling extra wiggly. Tobias couldn't be sure.

"No one gets to come unless I say so." Tobias tossed his shirt on the bed and whipped Noah's back again. "Understood?"

"Understood, sir," Noah hissed. He shrank away from the sting at first but then relaxed, arching upward. He took a very noticeable deep breath and released the tension as he exhaled.

"But you should feel free to yell and to beg. I rather like that part." Tobias walked around Noah and adjusted his own erection, giving himself a squeeze as he did so. "I like it a lot. God, how long has it been since I marked you? You poor thing, I've been neglecting you."

"Not neglected, sir, just..." Noah paused thoughtfully. "Used differently. More, please, sir?" Noah skin broke out in goosebumps as if he were already anticipating the next blow.

"You do ask so nicely." Tobias hit him again and frowned. "Not noisy enough." It did, however, make Noah's skin glow. Tobias crossed to the toy box once more and examined the selection of crops before picking one. It was supple and bendy, and when he whacked the bed with it, the sound was a nice, loud snap. "Better. Breathe, pet. This might hurt."

Noah nodded and took a very deep breath, which was followed by a long exhale. Everything about him seemed to lose tension and go slack; he even let his head hang loosely between his shoulders. "Ready, sir." Noah's voice was soft but encouraging.

Tobias lifted his arm and brought it down hard, the sound of the crop on Noah's ass filling the room. He heard Phan moan underneath Noah's cry, but Tobias didn't look, unable to tear his gaze away from the perfect red welt rising up. "Again," he said, lifting his arm and letting fly once more.

"Sir!" Noah didn't hold back his reactions, letting his voice fill the room as the crop landed solidly against his skin with a satisfying snap. His body shivered, and he arched and bowed with the sting. He lifted his head and cried out, "Thank you, sir!"

Smiling, pleased with both his submissive and with the marks he was making, Tobias kept at it, laying down stroke after stroke until more than half a dozen welts covered Noah's ass. "What do you think, Phan?"

Phan moaned again. "Beautiful, sir. He's beautiful."

"He is." Tobias had to agree with that. He looked at Noah, who was shaking and making soft sounds now that the cries had died away. Tobias tossed the crop to the side and knelt behind Noah to trace one of the welts with his finger. "How do you feel, pet?"

Noah hissed with the touch and started to speak, but his voice was rough. He cleared his throat and tried again. "I feel good, sir. Sore, sensitive. Grounded. Want more, please, sir."

Noah shifted and arched his ass into Tobias' touch. "I'm yours, sir. Don't stop yet, please?"

"Not stopping. Merely changing the torture." Tobias dipped his head and licked the welt he'd just touched. "Stay very still for me." He licked again and tried to remember what all he'd seen among the toys. Sometimes impromptu scenes were exactly what he needed; there was, however, no real substitute for his own inventory of items.

"Yes... sir." Noah moaned. Tobias could almost feel the way that his boy was fighting the desire to move under his touch. "So good, sir."

In the corner, Tobias could hear Phan shifting his weight. A glance told him that Phan was watching Noah so intently he probably didn't even know he'd moved. The tape keeping Phantom's cock against his thigh looked like it was uncomfortable enough to make Phan at least pay attention to himself, but no. Phantom did everything with such concentration sometimes that he could ignore even that.

Tobias licked Noah's welts again and stood up. "Stay," he said casually as he went to see what else he could find. Perhaps something soft. Maybe another crop? Maybe he'd just give in and find the lube, he wasn't sure.

Noah stayed, as Tobias knew he would, because he'd been told to stay. He stayed still, also because he'd been ordered to. But he wasn't quiet about it. "Love you, sir. It's so good to just be here and be yours," Noah said in a stream of consciousness, as if the words were just flowing from him.

Tobias dug down in the trunk and pulled out a wickedly huge dildo. "Hmm."

Phan whimpered.

"Not today, boy." He set it aside and made a mental note for Phan's benefit, then found another one that was slightly more realistic in size but had an interesting ridge and a button to vibrate the toy as well. "Now, this has possibilities." He took the toy and a second crop back to Noah. "What do you think, pet?" He didn't wait for a reply, merely lashed Noah's ass once more.

"Thank you, sir!" Noah shouted as his only reply. A red stripe stood out boldly against his skin.

"I do like to hear thanks." Tobias studied Noah's ass and tried to decide if he wanted to leave it at welts or if he wanted blood; he was in the mood to take as much as he could get, but Noah had to actually move around. "I think I'll have to settle for a few more of these and then just use you." He hit Noah again across the top of his thighs.

Noah cried out sharply. He was panting now, breathing through the sting. He rocked backward slightly as if begging to be used just exactly the way Tobias had in mind. "Yes, sir. Please, sir."

Tobias beckoned Phan to them. "Hold him up. That's it, understand?"

"Yes, sir!" Phan rushed to Noah and held him up, almost cradling him. "Yes, sir. Uh-huh."

Tobias looked at the dildo and abruptly changed his plans. There wasn't really room for a slow torture, not with the way his cock was aching. He was the Dom, he could do what he wanted. He could take his own pleasure. With a negligent toss, he got rid of the toy and opened his trousers.

He stepped around Noah's legs and presented his erection to Phan. "Wet me."

Phan's eyes went huge and his mouth opened automatically. Tobias wasn't sure if it was surprise or compliance; it hardly mattered.

Tobias caught Noah turning his head slightly to watch as Tobias pushed the head of his cock between Phan's lips. Tobias heard the boy moan, the low hum mingling with

Phan's own sounds. "Sir," Noah said softly, voice deep and full of need.

Tobias fucked Phan's mouth for a moment, his own eyes drifting closed. He'd really have to make a point of getting more head from Phan; maybe at his desk. His prick throbbed at the thought, and he pulled away. "Enough."

Phan made a soft noise of protest but fell silent when Tobias glared at him. "Yes, sir," he said with a squeak. He was breathing almost as hard as Noah.

His trousers still on his hips, Tobias fetched lube. "I'd really rather not damage you, pet." He would also really rather just plunge in. Noah would probably be able to take it just fine and love it. He was certainly in the right headspace for having it dry and rough, with only Phan's spit to ease the way.

"Yours, sir. Want you, sir." Noah wasn't being particularly still anymore. His hips rolled gently, up and then back and then down again as if grinding himself slowly against something invisible, and his cock leaked, leaving a small pool of liquid on the floor beneath him. Tobias tried to get a look at his eyes and found them glassy and unfocused.

He was beautiful. Noah was always beautiful, but when he was floating in subspace and offering everything up, he was stunning. Tobias' nature roared within him, demanding he claim what was his.

There was no need to deny either of them -- any of them. Without a word, Tobias tossed the lube aside, unused, and positioned himself behind Noah to take what he wanted. His cockhead pushed at Noah's body and demanded entrance.

Noah's body opened for him, and as Tobias pushed deep inside, Noah let out a long, relieved groan. "Oh, yes, sir. Thank you, sir," Noah stammered. Tobias felt Noah tightening around his cock, and the boy moaned again even before Tobias began to thrust.

There was very little doubt in Tobias' mind that Noah was going to hurt for a day or so. And if he was going to hurt, he might as well hurt for something completely worthwhile. He held onto Noah's hips and pushed in fast and hard, burying himself deep. "Hold on tight."

"Ah!" Noah reached out and tangled his hands and arms with Phan's for support. He pressed his head into Phan's lap, and his rough sobs and hungry sounds were muffled against Phan's bare skin. "Sir! Yes! Sir!"

Gritting his teeth to keep from embarrassing them all by coming too soon, Tobias fucked Noah with long, even strokes. He closed his eyes to block out Phan's face, hungry-eyed and staring, and wished he could block the sounds Noah and Phan were both making. Focusing entirely on his own pleasure, Tobias' hips rocked and his fingers dug into Noah's hips until he was about to burst.

Noah's back arched up hard and his breath grew tight. "Ring... ring, sir. Please! Please may I come, please?" His voice was raspy and thick.

"Not until I'm done." Tobias could barely speak himself, what with his orgasm barreling down on top of him. "Fuck." He closed his eyes tighter as Noah's body spasmed around him, likely the anticipation making him shudder. Tobias arched his own back and sped up, the friction of the dry fuck making everything sharp and bright. "Sweetheart!" He came in a rush, his pulse pounding in his temples.

"Oh, God, sir!" Tobias was dimly aware of Noah's sobs and the way that Noah's body continued to move against him. "Please, please, sir! Oh, fuck. Please!" Noah's head was still resting on Phan's knees; his shoulders shook and his skin was damp with sweat.

Tobias reached down and took the ring off Noah with a fast jerk of his hand. "Come for me," he ordered, wanting to feel it.

Tobias was barely able to get the words out before Noah's hips jerked. "Yes!" Noah's orgasm shook his entire body, rocking him between Tobias and Phan. His cries were a mix of gratitude and soft sounds of relief that lasted long after his erection was spent and his body grew heavy against Tobias' thighs.

"Good boy," Tobias whispered. He pressed kisses to Noah's shoulders and sighed, content. "Good boy, Noah."

Phan made a thoroughly pathetic noise.

"Oh, right." Tobias lifted his head. "You and I are going to find some time for a bit of knife play tomorrow. You can come now."

Phan gasped and shuddered. "Thank you, sir! Oh, God!" His hands scrabbled at the tape, but Tobias could see that it wasn't going to do him any good.

Tobias leaned slightly to the side and watched Phan's cock throb and gush, come streaking on his thigh and getting in Noah's hair. They were all going to have to shower.

Good.

"Very nice," Tobias said as he eased out of Noah. "Clean each other off for me, please."

Noah didn't miss a beat. He reached up to help Phan gently pull away the rest of the tape and then bathed Phan with his tongue, running it up Phan's thigh and then around the head of his cock.

"Oh." Tobias watched and grinned. "Nice."

"Very!" Phan gasped and wiggled, almost slithering on the floor to return the favor. "Best cleaning service ever."

Noah lifted his head and looked at Phan, and although

Tobias couldn't see his expression, Phan's grin said it all. Noah kissed Phan quickly and then pulled himself to his feet. "Towel," he mumbled as he made his way somewhat unsteadily to the playroom's adjoining bathroom.

"Rats." Phan cheerfully bounded to his feet and followed along. "I'll start the water, sir."

"Thank you." Tobias looked around the room as he stood up and smiled. Not bad for spur of the moment. He stripped off the rest of his clothes and headed to the shower, leaving the mess for his subs to take care of. After they'd tended to him, of course.

6

Thursday morning found them all back out at the farm. Tobias didn't have any interviews scheduled for the remainder of the week, and Noah knew that, as much as he liked his office at the club, Tobias preferred his quiet study in the country.

Noah himself didn't care much one way or the other; his ass was sore and his skin was sensitive and he was just happy to be of service wherever his Master wanted him. He'd been well used the day before and had been floating on the endorphins ever since. Everything was easier in subspace: no decisions to make, no stress, no worries. There was nothing he needed to do other than what he was doing right now -- keeping house with Phan.

He opened the oven and looked in, nodding at the way his banana bread was baking. It filled the kitchen with the warm, homey smell that had always drawn him into the kitchen as a kid to see what his mom was up to.

"Mmm." Noah hummed softly as he closed the oven. He crossed to the counter and picked up Mrs. M's recipe card, flipping it over in his fingers before filing it away in her cheerful yellow recipe box.

"She's got some really nice ones in there." Phan came up behind him and slipped an arm around Noah's waist. "I can't get the cookies right, though."

Noah leaned into Phan. He was always so warm and soft. "No? The oatmeal ones are pretty easy."

"The chocolate chip ones are always flat and dry. I think she put her baking soda in hot water first, but I can't make it work."

"I don't know that trick, either." Noah turned to face Phan. "Never got a chance to ask her to show me."

Phan's eyes filled up. "I did. And she showed me. But there's so much more, you know? Sometimes..." He sighed and let go of Noah. "I'll start the dishes, okay?"

Noah nodded. "Thanks," he replied, but wondered if he ought to say more. He let Phan move away to the sink, watching as Phan picked up a sponge and started in on the big mixing bowl. Noah missed Mrs. M, too. He missed her quiet, constant presence, her knowing looks, her kind smile. Though he'd never had quite the same relationship with her that Phan had. He looked away from Phan and wiped down the counter with a dishtowel.

"I wish I'd known her like you did."

Phan nodded, his head bowed as he washed the bowl. "She liked you a lot. She told me."

Noah smiled. "Well, that much I know. She didn't really make it a secret." He took the clean bowl from Phan. "How about I dry?"

Phan let him take the bowl and reached for the mixing spoon. "She was like that -- if she liked you, she made sure you knew. She said that the worst thing in the world was that people didn't know they were loved. So she made a point of being right out there with her affection."

Noah glanced sidelong at Phan, who, in contrast to Mrs. Miller, was generally more about saying things by not actually saying them at all -- this moment included. "I'm... sure you appreciated that," Noah goaded.

For a long moment Phan didn't say anything at all. Then he nodded, the gesture jerky. "She told me she loved me even before Sir did. She... she was the first person to love me since I was a child." His shoulders started to shake, and he put the mixing spoon back in the water.

Noah put down the dry mixing bowl and tossed his towel on the counter. "Oh, hon," he said quickly, slipping his arms around Phan's waist. "She might have been the first, but she wasn't the last."

Phan curled into him immediately, tears sliding down his cheeks. "She was like my grandmother, you know? I could talk to her about almost anything, and she just nodded and told me she believed in me. Every single time. She helped me so much, and I miss her all the time."

Noah nodded, hugging Phan close. "You do know that's completely normal, right, Phan? I mean, to miss someone that much? It just shows how much you loved her, and that's okay, you know? It's totally okay."

Phan nodded, his face still pushed against Noah's chest. "I feel bad, though. Because when there are too many people here, touching her things, I worry. What if they break her sugar bowl? And now that her room is gone, those things of hers are really important to me."

Noah winced a little. The gym that had replaced Mrs. Miller's bedroom upstairs had been his request. While he understood the impulse, he honestly thought it would have been creepy to keep her room the way she had left it, and truly believed that she would have wanted Noah and Phan to put their stamp on the house. Phan hadn't really protested at the time; he'd seemed sad, but they had all been sad then.

"I know, Phan. I understand, I do." Hopefully their plans to expand the bunkhouse would help. Noah made a mental note to ask his Master to get started on those renovations as soon as possible.

"I know." Phan's tears eased off but he sighed deeply, and didn't let go. "I do want to move on, kitten. I do. And I wouldn't want a museum for her. I think I just don't know how to grieve. I mean, I'm still learning how to feel, right?"

Well, that was true enough. It had been a long while before Phan had been able to accept the things he did feel as okay, before he stopped punishing himself for being happy and apologizing for wanting or needing just about anything. He wasn't raised with love, not the gentle kind that Mrs. M had obviously offered him.

"It's a lot to take in at once, huh?" Noah asked, just trying to help Phan find words to get some of this out of his system.

"It makes me kind of embarrassed," Phan mumbled. "No one else seems to hang onto things as long as me. It underlines how emotionally immature I am; it's like I'm thirteen."

"But that's a good thing, Phan. Most people forget their emotions after a while. Lose touch with them. You remember. You are honoring her by keeping her memory present. That's not something to be embarrassed about." Noah laughed softly. "Although you certainly have a teenage libido," he joked.

"Oh, and you don't?" Phan gave him a slightly watery grin. "I need to keep up with you so Sir doesn't go without."

"So, really, he's the one with the libido issues?" Noah put a little space between them, letting Phan get some air. "You know, Phan, everyone deals with emotions, with grief, differently. Don't be embarrassed, just be honest. Sir and I both appreciate that, and I'm sure Mrs. M did, too. You don't hide anything else." Noah glanced down at Phan's crotch, which seemed remarkably under control at the moment.

"That's kinda my defense." Phan rolled his eyes and looked around the kitchen. "I put it all out there, every bit of me, and don't give a flying fuck what anyone thinks, aside from Sir and you. And a few others. But this is different. It's... Elizabeth was different. There wasn't anyone like her, ever." He paused and made a face. "I'm going to have to talk to my therapist about this, aren't I?"

Noah couldn't help but grin. "Yep."

"Damn it. Dr. Brewer will be thrilled -- it's been weeks since she's had something to sink her teeth into."

Noah gave Phan's hand a squeeze. "So, you finished the dusting?" He walked over and shut off the oven as the timer started to beep.

"Not yet. I have to do upstairs. What's next on your schedule?"

"Well, I thought I'd bring a slice of the banana bread to Sir while it's still warm and then I'd get the vacuum out. We should think about dinner, too. Oh, and I think I heard Sir talking with Bradford about dinner out here... maybe tomorrow night?"

"For who?" Phan looked at him with a tiny frown. "I don't know if we have groceries for any more than about six people."

"I don't know. I'll ask. Hopefully just Master Bradford and Nikki." Noah pulled the hot bread from the oven and set it on a cooling rack. "Want a bite?"

"No, thank you. You're making me fat. And asking Sir is always a good idea." Phan nodded and went into the pantry. "There's enough things for breakfast if they stay and want pancakes."

"Fat," Noah snorted. "Right." He pulled out a knife and cut a thick slice, placing it on a plate. He cut it too early, he knew, and could almost hear Mrs. M chastising him about not waiting long enough for the crust to set, but this was how he liked it best, and his Master did, too.

"Put lots of butter on Sir's." Phan leaned in and sniffed. "Good job, kitten. She'd be proud. Except you cut it way too soon."

"I know," Noah winked at Phan. "I practically heard her say so." He headed for the refrigerator and pulled out the butter.

"I hear her all the time in this house." Phan put one of his hands on the wall and nodded, probably to himself. "All the time. That's why I love it so much."

Noah gave Phan a kiss on the cheek as he passed by. "It's really grown on me. I was such a city mouse when I met Sir." He pulled out a knife and drowned the hot slice of bread in butter.

"You're still a city mouse. So am I, I guess. But I love the way this house feels."

"Me, too." Noah picked up the plate and headed for the door. "I'll be upstairs with the vacuum in an hour or so."

"Not much sense in dusting, then. Maybe I'll polish the dining room."

"Not a bad idea, especially if we're having guests tomorrow." He winked at Phan. "You okay, hon?"

"I'm as okay as I ever am." Phan shook his head. "I'm fine. I'll wash the sink; you go take that to Sir before it cools."

"Thanks, hon." Noah left Phan and the sound of running water behind as he headed across the house to his Master's office, but he carried some of Phan's grief with him.

7

F riday evening, Tobias had Noah and Phan dressed for company in their best polished leather and silver fixings. Their collars gleamed and were on display, both of them wearing silk, open-necked shirts, and Tobias had them waiting at the door for their guests.

"Are we all ready?" he asked, straightening his shirt cuffs. Phantom had helped him dress, so Tobias was feeling particularly relaxed.

"Yes, sir," Noah said gently. He still seemed to be holding onto some of the euphoria of Wednesday's very worthwhile diversion. Tobias noted his perfect posture and the content expression on his face.

Phan nodded, his hands behind his back and his eyes down. His hair was artfully up, coppery peaks going where he'd gelled them to point. "All set, sir. The wine is breathing on the sideboard and your scotch decanter is on your desk."

"Good, good." Tobias opened the front door and stepped onto the porch just as Jorge pulled into the lane and started toward the house. "And there they are, right on time."

Noah and Phan hurried out to stand behind Tobias. Of

course Bradford was right on time; he made an art form of being practically perfect when it came to social graces.

"Good evening, Tobias," Bradford said as he stepped out of the car. Jorge waited for Nikki to climb out behind him and then shut the car door.

"Hello, old friend. Come in, please. Nikki looks well." Tobias nodded to Jorge, dismissing him, and held the door wide for Bradford and his boy.

Bradford nodded at Nikki, and Nikki answered quickly, bowing his head even deeper.

"Thank you, Master Tobias."

Bradford grinned in a way that Tobias knew meant he was joking. "I didn't get time to give him a good spanking today, so we'll hope he behaves."

Tobias had to laugh. Nikki was probably the most consistently well-behaved sub he knew. Even Noah and Phan would step out of line on occasion, but he'd never seen Nikki be anything less than exactly what Bradford wanted him to be.

"Well, I'll keep him away from bad influences, then." Tobias led the way into his office and crossed to his desk. "Have a seat. Noah and Phan have duties in the kitchen, but supper should be served shortly."

"Wonderful," Bradford sank neatly into one of Tobias' chairs. "Do they need Nikki's help?"

"I have no idea. I don't cook if I can help it. Noah?"

"If Nikki would like to help us set the table, sir...?"

"Perfect. Run along, Nikki."

"Pleasure, sir." Nikki stood and joined Noah and Phan.

"I think he'd actually prefer it anyway." Bradford smiled.

"He'd rather be with the rascals than with us stodgy Doms?" Tobias grinned and poured two glasses of scotch. "Drink?"

"Have I ever turned down good scotch?" Bradford reached for one of the glasses. "It is a good one, I hope?"

Tobias snorted.

"The farm looks marvelous, Tobias," Bradford went on. "When was the last time I visited? It seems ages ago."

"I'm not sure. So, yes. Ages." Tobias sat in the chair across from Bradford and leaned back. "Are things quiet at the club? Sorry I wasn't in much this week."

"You're not the least bit sorry, you liar." Bradford laughed. "The club was very quiet, actually. Noah's security equipment is in, the new calendar has been sent out, the staff remains top notch. I'm not even sure what they need me for anymore."

Tobias snorted. "I'm not even going to dignify that with a response. I noticed the membership applications are leveling off but renewals are up."

"Yes, isn't that nice? We have a full, happy membership." Bradford sipped his scotch.

"Happy is good. I value happy." Tobias smiled and sank farther into his chair. "I think that if we expand the guest services out here, the in-town teaching sessions might pick up, too."

"If they pick up too much more, you'll have to hire help," Bradford warned. "Your boys, especially Phan, seem quite overwhelmed enough without even more training on your calendar. Am I wrong?"

"Well." Tobias shrugged one shoulder. "Phantom's issue seemed to be more about what happens here and keeping it small. In town, he does quite well having Doms test on him. Not that I'm suggesting he do that any more than he is -- he only has the one body, and I'm quite fond of it. But I can see doing, say, an afternoon class on technique with a specific tool."

"What a wonderful idea," Bradford replied. The wheels were obviously turning behind those grinning eyes. Tobias wasn't sure if he should be excited or terrified by Bradford's slow smile.

"Of course; it was mine." Tobias took his usual tactic of bulling his way through. To give Bradford an inch was to give him several miles of lucrative interstate highway. "You'd have to pay me, of course. I'm on a fixed income, you know."

Bradford laughed. "Oh, my dear friend, you insult me. Of course I would pay you. In point of fact, you would pay yourself. It's your budget, after all. I'd just need to increase it accordingly."

"Have I ever told you how much I love the way you think? When you're agreeing with me, I mean." Tobias sipped his drink and looked around his office. He loved this room; of the whole house, it was probably the one he'd marked the most as just his. There was the bedroom, of course, and the safe room, but the office was a public face, and one he was comfortable showing to everyone who walked in the door, in the lifestyle or not. The stables were an entirely different case -- very much him, but certainly not for the general public. "You know, I think this room is the only place in the house where you fit in just perfectly."

"Provided I'm agreeing with you." Bradford sipped his drink and grinned. "Are you suggesting I'm too overbearing for farm life?"

"Yes. Also, you're too neat, and possibly too prissy." Tobias set his glass down. "But that's okay; you're exemplary at what you do. Will you be taking a class or two from me? Merely to foster goodwill among the Doms, I mean." Oh, that would be fun.

Bradford raised an eyebrow. "Was that a dare?"

"If you'd like it to be." Tobias beamed at him, delighted with the idea. "I'd love to help you brush up on some skills."

Bradford set his empty glass down on Tobias' desk. "Very well, your first class will be in the nuances of... the tawse, hm? And I'll attend. It's not an instrument I use with Nikki, so I'm sure I'm rusty."

"Phantom will be delighted. Or not -- I'll have to check with Dr. Brewer." Tobias frowned slightly. "The tawse might not get a lot of people in. Now, if you want a larger audience, we can move to knives. After Phan heals a bit. We had a good week."

"Knives... now, there's a thought. And I do hope you'll show off those marks for me. Knives it is. Pick a date and I'll get the word out."

Tobias looked toward the door and raised his voice to call, "Noah! A moment, if you're able to come without dinner being ruined!"

Bradford raised an eyebrow as they waited for Noah to appear. It was only a few moments.

"Sorry if I kept you waiting, sir, I had a dish in my hands when you called." Noah hurried to his knees beside Tobias' chair.

"You did fine, pet. Now. Please refresh my memory about my schedule for, say, the next three Wednesday afternoons?" Tobias carded his fingers through Noah's hair.

"Yes, sir. You generally like to keep Wednesdays open as you spend them at the club catching up from the weekend. I don't believe you have any set plans in the next month or so, but two weekends from now is another group session here, and so you might be particularly busy the Wednesday after that."

"Who needs a day planner?" Bradford snorted.

"Not me. I have a Noah." Tobias smiled and petted Noah

again. "Sometimes I do ask him to write it all down for me, though. So, Wednesdays may or may not work, as he's right - - that's my catch-up day. Noah, if I were to have a teaching afternoon at the club, what day would you suggest?"

"Well, sir, we're often in the city Thursday and Friday when you have appointments. Maybe a Thursday afternoon?"

Tobias looked at Bradford. "A class wouldn't take much prep, just a booked room and an hour or so for me to gather and order my thoughts. Say, this coming Thursday?"

"Oh, good lord. Nikki!"

Nikki appeared even faster than Noah had. "Sir?"

"Do you happen to know my schedule for Thursday?"

Nikki nodded. "Your two p.m. cancelled; the afternoon is open, sir."

"Thank you, Nikki." Bradford looked at Tobias. "There you are, I'm open after two p.m."

"Who needs a day planner?" Tobias smirked. "Phan!"

"Coming, sir!" There was a clatter and the sound of Phan's bare feet on the hardwood. "Here, sir!"

Tobias tried very hard not to laugh. "Good boy. Now we're all together again. Show Master Bradford your shoulders, dear."

Phan preened visibly as he turned and shed his shirt. Tobias' name stood out in red lines like cat scratches on the skin.

Bradford actually stood to get a better look. He studied the marks critically for a moment and then sat down again. "Tobias, I do believe you are as completely full of yourself as I am. No wonder we're such good friends. Nice work."

"Thank you." Tobias let Phan leave his shirt off. "So, Phan. We're going to do it again, with an audience. Next week."

Phan turned around and though his eyes were downcast his smile was huge. "Thank you, sir!"

"I'll have to have a discussion with Nikki," Bradford said. "We haven't used sharps between us yet, and I don't know where he stands on the practice. If not Nikki, I'll bring someone else on whom I can practice. Nikki, remind me to get the word out tomorrow."

"Yes, sir." Nikki's voice gave no indication whether he would be joining Bradford or not.

Tobias looked at his boys and nodded. "Supper, please. That's all for now."

Everyone got up and left in a rush, leaving Bradford and Tobias to grin at each other before following them. "We are lucky bastards, Tobias," Bradford remarked getting up from his chair.

"We planned it this way," Tobias reminded him. "From the time we were hanging out with Luca, learning from the best. Yes?" He got up as well and made sure the scotch was stoppered, ready for later in the evening.

"And now we're the best, yes."

"We are, indeed." Tobias led him into the dining room, and they decided between them to let the subs dine with them, even allowing them to sit at the table for a change.

Phan and Nikki didn't seem terribly comfortable with it, but they did their best. It never failed to intrigue Tobias how Phan resisted things like sitting at the table when they had company.

Dinner was wonderful, mostly due to Noah doing all the cooking and Phan doing the helping.

After the dishes were cleared and all three of the subs were taking care of the chores, Tobias came to the real reason he'd invited Bradford out to the farm. "So, shall we go and look at the guest house and come up with a few design ideas?"

"Ah... I knew there had to be an ulterior motive." Bradford stood, looking a little uncomfortably full. "My goodness, dinner was delicious."

"Of course. That's why Phan's looking so healthy these days." Tobias headed to the hall to get his coat and the keys. "Right, Phan?"

"Right, sir. Healthy. Not fat."

"Just so, Phan. You look marvelous." Bradford stopped on his way out and added. "And so do those marks." Tobias saw him wink at Phan before they left the room together.

"You're going to make him trip if you flatter him too much." Sure enough, Tobias heard Phan squeak and a chair fall over.

"I don't flatter, Tobias, you should know better. I only tell the truth. He does look marvelous, and he's one that needs to know that. It's remarkable, really. I was concerned about this triad of yours." Bradford waved his hand vaguely in the air before continuing. "Supportive and hopeful, but naturally concerned under the circumstances. I'm thrilled to see I had absolutely nothing to worry about."

Tobias smiled as he fetched his keys. "We're disgustingly happy, really. Even Phan's current issue is relatively minor. I put a large part of his healing on Noah; I couldn't have done what he's had such success at."

"It's a peer thing. These boys are smarter than most people give them credit for, I think." Bradford followed Tobias outside and down the dirt and gravel road to the barns.

"They are. But then, I tell you things I couldn't tell them, so there we are. And here we are." Bradford had seen the bunkhouse before, of course, but without this purpose in mind. Tobias unlocked the door and let him into what was essentially a large building of bedrooms. "So."

"It's... rustic," Bradford offered uncertainly. He moved down the hall, looking in doorways.

"It's functional. We need to make it functional, welcoming, homey, and comfortable." Tobias opened doors to bedrooms. "The rooms are big. We can either add on or lose a room or two to make a kitchen and lounge."

"Well, there's no reason why you can't put two Doms together in the larger rooms so you don't lose numbers... but a kitchen is a must, a second bathroom for sure, possibly even three. Ah." Bradford stopped in a bedroom at the back of the house that had a window that looked out over the back end of the property. "A lounge in here? You could even push it back and enlarge it, open it up with some french doors to a patio... maybe a grill, a hot tub. Hm?"

"Um. I don't want a hotel, Bradford."

"Okay, so skip the hot tub." Bradford shrugged.

Tobias rolled his eyes. "Okay. So you come here for a weekend retreat with your boy, a place where you can really put him in subspace and have him stay there for a couple of days. Do you want to share a bedroom?"

"Mmm. No. Good point." Bradford looked up. "Maybe add a story?"

"Yes, maybe. Bedrooms up and common areas down?" Tobias looked around, picturing pine and hardwood and white wash. "That could work."

"That would be logical. You could even keep a couple of the downstairs rooms, too. Maybe add a library or a quiet room down here for those that want quiet but don't want to hide out in their rooms."

"Oh, very nice. Like my safe room, maybe. I could incorporate that into the weekend session talks." Tobias looked down the narrow hall. "This needs tile and to be widened. Are we rich enough to do this?"

Bradford snorted. "In the short term, it might sting a bit, but long term, well, these weekends aren't cheap. It'll get paid for." He looked around. "It needs better lighting, too."

"Skylights, bigger windows, white walls. We need texture, too. Are there any artisans at the club?" Tobias' palms were starting to itch like they did when he was planning new things for his stables.

"Mike is a carpenter, and I think Scott does mosaic work. Hmm."

"Any painters? Sculptors? I'm not so much concerned with the carpentry, but the art might be nice to have done in-house, so to speak."

"You mean like Phan?" Bradford looked at Tobias.

"Well, yes. But he can't do a whole house. I'd never see him again. And fabrics would be nice to have."

"I'll have to look into it, I don't know off the top of my head, but I'm sure there must be someone. You know who would know? Nikki. He pays attention to that sort of thing. I tend to care more about what they do in the club than out of it."

"Oh, very good." Tobias nodded firmly. "So, next week we'll get the designers out?"

"You are in a hurry, eh?" Bradford headed for the front door. "I'll try to have someone here on Monday."

"Well, I'd rather not have Phan go to pieces, is all. Besides, we'll lose the weather if this goes on too long."

"Understood. It's not an outrageous project. A dedicated crew can have it done in a few weeks."

Tobias shook his head and grinned. "Isn't it fun, old man?"

Bradford laughed. "It is! And who are you calling old, Grandpa?"

"I'll have you know that not only have I never sired, you're clearly slipping. You're older than I am."

"I don't think I need to be reminded which one of us is the more mature."

"Clearly you do." Tobias grinned and pointed at himself. "Mature. You're merely old."

"If I were younger, or for that matter if you were, I'd call you out for that insult." Bradford laughed. "Tonight I'll settle for more of that very fine scotch."

"Excellent choice, my friend." Tobias left off the old as a boon. "I'd hate for us both to be embarrassed in front of our younger lovers." Laughing, he led the way out of the bunkhouse and back toward the very fine scotch.

8

T obias had to hand it to Bradford -- he got almost as worked up about improvements and expansions as Tobias did. Within days, the designers had been through, the permits obtained, and the basic rebuild begun. Of course, none of the choices about tile, flooring, colors, furniture, or cabinet doors had been made, but there were building plans and things to construct while Tobias made lists of stuff he wanted.

"Noah," he said as he marked yet another cabinet front in his catalogue, "Phan said he was going to go to the club after therapy, didn't he? We should probably meet him there for dinner."

"Yes, sir. I think that would be a very good idea," Noah replied without hesitation. "He had big things he wanted to discuss with Dr. Brewer this week." Noah set a fresh cup of coffee on Tobias' desk and went to his knees.

"Did he?" Tobias nodded and put the catalogue down. "I don't suppose it has anything to do with that surprise he's been working on every time he vanishes into his bedroom?" He shook his head, his rueful smile falling away. "Actually, he told me he wanted to talk to her about grief. I assume he's spoken to you about it?"

Noah sighed. "Oh, good," he said, sounding relieved. "Yes, we talked about it a couple of times. I'm glad he told you. He is really having a hard time sorting out his emotions -- the whole thing with Mrs. Miller and the house."

Tobias rolled his eyes. "He didn't precisely tell me anything, actually, other than he wanted to talk to Dr. Brewer about grief. However, Phan is hardly a closed book to me. Has he said anything to you that I should be aware of?"

"Oh. Uh... well?" Noah shifted uncomfortably. "He didn't exactly tell me I could talk to you about it, sir, but he misses Mrs. M. A lot. For a lot of reasons."

"That's why I asked you specifically if he said anything I should be aware of, Noah." Tobias frowned slightly. "I wouldn't ask you to break confidences, but you know as well as anyone what my position is where Phan is concerned. The usual rules of secret keeping simply don't apply."

Noah nodded. "Yes, sir. I would have come to you right away if I thought there was something you needed to know. This time, I just think he doesn't know how to cope with his feelings. He's not exactly used to coping, he's more used to denial, so... Sir? He said that he felt that Mrs. M was the first person to really love him and tell him so since he was kid. He lost a lot more with Mrs. M than I'd realized."

Tobias sighed and picked up his coffee mug. "I know. At least, I thought I did. Perhaps I was too lost in my own feelings at the time to really pay attention. He wasn't mine then, but I should have known. The two of them had a very special bond."

"Dr. Brewer will help him sort it out, I'm sure." Noah

leaned gently into Tobias' leg. "Should I make dinner reservations, sir? Do you think he'll even want dinner?"

"He may not want it, but he'll eat." Tobias ran his fingers through Noah's hair. "Even if I have to order him to chew. How are you doing, pet? There are a lot of changes going on."

"I'm fine." Noah shrugged. "Mostly. I'm still a little thrown by doing so many different things with my time: serving you, working the club, volunteering at the Y, weekend seminars, spending nights on the farm and some at the townhouse. I'm feeling pulled in a lot of directions, but I'm trying to let go of the big picture for now and concentrate on day to day until it all becomes routine again, you know? Just wake up every morning and go from there."

"Hmm." Still petting Noah's hair, Tobias asked, "Do you need more structure, do you think? Are you too busy?"

"I've always done well with structure, sir." Noah was leaning more and more into Tobias' touch, clearly enjoying the attention. "Before Phan joined us, I had a very set schedule that we'd worked out between us, and that worked really well for me. I never had to think about what was happening tomorrow. I don't know if I'm too busy or just trying to do too many things. Right now, though, I don't even know what I'd give up if I had to."

"I don't want you bored." Tobias frowned slightly as he thought. The service to himself was the whole point of... well, everything, so that was staying. Obviously. The volunteer work was essential to Noah as a person. The club work was something Noah also needed to keep from feeling like he was merely Tobias' toy. "All right," he said slowly. "I've added this knife play class on a whim. We'll give that one try this week, and then you and Phan and I will sit down and draw up a consistent schedule for a month or so. We'll be in town during the week mostly, I think -- I'm meddling for Brian, among other things."

"Thank you, sir." Noah lifted his head from Tobias' knee and grinned. "I think it's great that you're doing that for Brian, sir. He's such a good person and a good sub."

Tobias snorted and grinned back. "He's a brat and far too eager to get spankings. But you're right -- he's a good person. I'll try to meddle discreetly. Maybe after supper?"

"After supper," Noah nodded. "He's young, and he likes to have fun. He's no more over-eager for spankings than, say, Phan is for sex."

"Ha! Good point. I'll see if I can find Hayden for an after-dinner drink, then. Speaking of Phan and sex, I might keep you two restricted for a week or so. Just because I can."

Noah laughed. "That sounds like a horrible idea, sir."

"Fabulous! Go and call the club, get us a table, pet. Make sure it's in Brian's section." Tobias smiled to himself, looking forward to the games he could play.

Noah stood, shaking his head at Tobias' glee. "Yes, sir. Brian's section."

Tobias merely kept smiling.

He was still smiling when they got to club and he collected Phan from where he was drinking coffee in the bar. "Dinner, boy. But a word in my office first."

Phan nodded and stepped immediately to heel, pausing only to kiss Noah's cheek.

"I hope that was decaf," Noah whispered to Phan as they greeted each other. It was quiet enough that no one else would hear, but not so quiet that a Master who knew his boys well would miss it.

Tobias ushered them both into his office and sat in the big chair. "Come here, boy. Just for a minute."

Phan came to him, slightly vibrating but eager to crawl

into Tobias' lap. "Hello, sir. Did you have a good day?" He buried his face in Tobias' neck and kissed him before settling -- more or less -- into a cuddle.

Noah rolled his eyes and Tobias had to agree with him. Phan was wound up.

"I did, yes. So did Noah. But what I'd like to know is if your therapy session today was helpful or not, and if you and I need to have a longer talk about it later on this evening."

Phan was nodding his head eagerly through the first part of Tobias' speech, but by the end was shaking it. "Therapy was good, Dr. Brewer was good. I had to talk out some stuff and I needed to draw some stuff, and I have to write some stuff for next week, but it's stuff I can handle on my own, sir."

"You're sure?" Tobias was a little doubtful, but he fully accepted that his need to know was often slightly bigger than what reality actually allowed for.

"I'm sure, sir. Dr. Brewer gave me homework and some stuff to think about. I promise it'll all be okay." He wiggled. And then twitched.

Tobias glanced at Noah and shook his head dramatically. "All right, then, if you say so, Phan. Noah, I think it's time we went to eat before Brian gives away our table. Phan's a little... uh, caffeinated. I can feel his bones shaking."

"Oh, dear." Noah laughed sympathetically and held out his hand. "Come on, hon. Time to go to the dining room."

Phan kissed Tobias' cheek soundly and bounded to Noah, not unlike Tigger, though the springs were in his legs and not his tail. Hand in hand, the two of them waited for Tobias, who got up and gave them both a pat on their bottoms as he went past them. Phan giggled.

"Okay, time to dine. Be good, boy."

"Yes, sir!" Phan chirped. He'd definitely had caffeinated coffee.

"Sir!" Brian appeared from around a corner and skipped up to them, a definite spring in his step. "Your table is ready, sir."

Tobias rolled his eyes. "I assumed so, pup. Let me guess - - you put me right in the middle."

Brian showed off his dimples and gestured to the table. "You're stunning, sir. You need to be shown off."

Tobias had to laugh. "Water for three, Brian. And I'll take a menu tonight, thank you."

"Right away!"

Brian skipped off again and Tobias sat down. "Floor," he said, and both his boys sank to their knees. "Who wants what to eat?"

Tobias looked down at them. Both of his boys were very precise with their posture and their eyes. It was hard to mind being seated where everyone could see just how well behaved they were. He happened to catch Noah glancing at Phan briefly, but Phan didn't seem like he was about to offer up any suggestions.

"Thank you, sir. Something light for me, please, sir? A salad, maybe with some chicken, something like that?"

"That sounds nice." Judging by the nature of the order, it sounded like Noah was hoping to play, too. Tobias smiled to himself. "Phantom?"

"Dessert! Sir."

Tobias looked at Noah. "It wasn't decaf."

"Evidently not, sir." Noah grinned enough that Tobias could see it, but didn't budge a muscle otherwise. "Sir has a plan for us, Phan," he continued, softly. "You might change your mind about the dessert when you hear it."

Tobias saw Phan's shoulder twitch just once. Really, for all that he was a devil in leather, Phan had amazing control. It made him a wonderful submissive when he gave it up. "I see, sir. In that case, I'd like a lot of vegetables. Please."

"Now he's sucking up."

Phan tittered.

"Wow, how many cups of coffee did you have?" Tobias asked curiously.

"Three, sir."

"Oh, my." Tobias rolled his eyes, then looked around the dining room. "I don't suppose anyone here happens to have shackles? No? Phantom, go upstairs and get wrist and ankle cuffs, wide leather. With D rings and chain. You're going to be still if it makes us both ache."

"Yes, sir!" Phan bounded up and ran out of the dining room at full speed.

"I thank all the saints that you're a good boy, sweetheart."

"You just made his day, you realize, sir," Noah replied with only the slightest hint of sarcasm in his tone. "As for me, I'm just loath to misbehave when dinner is on the line."

"Oh, but you get to have sex tonight. He does not. Well, unless he has an emotional breakthrough, in which case I may relent a little for kissing and snuggling. He knows he's not allowed to have coffee after noon."

"Ah. I do generally try to stop short of actually breaking rules outright, sir," Noah conceded. "And thank you, sir, I'm looking forward to the evening even more now."

A jangling sound suddenly drew their attention, and Tobias look up to see Phan hurrying toward him, arms full of leather and chains. Everyone else was looking, too, and grinning. Tobias stood up and sighed for show. They did have a certain image to project.

Phan held the cuffs out and studied the floor. "The items, sir."

"Thank you." Tobias took the armful of restraints and pointed to Phan's usual spot next to him. "Facing the room, not me."

Phan's sigh was likely the real thing. "Yes, sir." He knelt down and held his wrists out behind himself.

As Tobias crouched down to fasten the cuffs on his wrists, he gave Phan's shoulder a bit of a pat. "Tell me why we're doing this."

"Because I broke a rule, sir. So I face away from you. I'm being cuffed and manacled because I need to be still and to calm down."

"Correct." Tobias moved on to wrap the heavy leather cuffs around Phan's ankles. "I'm going to short chain you, too. You'll have to balance carefully."

"Yes, sir." Phan's enthusiasm dimmed considerably. He was going to have to actually work and pay attention.

"You will eat every bit of food I put in your mouth."

"Yes, sir."

"And you will apologize to me later for having to work with you in public due to your rule breaking."

Phan drew in a shuddering breath and let it out slowly as Tobias chained his bound wrists to his bound ankles. "Yes, sir. Of course, sir."

With a nod, Tobias stood up. "Brian."

"Sir!"

Tobias rolled his eyes. "You have far too much energy, pup. I'll have a very large Greek salad, the rosemary lemon chicken, a side of green beans, and a pitcher of water, thank you."

Brian nodded and scurried off, and Tobias sat down again, ignoring both Phantom and everyone watching.

"Would you like to sit at the table?" He touched Noah's cheek gently, caressing his jaw. "You may, if you wish."

Noah checked his posture, straightening a bit more and looking straight ahead instead of down. The honor of sitting at the table with his Master clearly wasn't lost on him, though by the way he looked at Phan before he answered, Tobias thought perhaps he was torn between accepting and supporting his brother-sub. In the end, however, he did accept.

"Yes, sir. Thank you, sir," Noah replied, remaining still as he waited to be given permission to move.

"Across from me, please." It was actually a practical arrangement, as Tobias would need to turn slightly each time he fed Phantom, and it would be less awkward for him if Noah was across the table instead of beside him.

"Thank you, sir." Noah stood, pulled out the chair for himself, and sat. He kept his eyes low, but if he'd looked around, he would have seen heads turn. Whether their thinking was approving or disapproving, Tobias didn't care; his particular relationships with his subs were really no one's business but his own. Noah, for his part, remained just as respectfully submissive as if he were kneeling at Tobias' feet.

Tobias allowed Brian to pour water and leave the pitcher, then leaned forward slightly. "I notice that the unsuspecting object of my meddling is in the bar this evening, watching TV and probably waiting for someone to end his shift."

"Really? Well, that seems very convenient, sir." Noah reached for his water glass. "It also explains Brian's extraordinarily good mood."

"It does, doesn't it?" Tobias absently petted Phan, just to make sure that Phan wasn't neglected or had the impression of being neglected. He was trying very hard -- he had to be in order to balance -- and it was Tobias' job to be his anchor. "I just hope he doesn't vanish while we eat, or that Brian doesn't finish while I'm trying to guide their lives, making the target distracted. I may actually have you and Phan wait in my office. Having me and both of you descend might be a bit much, don't you think?"

"It certainly would seem more calculated and less casual that way, sir, I agree. Plus, I think Brian is intimidated by Phan." There was a smirk on Noah's lips just before he sipped his water.

"Everyone is intimidated by Phan." Tobias snorted and looked down at the top of Phan's head. "So it does some good to have him shackled in the dining room sometimes. Perhaps."

Noah laughed gently. "I'm sure it does them some good to see that he's not actually perfect, sir," he agreed. "I recall having my own issues with Phan way back when."

"You mean those issues that led to our very first fight?" Tobias laughed and petted Phan again, then leaned back as Brian brought out a tray with their meal.

Noah remained silent as Brian set out the food, apart from thanking him politely before he left the table, and then said, "Yes, those would be the issues I was referring to, sir." He blushed a bit. "We've come a very long way since then, haven't we? Seems like a lifetime ago in some ways."

"In some ways. In others, not so very far." Tobias fed Phan a green bean. "Please help yourself to the salad; you may have as much as you wish. The beans are for Phantom, and you may have one third of the chicken. If it looks like I'll be longer in the bar than I anticipate, I'll have a snack sent to you both in the office." With that, Tobias helped himself to a bite of the chicken and concentrated on feeding Phan, knowing that Noah would take care of his own nutritional needs.

"Yes, sir. Thank you, sir." Noah picked up his fork and dug right into the salad; he was obviously hungry. "Maybe it just seems like a long time to me, sir, because of all the bad habits I've left behind."

"Maybe. Although if you'd saved a few, I might have more to do." He smiled as he said it, knowing Noah wouldn't even see a wink, as his gaze was downcast. "It's difficult to chain you to a wall when you've done nothing to deserve it."

"What happened to doing something just because you can?" Noah took a bite of his salad, grinning. "Or maybe," he continued, mouth full, "it's time to push limits again."

"The first is fun, the second is important." Tobias ate some feta and an olive. "Yes." He nodded firmly and gave Phan some beans, then his one bite of chicken. "You and I shall talk, I think. But later, perhaps on the weekend, when I have you chained to a wall simply because I can."

Phan nodded, too, and Tobias took a closer look at him. He was finally still, not even vibrating, and his eyes were vaguely dreamy. "Boy, you've done it. Good job."

"Thank you, sir." Phan didn't move, but he did smile happily.

Noah smiled in Phan's direction and then went back to eating silently. Possibly, he was pondering the chat they'd have on the weekend, but it was more likely that he was trying not to intrude on Phan's moment. He reached over and cut a bite of chicken for himself, which he chewed carefully.

Brian appeared just as the chicken was finished and whisked the plate away. Tobias saw Noah set down his fork, so he put the last of the salad aside.

"All right, then." Tobias glanced at his watch and gave

Phan one last pat on his shoulder before crouching down to undo the chain between Phan's wrists and ankles. "Well done, both of you. Noah, would you please take Phan to my office for me? He's a little subby at the moment, so curling up on the couch might be a good idea. Leave the cuffs on, though."

"Happy to, sir." Noah moved to Phan's side. "Come on, hon." He held a hand down to help Phan to his feet. "We'll wait for you in your office, sir. Good luck."

"Thanks." Tobias laughed and resisted the urge to roll his eyes at his boys in front of a room full of others. Instead, he lingered at the table for a moment while Noah and Phan left, gathering smiles as they went.

Then he stood up and grinned. "Mine."

The men at the nearest tables chuckled -- the Doms, anyway -- and Tobias left the dining room, crossed the wide hallway, and went into the bar.

"Dave, I'd like a Perrier, please," Tobias said, scanning the room for his quarry.

"Right away, sir."

Hayden had left his spot at the bar, so Tobias began to examine the tables one by one. He recognized everyone, apart from one or two subs, and knew something about nearly every Dom present. Hayden, however, didn't seem to be around at the moment.

Dave moved smoothly behind the bar, pulling an ice-cold bottle from the fridge and setting it on the bar. Beside it, he set a highball glass full of cubed ice and garnished with orange, lemon, and lime on a cocktail skewer with a curled up bullwhip adorning one end. "Your drink, Master Tobias."

Tobias sighed, wondering if he'd missed his opportunity, and turned back to the bar. "Thank you, Dave."

"Pleasure, sir."

"Dave, a ginger ale, if you please? Evening, Tobias." Hayden appeared beside the bar suddenly.

"Right away, sir." Dave got to work again.

Tobias smiled. "Just the man I was looking for. How are you, Hayden?"

Hayden raised an eyebrow. "That sounds ominous," he answered, smiling. "I've been a good boy, sir, I promise."

"Ginger ale, sir."

"Thank you, Dave."

Tobias tried very hard not to roll his eyes. It really was a useful expression, and he could see why Phan was so fond of it. "One of the hardest parts about having my reputation is that I can't actually look for someone without inducing trepidation," he said with a laugh. "Do you have time to talk, or are you waiting for someone?"

Hayden nodded. "You do have a reputation, although I have to say that I'm not intimidated by it so much as I am impressed." He picked up his ginger ale. "I have an hour or so -- I have a room reserved at nine. Shall we sit?"

"Perfect." Tobias led the way to one of the tables at the side of the room, taking his glass with him. "I suppose impressive is good -- I'd hate to be unreachable, however. I enjoy talking to people, and while I expect a certain amount of deference from the subs, I'd hope that any of the Doms would feel comfortable talking to me about anything at all."

"Well, I do have to say that your screening process is demanding and probably the source of a good part of that reputation, at least among the newer Doms like me. But I don't think you're unapproachable. Quite the opposite. If I had an issue, you'd be the first person I'd go to." Hayden pulled out a chair for himself and sat down.

"Oh, good!" Tobias beamed at him and made himself

comfortable. "Of course, I like hearing the success stories as well. Is your room at nine with someone you've played with before? I know you don't have a primary submissive, but I'm always hopeful for good matches."

Hayden nodded. "I've made arrangements with Brian. We've worked together before, as you know." He grinned. "We've reserved the Sultan Room; he's expressed a fondness for the pillow-covered floor."

Tobias laughed. "He likes soft surfaces after he's been spanked." He nodded to himself and smiled at Hayden. "It's nice to have someone take him seriously. He's been here for a long, long time, and I wondered if his energy was scaring people off."

"Mmm." Hayden nodded. "That can make things difficult. His energy is something we worked on last time -- being still, concentrating, putting his impulses to better use. He's a challenge, that's for sure, but I kind of like that about him. As you and I discussed, the heavy hitting tools really aren't my style. I'm more into bondage and domination than pain play. Brian seems to respond well to that."

Oh, this was going well -- for all three of them. Tobias nodded. "Absolutely. Brian's never really been one for pain, but he definitely needs to be dominated. He gets unsettled and upset if he's at loose ends for too long, I've noticed."

"I'm sure that's hardly an issue for him, he seems quite popular. Everyone I've spoken to says he's fun. He can't possibly have much time on his hands."

Tobias felt an eyebrow go up and made a concerted effort to bring it back down. That part wasn't really the nice and easy he was hoping for. "Oh, I don't know about that," he said casually. "There's a difference between playing at submitting and actually doing it, as you know. A few spankings can calm him, but it's not really where he thrives."

"He's a flirt, Tobias; playing is what he does. I can't imagine what it would take to bring him to heel full time. That would have to be one dedicated Dom."

"Well, yes. Of course it would. But it can be done -- look at Phantom, after all." He smiled broadly. "The rewards are intense."

Hayden regarded Tobias with interest. "Phantom is that scattered?"

"Oh, my God, yes." Tobias sometimes forgot that the new people didn't know Phan as well as the others. He looked around the bar, hoping one of Phan's interim playmates was about. "Eben?" He waved the man over. "Would you describe Phantom as calm and centered on a typical day?"

Eben snorted. "Only if you have him in chains," he said, shaking his head. "Otherwise, he's got the attention span of a flea on crack." Eben looked at Hayden. "Hi, I'm Eben, I don't think we've met."

"Hayden."

"Welcome." They shook hands, and Eben looked at Tobias. "Are you offering Phan around now? Because if so, I'd like to get on the waiting list."

Tobias stared, actually speechless for a moment. "No," he finally said. "But I'll let him know he's still popular. He'll be delighted, I'm sure." He'd float on that for days. "This is where I'm trying not to snarl 'mine,' I'm sure you both know."

Both of the other Doms laughed.

"Really, Tobias," Eben said in a friendly, jovial tone. "You're so possessive of those boys. You're too easy to tease."

"You have to admit he got you there, Tobias," Hayden agreed, picking up his ginger ale and taking a long sip.

"But can you blame me?" Tobias asked once Eben had excused himself and gone back to his own table. "That kind of domination, that level of deep trust with a submissive, with a lover, is an intense thing that needs to be protected and cherished." He sat back, smiling. "I don't mind being teased, as long as everyone knows that Noah and Phan are mine, utterly. They blossom under the care -- the same way Brian would open up under a consistent hand."

"I think your dedication to them is as respected as their dedication to you, Tobias. Nothing to worry about there that I can see." Hayden leaned forward a bit, resting an arm on the table. "I certainly look forward to working with Brian, I have to say."

"He seems just as taken with you." Tobias leaned forward as well, as if he were sharing a secret. "I've known that boy a long time, even spanked him once or twice. But I've never seen him as pleased as he's been the last while."

"You think so?" Hayden looked thoughtful for a moment and rubbed his fingers across his chin. "Hmm."

"Oh, absolutely. He's glowing." Tobias sipped his water and nodded hello to Logan as he came in, then turned back to Hayden. "Just something for you to think about. Of course, I wouldn't dream of pushing you into anything if all that you want is some casual play; but by the same token, if you and Brian have a connection you'd like to explore, I want to put myself at your disposal."

"Well." Hayden leaned back in his chair again. "I certainly appreciate your observations and your time. I hadn't considered the possibility of anything more meaningful with Brian. He's been here a long time, I know, so I naturally thought he was happy with things as they stood."

"There's content, there's happy, and there's thriving." Tobias smiled at him and lifted his glass in a toast. "This is for both of you, though. He can't really thrive unless it's something good for you both. But I do hope you'll consider things and see what you'd like to pursue."

"I'll consider it," Hayden promised, raising his glass as well and touching it to Tobias' before taking a sip. "I'll definitely consider it. Thank you."

"I'd be interested in--" Tobias broke off and smiled as Brian came in and stood a few feet away, his hands behind his back and his eyes downcast. "Well, another time. I think your companion is ready to take you away from me."

"Oh, no, sir!" Brian looked stricken at the tease. "If you and Master Hayden are busy--"

"Pup." Tobias laughed and stood up. "I was kidding, Brian. It's your night off, and I hope you enjoy it. I'm going to go and collect my boys, then see if I can annoy Master Bradford for a while. Thank you for excellent service at dinner."

"You're welcome, sir." Brian flushed pink and edged his way closer to Hayden, clearly wanting to get on with his night off.

Laughing, Tobias took his glass of warming water and headed to his office. He found it quiet and dimly lit, both of his boys kneeling in the center of the room, side by side. Phan was leaning slightly against Noah, and Noah's arm was wrapped loosely around Phan's back.

Noah raised his head at the sound of the door. "Hello, sir," he said softly. "Did you find Master Hayden?"

"I did. Wow." Tobias went in and closed the door all the way behind him, sealing them into a pocket of quiet. He crouched in front of them and tried to look at Phan's face, but the light was too poor. "Are you all right, dear?"

"Yes, sir. Just really, really calm. And a little hungry."

Tobias smiled and glanced at Noah. "Things okay, sweetheart?"

"Just fine, sir. Phan's really grounded and he needed some quiet after we left the dining room, so we've just been kneeling here together. We never quite got to the cuddle you suggested, but it's been nice sitting here thinking. It's been a while; I'd forgotten how soothing quiet can be."

"All right, then." Tobias left them there and went to his desk to check his calendar. "We have a pretty interesting day tomorrow. Bradford says there's been a strong interest in the knife play instruction. I'd like to talk about this with you both when we get home -- especially you, Noah. We may have found our boundary to push." He glanced up and smiled. "Time to dress, lovelies. I'll call for the car."

"Yes, sir. Come on, hon." Noah helped Phan to his feet. Together, they dressed, and then Noah took the shackles and chains back upstairs.

The car ride to the townhouse was quiet in a different way. Noah was frisky, Phan was snuggling, and Tobias sat between his boys, offering each some affection in turn. Fortunately, it was also a short ride, which meant they could get inside and get on with their evening all the sooner. Phan had mentioned he was hungry, so their first stop was the kitchen.

Tobias wasn't about to trust Phan at the stove in his condition; calm was good, but Phan seemed a bit too dreamy to be working around heat. Instead, he had Phan sit at the table and wait while he and Noah built some sandwiches. For all that Tobias enjoyed being waited upon, it was also nice to trade kisses with Noah as they sliced cheese and tomatoes.

He also let the entire matter of working with sharps drop until everyone was fed and ready to curl up for a while. After a bit of thought, Tobias rejected his bedroom and took them both upstairs. "Into the tub," he instructed. "No bubbles, but the jets will be fine."

Noah had a chuckle about the bubbles while the tub filled, and then he started the jets running. Tobias watched him as Noah stripped and elbowed Phan playfully before tossing all of their clothes into a pile; grabby hands made short work of Tobias' clothes as well, and moments later, Tobias had two naked boys next to him in his tub.

"What time is the seminar tomorrow, sir?" Noah asked. "Master Bradford told me the new security cameras are in."

"Yes, good." Tobias leaned back and let the water rush over his legs and around the small of his back. "We're to be at the club no later than one, but that won't be an issue -- we're going in for ten as usual. After lunch, we'll make sure the room is set up to my liking. Phan, I'll be doing some design work on your thighs."

Phan nodded and wiggled. Even in the water, Tobias could tell he was wiggling. "Yes, sir."

Tobias smiled, knowing Phan would be at ease and no trouble at all. "So. Noah." Tobias turned only his head to look at him. "I want to talk about sharps and your skin and your issue about being cut." It was part of their signed contract, due to a trauma Noah had sustained in a prior relationship, that any knife play had to be broached with Noah before a decision could be made about cutting.

"Me, sir?" Noah looked surprised. "I... don't know. I didn't realize you wanted to use me tomorrow, too. It's been a long time." Noah seemed a little unsettled, but he was also thoughtful, a state Tobias had seen before, and not unusual when Noah was trying to honestly evaluate his feelings. "I wasn't cut with sharps, it was an accident, and... it wasn't you."

"It wasn't me." Tobias nodded and let Noah work it

through for himself, lending support along the way. "It wasn't me, but that doesn't mean there isn't a block there. I'd like to work on that with you -- but I won't force you to start tomorrow, with an audience, if you're not comfortable with that." On the other hand, if Tobias did his job correctly, the audience wouldn't matter.

"It's been a while since we worked on something at that level." Noah leaned back in the tub, looking a little more relaxed. "I could do it. With you, I think I can do it. And I've never minded an audience." Noah grinned slyly, remembering the very public scene that Tobias once orchestrated in a nightclub parking lot. "As you might recall."

Phan snickered. "Thank God for that. Best show I'd seen in years."

Noah was definitely blushing now. He could almost hear the voices that had surrounded them; rough, rude comments pushing both of them to a breathless climax. Tobias had gone to great lengths to create a sense of recklessness in a very safe environment. "I don't think this will be that kind of audience," he said, shooting Phan a look. "They'll probably just disappear once I'm in a good headspace anyway."

"Not literally, I hope." Phan was grinning past Tobias at Noah. "I like watching people watch you."

"We all know that." Tobias shook his head. "Oh, by the way, did Noah pass on to you that you're both on restriction? No sex with each other for a week. Well, unless I explicitly direct it. No blow jobs, no orgasms. You can roll around all you want, but no one gets to come."

Phan blinked and his jaw dropped open. "No, sir. Noah didn't pass that along."

"Good." Tobias gave Noah a kiss. "I didn't tell him to, and

these things should come from me, anyway. Also, you don't get to come tonight, for drinking all that coffee. You'll both sleep in chains tonight, as well, on the floor." God, just listing it all off and putting them where they were supposed to be was making him hard.

"Understood, sir. Thank you, sir," Noah replied automatically. Neither of Tobias' subs ever gave him trouble when he set limits or collared them at night. Noah especially responded well to those orders that took away the need for him to make decisions, as willing to let Tobias take control as Tobias was eager to take it.

He was a smart boy, too, and hadn't missed the fact that he was not under the same restrictions that Phan was for the night. Tobias felt a hand slide down his thigh, and Noah spoke in a suggestive tone. "Are you comfortable, sir?"

"One can always be more comfortable, pet." Tobias smiled hugely. "Do you have something in mind?"

"Well, I was just thinking that I could help you be more relaxed for tomorrow. Make sure you sleep well." Noah's hand moved more deliberately, slipping across the top of Tobias' thigh. Strong fingers wrapped gently around Tobias' cock, and Noah stroked his thumb over the head.

Phan, after sighing deeply, scooted a little to the side and watched closely. "Can I help, Noah?"

Noah looked at Phan. "I think maybe you'd better ask Sir that question."

Tobias smirked and let his eyes close. "I stated the rules. Phan can't come. If Noah wants you to help, he'll tell you what to do. You'll wind up watching anyway, I'm sure."

Phan made a soft sound, but it wasn't a whine or a plea for mercy; it never was. Sometimes Tobias wondered if Phan would do just as well living a life of total denial. Then he remembered how enthusiastic Phan could be about sex and decided not to bother trying to find out. Why should he suffer, after all?

"Okay, Phan. Why don't you concern yourself with the things that are above water?" Noah suggested. "Like here." He licked across one of Tobias' nipples. "Or, maybe here." Tobias felt Noah's breath in his ear and teeth on his earlobe. "What do you think, sir?"

"I'm doing my very best not to think at all." Eyes still closed, Tobias couldn't help smiling and even moaning a little as Phan cuddled up to his side and sharp teeth tugged at the other earlobe. Nimble fingers swept over Tobias' chest, and it became very easy not to do anything but feel.

As Noah released his ear, the grip around his erection grew tighter. Noah started to stroke slowly and the sub's other hand cupped and tugged at Tobias' balls. "I'll beg you to fuck me, sir," Noah offered softly, giving Tobias' prick a tug. "Hard and long. Maybe here in the tub, maybe up against the wall in the hall, maybe in bed. Maybe all three."

"Maybe you'll beg there or maybe I'll relent there?" Tobias let his head fall back as Phan licked his way from Tobias' ear to his collar bone and then lower. He lifted his hips slightly, the water making it easy to slide through Noah's grasp.

Noah laughed, and his tone grew low and sultry. "Where you relent is up to you, of course, sir. I'm yours to use as you please." Without releasing Tobias' cock, he shifted and maneuvered a leg across Tobias' lap until he was straddling Tobias' knees.

Tobias lifted his head and opened his eyes as Phan's hand slid down to briefly join Noah's. Just for a touch, more a caress than a stroke, and then Phan grinned impishly at Noah. "Whoops."

Tobias snorted. "Naughty. I may let Noah pay you back

for that someday soon." He tried not to gasp as Phan's mouth attached to his nipple, licking and sucking. "At least one of you knows his place." Tobias reached for Noah's hips and pulled him a few inches closer.

"Mmm. Sir." Noah rolled his hips suggestively in Tobias' lap and leaned around Phan to draw a wet line with his tongue up the side of Tobias' neck. He slid even closer, almost close enough to trap Phan's head between them, before starting to rock rhythmically, so that the head of Tobias cock pressed against Noah's balls over and over. "Please, sir," Noah breathed against Tobias' neck. "Touch me. Fuck me, please."

"No." Tobias growled and slid his hands over Noah's ass. "Ask me again."

Phan's teeth scraped, sharp and hot on his nipple, making a line zing right to Tobias' balls.

Noah groaned. "Yes, sir. Please, sir, won't you?" His sub continued to move, the head of Noah's erection rubbed lightly against Tobias' abdomen, and Noah was starting to pant. "I need you, Master. Please? Fuck me."

"No." Tobias shook his head and moved his hands again, this time squeezing roughly. "I don't want to." No one ever said Tobias couldn't lie when he was playing. That was part of the fun of making up the rules. He pushed a finger against Noah's hole, but didn't do anything more than that; Noah would still be tender from the dry fuck.

Predictably, Noah arched his ass into Tobias' hand, begging with his body as well as his words. He continued to stroke Tobias' cock slowly but with a firm grip as the tub jets swirled warm water around them. "Sir. Anything. I'll do anything you say, sir. Please. Anywhere. Anything you want. I need you to want me."

Phan moved in the water and started licking his way

over Noah's chest, panting almost as loudly as Noah. Tobias smiled as he watched, then became suddenly aware that he was in danger of orgasming. The water was hot, but his spine was feeling tight and his balls were aching. Gritting his teeth, he peeled Noah's hand away from him. "Turn around and bend over," he ordered.

"Yes, sir." Noah nodded and moved quickly, sliding off Tobias' lap and turning as ordered. Bending over appeared to be a bit more of a challenge, but he braced his hands on the opposite side of the tub and spread his feet for balance, offering Tobias a superb view of his ass and balls. "Good, sir?" Noah asked. Tobias could see his fingers grip and release the edge of the tub anxiously.

Tobias looked at Phan and nodded. "Good, don't you think?"

Phan's eyes were huge. "Uh-huh. Good."

"Get him wet while I--" He hadn't even finished speaking before Phan had his tongue buried in Noah's ass. "That." Laughing and taking a moment to not only enjoy the view but to get himself under control, Tobias reached for the lube they kept by the tub.

Poor Phan was going to pay for his enthusiasm when he was denied orgasm himself.

"Fuck!" Noah cried out, and his elbows buckled. He recovered his strength quickly but not his composure. "Oh, fuck. Phan!" Tobias heard him moan, listened to his rough groans. "Sir. Phan! Sir!"

"That's two for me and one for you, boy." Tobias stood in the water and slicked his cock before tapping Phan on the shoulder.

"Sir." Phan was almost pitiful, reluctantly -- though quickly -- moving away. "Can I suck him?"

"Not this time." Tobias didn't want anyone to drown.

"Maybe next week." He didn't let Noah whimper more than once before he lined up and started pushing in.

"Yes, yes, sir! Oh, God," Noah stammered shamelessly, as if making sure Tobias knew just how badly Noah wanted. He spread his legs wider and pushed his hips back hungrily.

Noah's ass was tight, tight enough to make Tobias grateful that Noah was as far gone as he was; maybe he wouldn't notice if Tobias just gave it all up and came right then. But then there was Phan to think about. Tobias shoved his cock in hard, eliciting another cry from Noah, and looked over to where Phan was staring at them.

Phan's hands were in the water, but Tobias could see that he wasn't jerking himself off; he was squeezing hard and doing his very best not to come, not to break Tobias' orders.

"Oh, God." Tobias moaned and looked away, down at Noah's back and then lower at where they were joined. "Oh, God." He reached around and started playing with Noah's cock. "After me, sweetheart. My good boys." Eyes rolling back, Tobias let his hips move as they wanted, slamming into Noah again and again, chasing his orgasm.

"After. Oh, fuck." There was more than a hint of frustration in Noah's groan. "Yes, sir. More. More, please, sir!" Noah's back was beaded with sweat, his body rocked with Tobias' effort, and his arms were trembling. He was utterly submissive, taking every bit of energy Tobias had eagerly, but after that, words apparently failed him, and he had nothing left but whimpers, sharp cries, and long moans to offer.

Tobias had no more to give him, just his cock buried deep and his teeth scraping on Noah's shoulder. "Now. Yes, now." He groaned as he climaxed, his whole body tight and then tighter still as pleasure passed through him in long pulls. He held on tight, dimly aware that Phan had come to their side and was making sure they didn't fall back into the water.

Noah followed, his hips jerking back hard against Tobias as he came. The room was filled with their combined sounds: Tobias' long groan, Noah's relieved sobs, and gentle sounds from Phan. "Sir, sir, sir," Noah whispered breathlessly over and over as his body started to relax.

His chest tight as he tried to get his own breath back, Tobias eased them back into the water and let himself slip free of Noah's body. "Shh. Come here, sweetheart." He sat with his back to the side of the tub and urged Noah into his arms. "I've got you." Turning his head, he kissed Phan. "Thank you, dear."

Phan's mouth clung to his and then the slight figure curled in with them, though Phan didn't speak. Tobias let him get as close as he needed to be and hoped Phan's body would calm quickly.

"Thank you, sir," Noah managed to say between harsh breaths. Whatever headspace he'd been in, he'd managed to work himself into quite a state. He melted against Tobias' chest, eyes closed and clearly making an effort to get his breathing back to normal. The next thing he was able to say made them all chuckle. "Wow."

"True enough." Tobias made sure Noah wasn't about to slide under the water and nodded. "Wow." Beside them, Phan was blinking and breathing rapidly, but he'd stopped making little sounds of need. When Phan could breathe properly as well, it would be time to get out of the tub. "I think we'll all sleep well tonight."

"Mmm. Thank you, sir. I'm looking forward to it." Noah sat up a bit and looked at Phan. "Hey, you. You look good." Tobias saw him grin at Phan.

"Yeah, about to burst is a good look for me." Phan grinned back, though, his cheeks pink and his chest flushed.

"Get used to it," Tobias told him happily. "It's going to be a long week. However, if you're good tomorrow, I might play with you."

"He'll be good tomorrow. He's been practically vibrating about tomorrow." Noah sighed happily. "Mmm, sir, I feel as good as he looks."

"You look as good he looks." Tobias urged Noah to move. "The water is cooling, my darlings. Dry off, get something light to eat if you're still hungry, and then we'll go to bed. I need to inspect your chains and hand out bedtime spankings, too. My life is so hard, poor me."

Phan giggled and unstoppered the tub. "I'll do my best to make it up to you tomorrow, sir."

Noah shook his head. "Poor, overworked Master." He hauled himself out of the tub with some effort and retrieved a stack of towels. "Remind me to scrub this tub tomorrow, Phan. Assuming I can still bend over far enough."

"I can help you with that," Phan said archly, and Tobias rolled his eyes.

"Please don't make me start calling you two 'children.' The image is disturbing." He climbed out of the tub and let Phan wrap him in a towel. "I'll meet you both in the bedroom." Still dripping, Tobias left them to clean up and went to lock up the house.

It was going to be a good week; he could feel it in his bones. Good boys, good work, and the added joy of chains clinking at night. Things didn't really get a lot better than that.

9

The first thing Tobias did when he got to the club was ensconce his submissives in his office, both of them quiet and calm and more or less too far into their own headspaces to be out wandering around the building. There were things he needed to do before taking them upstairs, so he asked one of the security personnel to stand guard at the door, just in case.

Then he went to find Bradford.

Nikki opened Bradford's office door. Bradford was on the phone but waved Tobias in with a smile. "Yes, that's what I'm looking for. Well, really it should be something discreet -- could be mistaken for Ivy League or a retired firefighter or something unless you know what you're looking at. Mmmhmm. Mmmhmm. Yes." Bradford gave Tobias the thumbs up sign, grinning smugly. "Perfect. I'll come take a look at what you've got in mind tomorrow. Afternoon is fine. Thank you." He hung up the phone. "Remember a while back we were discussing member lapel pins? I believe I've found someone to make them."

"Really?" Tobias laughed softly as he seated himself. "As

long as we don't need a secret handshake, too. One pin for all members, or will there be a slight variation between Doms and subs?" Taken to extremes, there could be many variations, which might be over the top. Still, it would be good to know who you were talking to, in general terms.

"One for Doms and one for subs, of course, though I don't plan on creating our own version of the hanky code if that's what you're worried about." Bradford looked Tobias over critically. "Hmm. No, that's not what you're worried about. What's on your mind?"

Tobias raised an eyebrow. "My mind, I admit, is rather taken up with this afternoon's demonstration. Class? Lecture? What are we calling it, anyway?"

"It's a seminar. That way it can be as hands on -- or off as the case may be -- as you feel comfortable with. We have good attendance, and the Doms who have regular subs are bringing them. Oh, and I might not have mentioned there will be two Doms who are currently prospective members. I asked Nikki to leave their files on your desk. I assume you saw them?"

"Not if they were put there this morning. I just got here. How many people is 'good attendance'?" He trusted Bradford not to overfill the room -- what good would it do if no one could see? -- but he might have to adjust his planned teaching style if there was more than an intimate gathering.

"Fifteen Doms, not including myself."

"Jesus Christ." Tobias stared at him. "Where are we doing this, the dining room?"

"The banquet room, where we had the boys' collaring. Plenty of room there." Bradford didn't seem at all concerned about the numbers. "Too many Doms for your liking?"

"About three times more than I expected, honestly." Tobias frowned to himself as he reworked segments of his presentation for a larger crowd. "How on earth are they going to see everything?"

Bradford frowned. "I had thought they would sit in a semi circle, two deep. You hadn't mentioned an attendance restriction. Tobias, would you prefer that I split it into two sessions? We can do one this week and one next."

"I didn't even think about numbers because I'd assumed that no more than four or five of them would be able to take time off during the middle of the week on such short notice." Tobias glared at Bradford. "Don't say a word to Phan about that, either. He'll tease me until I have to thrash him."

"I think you're forgetting two things, my friend," Bradford said, running his fingers through Nikki's hair absently. "For one thing, it's your class, not some random how-to demo. And secondly, are you aware of just how large our membership is at the moment? Do you know how many active Doms we have right now?"

"About fifty regulars? More than that again on the rosters that show up once or twice a year?" Tobias guessed blindly. "And your first point is why I don't want Phantom to hear about this. I shudder to think what he'd say, in that gleeful little wiggly way of his." He did, actually, shudder. It would be horribly embarrassing.

"About seventy-five regulars, another twenty or so who show up at least once a week for dinner and to play, and another fifty or so who show up mainly at the parties and social events. And with your weekend seminars and now these weekday demonstrations being open to non-members, we're not a small organization serving a few kinky guys anymore, Tobias. We're an active, profit-making business. Fifteen attendees is a drop in the bucket."

Tobias gave him a long look. "I think I want better booze in my office. God." He pinched the bridge of his nose. "Okay, today we'll leave as is -- these men did take time off. The next one, if we do this again, we'll cap. How does that sound?"

"Fine with me. It's your show, Tobias. But if you want better booze, that will have to come out of your budget." Bradford grinned and leaned forward across his desk. "We're doing very well, my friend. Maybe we should treat ourselves to a vacation this spring. I've yet to take Nikki anywhere."

Tobias glanced at Nikki. "Cruise, maybe? Or we can rent a private property somewhere warm. Oh, Greece. Let's take them to Greece."

Nikki was sitting still as stone, but it was clear that he was listening intently. Bradford followed the boy's gaze and smiled at him. "Greece is a lovely idea. A perfectly wonderful idea. What do you think, boy?"

"I think it sounds amazing, sir." Bradford's sub was grinning widely now.

"Well, Tobias, you might be on to something. Noah will look splendid tanned and kneeling on a beach, and Phan... well, Phan probably sunburns. Better take out some stock in sunscreen."

"Phantom is a delicate little orchid who will stay in the shade and mix our drinks and make our lunch. Oh, I do think we've got our autumn planned, good for us." Tobias smiled just as widely as Nikki. "Naked Mediterranean frolics. Lovely. Now, I just need to get through today. Tell me, do we have particularly good resolution on our security cameras? We may be able to use them somehow to get good detail shots of Noah and Phan as I mark them up to varying degrees."

"I'll do you one better. I have a video camera we can set up and perhaps place a few monitors around the room. Let me just make a call..." Bradford picked up the phone.

"Shiloh? Hello. Can you arrange for a video feed in the banquet room for our gathering this afternoon? Yes, monitors, and we might as well record it for the library. Perfect. Thank you." He glanced at Tobias. "Done. Anything else?"

"Not that I can think of." Tobias stood up. "Lunch? My boys are in my office; Phan's anticipating and Noah's so deep into his headspace that I think the waves of calm are what's got Phan quiet. It's fascinating, really."

"Sounds it. I'm continually fascinated by all three of you." Bradford grinned. "I'm up for some lunch, sure," he added, standing. "Come, Nikki, darling."

"Do you mind if we eat in my office instead of taking them into the dining room?" Tobias opened Bradford's door and headed down the hall toward his own. "Something light ought to do it."

"Not at all. I never get to actually eat when I sit in the dining room anyway; someone always has questions for me. Shall I have Nikki get us some salads?"

"Perfect." Tobias nodded his thanks and then took a moment to thank the security guard, Andrew. "They were good?"

"Of course, Master Tobias." Andrew smiled. "Not a sound." He inclined his head and left, presumably going back to his regular duties.

Tobias opened the door and left it open for Bradford, who was quietly instructing Nikki. In one corner, Phan was kneeling and waiting, just as he'd been when Tobias left him there. In the middle of the room, Noah knelt on a cushion. They were both wearing casual clothes, mostly so they'd be warm, but the shirts were low enough that their silver collars were on display. "Well done," Tobias said softly. "Are either of you hungry?"

Noah took a second to answer, as if being pulled back to reality by Tobias' words. "No, thank you, sir," he said, not moving a muscle.

"Phan?"

"Cheeseburger?"

Tobias snorted. "You're first up, pretty boy. Just remember that. When I'm done with Noah, I want to scoop him right up and do all the aftercare, no pausing. You're going to be marked all to shit, and I'll be having Nikki clean you. Do you still want a cheeseburger?"

Phan's head tilted to the side as he considered. Then his stomach rumbled, loudly. "Yes, please."

Smiling, Tobias went back to the door. "And a cheeseburger, please."

Nikki nodded. "Yes, sir."

"Get something for yourself, Nikki," Bradford added. "Eat well. We may not have time for a sit-down dinner tonight."

"Yes, sir. Thank you, sir."

"Run along."

Nikki disappeared quickly.

"Noah must be deep if he's not eating," Bradford suggested, stepping past Tobias and looking the boy over.

"Deep, and about to try something new, facing a barrier. I'll make sure that he has a wonderful supper later on." Tobias sat down and pointed to Phan's usual spot. He'd take some time to love on Noah after the rest of them had eaten, before they went to the banquet room.

As they ate, Tobias and Bradford went over the last few details for the afternoon, and Tobias kept a close eye on both of his submissives. Phantom seemed cheerful and cooperative. Noah seemed to be safely aware of what was going on but very calm and centered, which exactly what Tobias needed. If Noah went so far into his headspace that he grew lax and unresponsive, too calm, Tobias would need to bring him up a little. With a new tool, and one as serious as a scalpel, Tobias needed to know that Noah's reactions were going to be quick and clear so Tobias could react with Noah to make the experience both safe and powerful.

When the meal was cleared away, Bradford and Nikki took their leave. Tobias assumed that Bradford was going to greet the guests; Tobias hardly had time to do it, after all, and playing the charming host was one of Bradford's special talents. With a few quiet words, he had Phan get changed into a simple linen garment that was barely more than a loin cloth. For Noah, he had loose cotton pants, closed with a drawstring. He wouldn't be using Noah's legs and saw no reason to tempt himself with that much unmarked skin.

"Are we ready?" he asked quietly, looking down at them as they knelt together.

Noah nodded slowly, not giving Tobias any outward sign that he was feeling anxious. "Ready, sir."

"Yes, sir." Phan smiled and reached out to take Noah's hand. "Me first, kitten. Then Sir can love on you a lot after it's all done."

Tobias saw Noah give Phan's hand a squeeze. "I'm fine. Sir will take care of me. And I know you'll be amazing as always."

"Of course he will be -- he has to be, this is his kink of all kinks." Tobias grinned and straightened his tie. "Phan loves to show off."

Phan shrugged and somehow managed to look modest. "I do. It's true."

"This should be a very successful day for you, then, sir," Noah replied. Tobias had a feeling that if Noah'd had permission, he would've given Tobias a wink and a nudge to go with his remarks.

"I'm counting on it." Tobias nodded and turned on his heel. "Come, boys. Let's go and teach a lesson." He started walking, pleased when both subs fell into step right at his heel before he even got close to the office door.

The three of them took up the entire width of the hallway as they walked to the banquet room; it was a very good thing that no one was coming toward them, because Tobias wasn't going to shift from his path for anyone or for any reason. He was as deeply into his headspace as Noah was, just as he was supposed to be.

Smiling about that, he walked through the door and led his boys right to the middle of room, not looking around and not hesitating. "Good afternoon."

Bradford was standing across the room, speaking casually with one of the Doms, and he quickly excused himself and met Tobias in the center of the room. Everyone settled into seats, some with subs at their feet.

"Gentlemen, you all know Tobias Vincent, so I'll skip the introductions and just say that this is the first of what we hope to be a series of seminars that Tobias will offer. Please be ready to give us some constructive feedback when we're through today. Also, out of respect for Tobias and for his subs, who will be part of his demonstration, please hold all comments and conversation until Tobias opens the floor to questions. The rest I'll leave to the Master." Bradford touched Tobias on the shoulder as he left the floor and took a seat where Nikki was kneeling beside an empty chair.

Tobias grasped Noah's wrist gently. "Go and sit with Master Bradford until I call you, pet. You can watch Phan, if you wish, but you don't have to. Be calm."

Noah nodded and whispered, "Yes, sir." He went and

knelt beside Nikki, and Bradford acknowledged him by giving his shoulder a light squeeze before turning his full attention back to Tobias.

Tobias gestured to the low table they'd had made up as a bed, and Phan sat on the edge. "This is Phantom," Tobias said as he looked around at the assembled men. "Most of you know him, I believe, and some of you have known him for years. He's mine."

There was a soft round of laughter as Tobias stated the obvious.

"Phan's got a lot of experience with sharps." Tobias moved around to stand behind Phan, making sure everyone could see Phan's chest. "He's scarred in several ways from years of being whipped with... well, with just about everything, honestly. He's been caned so hard he's got scar tissue on his upper thighs from it, and he's got bull whip marks. But if you look closely, you can tell which fine lines are from knives and quills." Tobias allowed himself to smile. "And if you're very close to me, or to Phan, you'll be able to figure out which marks are mine -- aside from the obvious, of course. The rather large 'T' on his hip is a bit blatant."

Everyone laughed again, and there were a few comments. One man tilted his head as if reading the 'T' for himself. Tobias heard Bradford snort and looked over to find him grinning, but Tobias followed his own rules and said nothing out loud.

"So, today I'm going to use Phantom as a bit of a canvas. He's used to sharps, we've done this before, and he's got lovely, lovely skin. I'm going to scratch him, write on him, and even draw on him, working with a variety of tools as I go." He urged Phantom to lie back and launched into the safety issues of working with sharps, right from the first aid kit to sterilizing scalpels to how much blood was too much.

Phantom blessed them all with an extremely obvious erection and a broad grin.

While he talked, Tobias looked around the room, meeting the eyes of various Doms, some of whom he knew well, a few of whom he'd met once or twice, and the two prospective Doms Bradford had told him about but whom he'd yet to meet. Everyone seemed interested and attentive, and why shouldn't they be, really, with Phan putting on such a lovely display.

Even Bradford listened closely. The fact that Nikki was with him meant that they'd had their talk and Nikki either decided he was interested, or at the very least decided he wanted to learn more. One way or the other, they were in the right place.

Noah knelt still as stone with his eyes on Phan. It was hard to guess what that meant; either he was calm enough that he felt he could participate somewhat, or he was anxious enough that he felt he needed to see what would go on for himself.

"One of things I've been doing with Phantom is using knife play as a reward." Tobias held up his scalpel, letting the light flash on its blade. "It works for us that way, as it takes Phan very deep into subspace, almost as deep as pain. It may not work that way in your relationship, of course. However, I'm not here to lecture anyone on their relationships and what they should use a given technique for -- I'm here to demonstrate the technique itself. Phan, roll over."

Phan flipped himself over, taking a moment to ruefully adjust his cock.

Tobias pointed to Phan's shoulder blade. "Once upon a time, Phan had an identity crisis. I scratched his name into his skin with a toothpick. Every night for a month I wrote his name on his shoulder, over and over. It's there now, scarred into him, and I didn't once draw blood."

Tobias set the scalpel down on Phan's spine and ignored the very, very quiet sound Phan made. "A toothpick can be just as effective as a knife." He pointed to a small table by Phan's head. "Feathers, pins, needles, sticks, knives and razor blades. If it's sharp enough to cut you by accident, and if you can make it clean, you can use it to mark your sub."

Phan nodded and Tobias watched the scalpel on his back rise and fall as Phan's breathing picked up. "Okay, boy. Let's show them how you do." He reached down and picked up the scalpel. "Who are you?"

"Phantom, sir."

"Phantom, who?"

"Phantom Shaw, sir." Phan's hands were squeezing the cloth underneath him rhythmically.

"And what are you?"

"I'm your sub, sir. I live to serve you and make your life full and happy."

Tobias smiled, unable not to. "Yes, boy. You do that. Roll over, please, I'm going to write all over you."

"Thank you, sir!" Phan rolled once more and his erection pushed the fabric covering him away.

"Thank me later. Don't come until I say so."

To his credit, Phan didn't snort at the instruction. Maybe it was because of the audience, or maybe he just thought he'd best not risk Tobias taking even the hope of orgasm away. "Yes, sir!"

Tobias made sure the cameras could pick up what he was doing, and then he began to draw.

10

I t was a full twenty minutes later when Tobias gestured for Nikki to come and fetch Phan. He was raw, still bleeding in a couple of places, and covered in come. Tobias thought Phan could probably have floated all the way to the corner where Nikki would tend to him, he was so relaxed and happy.

"Shall we take a short break?" Tobias asked Bradford, sympathetic to the number of men who were filling the room with heated intensity. "Or shall we carry on?" He'd avoided even looking at Noah until then, needing to focus on the skin he was marking.

Bradford stood. "Why don't we take a short break and allow everyone to get some water and see to their subs. That was a very intense display, hmm? Gentlemen, five minutes, please."

The room erupted in chatter, Doms talking to their subs and to each other, some of them getting water from the table of refreshments in the corner. Bradford left Noah kneeling just as he was and approached Tobias. Noah's eyes were still on Phan where Nikki tended to him.

"Impressive," he said, smiling at Tobias.

Tobias shook his head. "Just technique on a subject who knows exactly what to expect. Impressive will be guiding Noah through a taste of the same."

"Well, then, I look forward to it." Bradford leaned around Tobias and took a look at Nikki and Phan. "Nikki seems intrigued. I promised him we'd talk about it tonight after he's had a chance to digest things. He tends to idolize your boys, so I want to be sure he's making a good decision for himself."

Behind them, men began to take their seats again.

"He's more than welcome to talk to either of them at any point. They'll be honest with him -- Noah, especially." Tobias nodded once, slipping back into his role, though he hadn't entirely left it. "Thank you for having Nikki take care of Phan for me."

"My pleasure. And Nikki's, too, I'm sure." Bradford inclined his head and then headed back toward his seat and Noah.

Tobias looked around the room and silence fell almost instantly. It was rather impressive, and a little alarming. Perhaps he'd better start taking care to keep his notoriety in check a bit more effectively. "Thank you," he said quietly. "I hope that you all learned at least one thing you'd like to try or even merely discuss. And I'm sure Phantom appreciates your kind attention as well."

Again, there were smiles, but the room seemed almost eager to move on.

"Now I'd like to... well. You've all met Noah, I'm sure. Noah hasn't been marked this way before, so we'll just see how this goes, shall we? Sweetheart, come to me, please."

Noah stood up and went right to Tobias, likely not even noticing the supportive hand that Bradford had hovering beneath his elbow in case he was unsteady getting to his feet. Rather than kneeling again, he presented smartly, awaiting instruction.

Tobias put his hand under Noah's chin, cupping his jaw gently. "Are you ready?" he asked softly.

Noah nodded, and Tobias felt him lean slightly into the touch. "I'm ready, sir."

"Okay." Tobias leaned in and kissed his cheek. "Lie down, please. On your stomach. You can turn your head to look away from the others if you want."

"Yes, sir."

Tobias watched Noah move, watched him climb up on the table and lie face down. Noah took a few seconds to get comfortable and then let his arms rest down his sides. Tobias noted that Noah did choose to turn his head away from the watching audience, and his breathing seemed a little quicker than it ought to be, but there was no indication that the boy was about to panic.

"For the first time, we need something special," Tobias said quietly. He kept his voice low and soothing, just as if they were alone at home in the stables. It was a scene like any other, and the people in the room were filtered out like so much distracting white noise. Noah was all that mattered. "A quill would scratch like a cat. I'm going to use a blade on you, pet. It will be smooth, cold, and then warm. I won't tear your skin, and I won't go deep enough to scar. Not this time. Do you understand?"

"I understand, sir. Thank you, sir." Noah took a deep breath, and Tobias could tell he was working to stay in his headspace and to stay calm.

Tobias glanced to the corner to make sure Phantom was all right with Nikki, then he selected a new scalpel from his case. "Soon, Noah." He stayed where he was beside Noah and stroked one hand down Noah's back. "Not until you're calm. I'm right here. You're safe, pet. I won't ever damage you."

Eyes closed, Noah seemed to be concentrating hard. "I know, sir. I trust you, Master. I want to please you." Tobias knew that his boy's words were said as much for Noah's own benefit as Tobias', and they seemed to do the trick. Noah's breathing settled out and his shoulders visibly relaxed.

"That's it," Tobias whispered, petting him again. "Good boy. That's it." He rubbed his hand along Noah's shoulders from left to right, feeling the smoothness of his skin. "Just a little today. Just to mark you as mine; so you'll feel how proud I am." He touched the spot on the nearest shoulder blade where he was going to make his initials, then swabbed it with an alcohol pad. "Good boy, Noah."

Slowly, carefully, Tobias began to work. He listened only to Noah's breathing and felt only Noah's body under his hand as he rested the scalpel and watched the skin part under it. His blades were sharp; sharp enough for fine curves, though he wouldn't do any on Noah's back.

Not this time.

The down stroke of the T was done before the blood had even risen to the surface at the top of it. "Good," Tobias murmured again.

The only sound Tobias heard from Noah as he moved the blade was a soft hiss, and he noticed, with quick glance at the boy's face, that Noah's brow was creased. Otherwise, Noah was perfectly still.

His skin slowly beaded red where Tobias had made the cuts, and the flat area around Tobias' fingers felt warm and a little damp with sweat. "Thank you, sir," Noah replied steadily.

"You're welcome." Tobias examined the completed T

critically and moved on to the V. "It won't even itch tomorrow." He etched the V into Noah's shoulder and watched it turn red. "Would you like more?"

Noah opened his eyes and blinked a few times. He was wearing that floaty expression that Tobias had seen many times before. "I'm fine, sir. If you'd like to do more, I... would like to try."

Tobias smiled and started cutting again, drawing a very small border around each initial, making them more than just thin lines. He added depth using straight lines and paid close attention to Noah's breathing and his temperature; endorphins could have him asking for more than his body was actually capable of, but they weren't really in danger of that. Often it would take an hour or more in a tattoo artist's chair to get to that point.

The real goal was to do only so much as the blade would allow, and to give Noah a taste. There was a real fear of knives in his boy, Tobias knew, and he had to approach that very carefully.

Finishing the last line, Tobias reached for another cotton pad and the sterile water. "Shhh. Cold now." He pressed the wet cotton to Noah's shoulder and glanced at Bradford, hoping that was enough of a signal that they needed a few minutes.

Bradford nodded once and stood, taking his cue. Years of friendship and shared interests had made them able to read each other well, and Tobias was particularly grateful for that right now.

"Gentlemen," he said smoothly. "It's time for another short break, let's say fifteen minutes? Feel free to leave the room and help yourselves to refreshments. Tobias will open the floor to questions shortly."

Bradford gave Tobias another nod as everyone began milling around again, and went to check on Nikki and Phan.

Under his fingers, Tobias could feel Noah's increased heart rate. He watched Noah closely as his boy took several deep breaths. "Very cold, sir," was all Noah said, and the emotion in his boy's voice seemed complicated and difficult to read.

"It'll warm." Tobias spoke soft and touched Noah's hair. He lifted the compress and changed it for a fresh one, taking away the worst of the blood. "How do you feel?"

Noah roused a little more, moving his shoulder slightly under the compress. "Strange, sir. Floaty, which is good I guess, and something else that's hard to describe. Relieved, but still... a little nervous. I feel like I need to see it. I'd really like to see, sir."

"Well, let's see if we can do that." Tobias left the compress on him and reached for his phone. "This'll have to do, sweetheart, until we can look at the recording." He lifted the cotton pad and took a photo, then passed the phone to Noah. "See? Small and innocuous."

Noah held the phone and looked at it for a long time before saying anything. He ran his thumb over the picture as if he could touch Tobias' handiwork. "Wow," he breathed. "It felt like so much more than that. Bigger. It's... neat." He smiled and handed the phone back to Tobias. "Thank you, sir."

"You're welcome, sweetheart." Tobias leaned down and kissed him gently. "I'm very proud of you. Are you ready to sit up?"

"I think so, sir." Noah let Tobias help him roll over and sit up, and while he seemed fine, Tobias allowed Noah to lean on him for a moment of comfort. Bradford joined them.

"I've checked on Phan. He's on cloud nine over there, as you might imagine. Nikki's got him all fixed up."

"Thank you, Bradford. We really appreciate it." Tobias petted Noah's hair and smiled at him. "Good boy. In a moment or two, I want you to go and curl up with Phan. I need to answer some questions, but I'll be right here, and then the three of us can go home for the evening."

Tobias felt Noah nod against his chest, and then the boy straightened up. "Yes, sir." Noah slid off the table to his feet and looked over at Phan before slowly moving away from Tobias. Slow, yes, but steady.

"That seemed to go well," Bradford offered.

"Did it?" Tobias smiled a little ruefully. "I admit I wasn't paying attention to anyone but Noah after he got up here. Did I bore anyone?"

Bradford snorted and shook his head. "Bore? You've got to be joking. Could hear a pin drop in here. No one moved. Everyone went on that journey with you, trust me."

Tobias looked over to watch Phan gather Noah up and start whispering to him. "That's good to know. I suppose we should give them all a chance to grill me, yes?"

"We should," Bradford said, waving for Nikki to join him. "Even I have a question or two. Brace yourself." Bradford winked at Tobias before calling the room to order. "Gentlemen, shall we finish up with your questions?"

11

"I'm okay," Noah replied to Phan's worried whispering. "I'm good." How good remained to be seen, as he still didn't have a handle on his own emotions yet. They were floating somewhere outside of him, along with the sting of his Master's blades and the irrational fear he'd fought to let go. But little by little those feelings were coming back to him. "I'm just kind of..." Noah shrugged.

"Floaty," Phan offered.

"Yes."

"That's okay. Floaty is good." Phan kept petting him gently. "It can be pretty intense. Do you hurt?"

"The skin on my shoulder kind of burns all over and it feels really tight, like something might tear if I move too fast." But the hurt itself wasn't what was sticking with Noah; it was something else. He'd been physically hurt plenty of times before in all kinds of scenes with his Master. That was the nature of what they did, who they were. It wasn't the pain itself but the kind of pain, and the way it was inflicted. "It was intense," Noah said, thinking out loud. "But not like a flogger or a bullwhip kind of intense, you know?"

"Uh-huh." Phan's fingers carded through his hair. "It's not the same -- no thump, no sudden surge of pain. Just the slow, steady coldness turning hot. For me, it's like I can feel pressure being let out of my skin."

"It's just so quiet. There's no noise, nothing slicing through the air or snapping against my skin. Just breathing and Master bending over me, nothing for me to do but lie there. The focus gets so narrow." Noah shook his head as if trying to shake something more coherent out, but the whole experience was so new for him. "It wasn't at all what I'd expected."

"Can you tell me what you expected?" Phan's voice was low and soothing, calm. "Was this better than you'd feared or too different to compare?"

"I really don't know. My only experience with blades was with David as punishment. It was quick and cut deep and then it was over. And he was usually angry. I wasn't expecting that, of course, but I guess I was thinking of blade work as more... I don't know, really. More painful? More immediate. It's hard to explain."

"It's two different things -- like the difference between being spanked for being bad and being spanked because Sir wants to see a rosy bum." Phan laughed softly. "So it really is a new experience for you to process. I love it, personally. The narrow focus really keeps me where my head should be, and I find it incredibly erotic."

"Really? I hadn't noticed. Not at all." Noah wasn't sure how he felt about it, yet. "It was intimate for sure, and it definitely held my attention. Kind of like when Sir restrains you and just talks and talks, and the only thing he wants you to do is listen. Only with a bit of a sting."

"Did you feel safe?"

"Yes." Noah nodded. Whatever he was feeling, he was certain of that. "I trust Sir. I always feel safe. If I don't, I use my words." There was a time when he might have been hesitant to do so, but not anymore. He knew how much his Master counted on him to be honest, especially at their level.

"Well, that's what's important." Phan kissed him softly. "Every time we try something new, it has the potential to be scary or too much or maybe even just not something we like. You did great, you know. Trying something new like this for the first time, in front of people, is brave."

"I didn't even remember there were people there," Noah explained. He looked at Phan, curious about something else. "What does it feel like, the things he did to you? Deeper cuts, cuts that mark? Scratches? Do you find all of it equally good?"

Phan grinned at him. "You know me, kitten. Hit me harder and I'll be all the happier. But, yeah. I like the scratches, I like the way he takes months and months to scar me. I like to bleed. Mostly, though, I like the headspace and the way we get so completely tied into each other when it's happening."

"I did feel that." Noah nodded. "Tied into him. He was so still and so focused on me; his hands were gentle and not at the same time. Kind of like with the sensory dep work we do. It was wild. I guess I'd need to try it again to see if it's something that works for us. I get that kind of tied-in feeling with some of the role play we do -- like we both have to read each other so carefully." Noah remembered one particular role play scene that involved being bound with a lamp cord; that day he held onto as one of their best scenes ever. Sir had been so immersed in his role, and they'd walked a very fine line together. It had been amazing.

"When you want to try it again, all you need to do is say so. Sir will do anything we need -- and this is one of those things he likes, too." Phan was smiling and snuggling in. "A lot, at least for me. He says it's easier on his arm."

"I imagine so," Noah laughed softly. "I know we'll talk about it later, so I'll tell him then." He leaned on Phan as much as Phan was leaning on him and looked over at his Master, who was answering questions from other Doms. "He is so happy right now." Noah smiled. "So in his element, so excited that his passion is appreciated by someone. I love it."

Noah wondered if glancing at his Master's back halfway across the room was technically breaking the rules. Not sure, he dropped his eyes again quickly.

Phan chuckled softly and sprawled a bit. If anyone could look indolent and obedient at the same time, it was Phan. "It didn't suck, is what you're saying?"

"It didn't suck, no." Noah poked Phan in the side. Somehow, that phrase summed up the experience better than all of Noah's babbling about it. "It didn't suck at all. Did you look at it? I know it's not anywhere near as cool as yours, but still. I'm proud of it."

"It's beautiful." Phan said it in the voice he reserved for very serious matters. "It is. You're beautiful and his initials on you are beautiful. I couldn't imagine anything else going into you this time, the first time. It's right."

Noah nodded, feeling surprisingly emotional all of a sudden. Not just about the truth in what Phan said, but about the fact that Phan got it. He was quite possibly the only person in the world that really could understand things completely from Noah's point of view. Noah was absurdly grateful for Phan in that moment. "Are you trying to make me cry in front of an audience?" Noah smiled to cover up some of what he was feeling, but he doubted Phan was fooled.

"Nah. Well, maybe." Phan smiled and kissed him again, petting his hair once more. "I love you, Noah. Even if you never do this again, I'm glad you did today. Now you know, and you'll understand when he does it to me."

Noah nodded, sighing at Phan's gentle touch. "It's good. It's all good. Thanks, hon. You're amazing."

Phan nuzzled against his jaw. "I know. Modest, too. Oh, good, people are getting up. Maybe we'll get our Master back. I want to go home, you know? Dinner, bed, snuggles."

"That all sounds perfect." Noah did a quick check of his headspace, not wanting the first thing that came out of his mouth in front of his Master to be something stupid. The stupid stuff was better left to Phan, who seemed to get away with it more often than Noah did. His shoulder still stung, more than he'd thought it would; just enough that he knew he'd be thinking about this for the next few days.

12

Tobias got his little family home as quietly and quickly as he could without insulting anyone by rushing away. He thought he had some leeway, given that the Doms all understood that both Phantom and especially Noah needed him in the aftermath of the seminar. Bradford went out of his way to clear the decks, seeing to the guests and making sure that Jorge was waiting with the car as soon as Tobias had his submissives dressed for public.

The ride home was free of any catastrophe, and it was only late afternoon when he took Noah and Phan to the huge bathroom upstairs so he could give their wounds another good look in the best light they had. He kept Noah close to them as he went over Phan first, thinking that, given the sheer number of cuts, words, drawings and scratches he had, he might need a bit more physical care. Emotionally, he wasn't in the least worried about Phan.

"What shall we have for dinner tonight?" he asked them both as he dabbed at a still-oozing cut on Phan's chest. "You -- no lifting for a few days."

"Yes, sir." Phan nodded, his eyes drifting closed. Even tending to the damage made him hard.

"Macaroni and cheese and chocolate milk shakes," Noah offered from where he was kneeling a few feet away. The boy must have felt Tobias' raised eyebrow and incredulous look, because he quickly went on. "Okay. Maybe meatloaf and mashed potatoes? You know, comfort food."

Tobias smiled. "All right. Comfort food. Can either of you make Mrs. Miller's mac and cheese? If we're going to do it, we have to do it right."

"Phan can," Noah answered. "Well, usually. I'm not sure it's safe to trust him around a hot stove right now."

"Better me than you," Phan said without heat, his voice calm and teasing. "I can make it, sir. I think we have everything. Oh, and dinner rolls, too. Mmm, hot rolls with butter."

Noah practically swooned where he was kneeling. "Mmm. Butter."

Their comfort food was going to make him fat. Tobias shook his head ruefully and admitted to himself that it sounded wonderful. "Okay, dear." He kissed Phan's shoulder and let him up. "You go start that, and we'll be down in a little while."

Phan rolled to his feet, his chest, back, and thighs red with marks. He had to sting, but he walked as if there wasn't any damage at all, his cock still half-risen. "Yes, sir." He paused to kiss Noah and then left them.

"Your turn, sweetheart." Tobias got a fresh bandage and the antibiotic cream ready. "How are you doing?"

"I'm still processing, sir, but I'm fine. I'm just... not sure of anything yet. It was a completely different experience than I had expected."

"They often are." Tobias got him turned around and

carefully peeled off the bandage. The cuts looked fine and likely only needed air in order heal up. "I'm going to leave this open with just some more cream on it. Do you want to talk about it?"

Noah nodded. "Phan and I talked a little, too, and he was really helpful. I think I'm mostly still thrown by how quiet it was. And instead of a sting, it was a slow burn... I've just never experienced anything like that. I... think I want to try it again. Maybe something deeper?"

Tobias considered that while he dabbed cream carefully onto his initials. "Deeper as in longer, or deeper as in deeper cuts? I'm not sure if I'm ready to scar you yet."

"Honestly, sir, I'm out of my depth here, and I think you should decide what you think is best. I just know I want to try it again sometime. I feel like I'm exploring this blind -- I don't know what the next step should be."

"Very wise." Tobias finished with Noah's shoulder and moved them around so Noah was mostly in his lap. "This is one of those things where I lead, then. I'll pay attention to you, and we'll go slowly. Just like always. I'm so proud of you, do you know that? You've come so far from the man who said he wouldn't use a safe word."

"I don't even know that person anymore. I can't imagine taking risks like that, making the kinds of bad decisions I used to make. You've taught me so much about the lifestyle and about myself." Noah shrugged and then grimaced at the sting, and Tobias did his best not to chuckle at his boy. "Believe me, that man had no idea things could be this good."

"But that man was special, too." Tobias rubbed his jaw along Noah's. "So eager to please, so full of wanting, so desperate to find the right path to follow."

"I guess you liked him well enough." Noah grinned and kissed Tobias gently. "Thank you, sir."

"I liked him just fine. I like you more, though." Tobias took a second kiss and then a third. "So. Are you ready for supper? I think the three of us should watch a movie later and go to bed early."

"I can't remember the last time you made it through an entire movie, sir," Noah teased. "I think the last time we got, what, twenty minutes in before we had to go to bed?" Noah slid off his lap and displayed, waiting to follow Tobias downstairs.

"Movies these days are far more boring than my bed." Tobias laughed and left the bathroom, glancing around the playroom as they went through it. "We need to redo the inventory in here next week, pet. Then the entire stables. If I'm going to have more and more people out there, I want it all neat and sure."

"Yes, sir. We have lists for both places. I did the one for the farm a while back, and Phan did one for here shortly after we moved in. I'm sure they won't be difficult to update." Noah fell in step behind Tobias easily. "I was thinking we should check the condition of your library table at the stables, too; it sounded a little creaky last weekend. How much longer before the renovations to the bunkhouse are done?"

"Another few weeks -- the tile mason we want is busy. I'm in no rush, really; I'd rather have Phan all settled before we do another large weekend. I think there's a small party of guests the weekend after next, though, just two couples. We'll make do."

As they walked down the stairs, Tobias could already smell onions cooking and hear Phan humming to himself.

"Maybe you better make sure he doesn't try to do too much in there."

"I'll check on him. He's probably eating all the cheese. Take your time, sir. It takes a while to cook."

"But so, so worth it." Tobias laughed and kissed Noah on the nose. "I'm going to take a shower and put on something a little more casual. Off you go."

Noah grinned. "I like the tie, sir," he said as he walked away. "It's a useful item."

"That's why I never throw one away, pet. Even if they're hideous. Those ones just wind up in the toy boxes." The one he was wearing would be put away properly, however; it was rather nice. Still smiling, Tobias went into the master bedroom and set about relaxing for an evening at home.

He spent longer in the shower than he'd anticipated. The water was fine and he washed quickly, but his thoughts wouldn't settle. Belatedly, he realized he was still riding a bit of a high. He indulged himself, knowing that he had to process as much as Noah or Phan did. The scenes replayed themselves for him, from greeting to questions, and once more Tobias felt a wash of pride. His boys really were wonderful.

Clean and dry, dressed in soft jeans and a cotton T-shirt, Tobias followed the smell of supper right into the kitchen. Fresh bread and cheesy onions and garlic called to him as much as his lovers.

He was treated to a view of Noah's ass as he bent over to retrieve dinner from the oven. Phan was busy mixing something in a blender that looked suspiciously like chocolate.

"Oh, sir. Just in time." Noah sat the dish of macaroni on a hotplate in the center of the kitchen table. The table was set, so the boys must have decided the dining room was too formal for Mrs. Miller's comfort food.

"That looks fantastic." Tobias admired the crispy top on the mac and cheese, then went to peer at Phan's blender. "Milkshakes?"

"Yes, sir." Phan wiggled. "Ice cream, chocolate, milk, and a frozen banana for kicks. So thick I might hurt something sucking it up."

"Don't do that." Tobias gave him a pat on the bum. "I need you able to suck later on."

Phan wiggled harder.

Noah laughed. "With me, you suggest a movie with subtext, but with Phan, you take the direct approach. Fascinating." He set three pint glasses on the counter next to Phan. "What do you suppose that means, Phan?"

Phan grinned and bumped his hip on Noah's. "Means I don't do subtle."

"True." Tobias watched Phan attempt to pour what was really merely soft ice cream into the glasses. "You're a bit more refined, Noah."

"I'm refined sugar." Phan laughed and finally resorted to using a spoon to make the ice cream flow into the glasses. "Dinner is served!"

"I'm starving." Noah picked up two of the glasses and set them on the table. "Come sit, sir." He pulled out a chair and rested his hands on the back of it.

Tobias sat and let Noah push his chair in, feeling oddly amused by the gesture. He reached for the serving spoon and dished out huge portions for all three of them. "I'm rather hungry myself," he said with a grin. "You two can debate what movie we should watch, if you want. I'm going to eat." He grabbed a hot dinner roll and did just that, completely uninterested in whatever movie he'd wind up ignoring anyway.

Everyone ate well. Noah had a second serving and his entire milkshake and didn't look at all like he was going to explode. He took so long to eat that Phan started clearing the table before he was finished.

"Want help with the dishes?" Noah asked, finally bringing Phan his plate.

Phan was standing a careful distance from the counter, and it was pretty clear to Tobias why. "There's not much room at the sink," Phan answered quickly.

"What movie did you all decide on, then?" Tobias asked. He'd heard three or four mentioned and then a lighthearted argument about sappy romances, but had decided to stay out of it in favor of his milkshake.

"Phan wants porn," Noah said simply. "So I suggested we just skip the movie altogether. Phan, as you can probably tell, seems to like that idea." Noah reached with one hand and put his plate in the sink but his other hand slipped suspiciously between the counter and Phan's hips.

"I love it when you do all the work for me." Tobias watched as Noah played, the view particularly loved for the way his name was all over both of them. "Mind your restriction, however." He'd let them get to desperate and then make them wait -- or maybe not. He had yet to decide. Either way, he sprawled a little in his chair and let them entertain him.

"Restriction," Phan echoed. He said it, but it was pretty clear his attention was somewhere else entirely.

"Restriction. Of course. Does that mean you want me to stop?" Noah asked Phan, his fingers stroking slowly down the length of Phan's erection. He was clearly avoiding too much contact with Phan's back, but his lips sought out a clear patch of skin between Tobias' intricate designs.

"I'm not insane." Phan moaned softly and looked like he wanted to lean back into Noah. "Don't stop. Touch me."

Thankfully, Noah had as much showman in him as Phan when it came to Tobias, and he made sure that he didn't block Tobias' view of anything. He continued to stroke Phan slowly, and his lips explored every bit of unmarked skin he could find on Phan's back and shoulders.

"Oh, God." Phan shuddered a little, and Tobias saw the little hint of teeth that Noah used. The small amount of cloth covering Phan wasn't doing its job at all any longer.

"You better pause, Noah." Tobias unfolded himself from the chair and walked toward them, grateful that his jeans were roomy. "Sometimes, Phan, it's better to approach slowly rather than race to the finish line. Especially when the finish line can be moved farther away."

Phan whimpered and nodded. "Yes, sir. No racing, sir."

Noah took a step away from Phan and stood with his arms at his sides and his eyes low. "It's my fault, sir. He tastes good." Despite his apologetic words, Noah was grinning and didn't look the least bit contrite. "And his marks are beautiful."

"Of course they are." Tobias couldn't help leering a little at the marks. "Enticing, even. But Phan is in danger of going too fast, so I suggest you concentrate elsewhere for a while."

"Mmm." Noah stepped past Phan and closer to Tobias. "Elsewhere. Yes, sir." He reached slowly for Tobias and ran warm hands up under his T-shirt. "Will here do, sir?"

"Oh, no. Well, maybe. But I was thinking about something a little farther south." Tobias wished he'd gotten a little closer to the counter; Noah had very clever fingers.

"I can help!" Phan all but scurried to Noah's aid. "Sir. I can."

Noah pushed Tobias' T-shirt up and off over his head. "He could help."

"He could get me a chair." Honestly, he'd just left his chair. How annoying. But Phan was fast and there it was again -- too bad Phan was between it and Tobias.

"Or," Phan suggested, standing behind Tobias and helping Noah with his exploration of Tobias' chest, "You could just lean back a little. I won't let you fall."

"I know you wouldn't." Tobias knew very well that he could count on either of them, always. "But I don't want to rub your cuts open, dear."

"You two duke it out. I'm busy." Noah slid his hands lower and worked Tobias' jeans open slowly. First the button, and then the fly. "Very, very busy," he continued, sinking to his knees.

"Here is just fine," Tobias said immediately. He'd be damned if he couldn't keep his balance while getting blown.

Phan giggled behind him. "Noah, don't rush."

Fingers pushed at Tobias' jeans until they sat low on his hips and Noah's lips were so close to his skin, he could feel Noah's breath. "Never rush a good thing. Sir taught me that. Didn't you, sir?"

"I certainly hope so." Tobias looked down at his head and then shifted his hips a little. "There could be exceptions, though."

Again, Phan giggled. "Different rules." His fingers splayed over Tobias' chest and teased his nipples.

"Pretty much." Tobias grinned and willed Noah to move a fraction to the left.

Noah's tongue grazed over the base of Tobias' cock and

continued outward toward his hip bone. "Different game, too," Noah agreed, circling Tobias' hip bone with his tongue.

"I think I could like this game." Tobias took a steadying breath and stroked his hand down Noah's neck.

Phan's hands moved. One kept teasing at Tobias' nipple, but the other slid down, over his abs and across the hip that Noah was neglecting. "Noah comes up with some lovely games. He really does."

"This one is called, 'See how long it takes before Sir's knees give out.'" Noah followed his tongue with his teeth. "It's a classic. One of my favorites." Noah's teeth dragged across his hip bone and back toward his belly.

"I like it, too," Phan put in as he slid his hand over to the base of Tobias' cock. "As much as I like this, I think."

Tobias gasped. "Boys."

"You got him, Phan?" Noah moved beyond Phan's grasp and lower, to tease at Tobias' balls with his tongue.

"Uh-huh." Phan licked at Tobias' shoulder blade. "I sure do." He stroked slowly, and Tobias' hips twitched. "He likes that, kitten. Do it again."

Tobias closed his eyes, trusted Phan, and went with it. What else could he do, really?

Noah painted Tobias' balls with a hot tongue before gently pulling one and then the other into his mouth. His hands slid up Tobias' legs and wrapped around his thighs. Teeth followed, gently nibbling here and there at the tender skin. "Sir," Noah breathed huskily.

Even with his eyes closed, they rolled back in his head. Tobias could feel himself breathing more heavily, and he had to make some fast choices about how, precisely, he wanted to get off. They were all a little too tired for a full-out hedonistic orgy -- at least without a nice long nap. There was, however, the middle of the night, and he could wake them up again. "Suck me, Noah," he growled.

Noah made no move to obey. "Is that an order, sir? Or a suggestion? Or maybe you're begging. Sometimes it's hard to tell."

"Just for that, you don't get to fuck Phan. Now, suck me."

Phan growled.

"Wow. I didn't even know that was on the table, sir, with our restriction and all. Sorry, Phan." Something about Noah didn't seem sorry. Probably the part of him that knew if it had been on the table once, it would be again. Damn smart sub. He didn't waste any time, though, and swallowed Tobias' cock into his mouth, along with a couple of Phan's fingers.

"Hey!" Phan jerked a bit behind Tobias, and then he did it again with a lot more deliberation. "Ohhhhhhh."

Tobias couldn't blame him. Fingers and cock both were getting a nice tongue bath and suck, and Phan had somehow managed to get his dick to rub along Tobias' ass in a way that he clearly liked. Tobias would have told him to cut it out, but it felt really good -- not as good as Noah's mouth, but good.

Tobias put his hand on the back of Noah's head and started thrusting, gently at first. He fucked Noah's mouth in long strokes and gasped when Phan's hand tightened. "That's it," he whispered. "Just like that, sweetheart. Take it."

Noah's fingers grasped Tobias' thighs and his throat opened wide. Now and then he was able to swallow and everything around Tobias' erection tightened up, but otherwise Noah was completely motionless, taking whatever Tobias chose to give.

Growling, Tobias sped up, spurred on by the supplication. Phan's fingers tugged and twisted at his nipple until it ached and felt hugely swollen, but it was a distant sensation compared to the heat in his balls. He shoved into Noah's throat, and the next time Noah swallowed, Tobias roared and came, his cock throbbing as he spilled.

Phan's thrusts were growing frantic against him, and Tobias was dimly aware of the dampness he was leaving behind. "Go," Tobias told Phan. He reached back and tugged Phan away from him and around his body. "To Noah." He stepped back, shaky and unsteady, to the chair. "Both of you. Go ahead."

Phan pounced.

Noah fell over backward on the kitchen floor with Phan on top of him. "Hot, hon?" Tobias could just see his grin.

With another, rather adorable little growl, Phan started rubbing on Noah. "You tell me, Mr. Hard Enough To Drill My Thigh. This aching?" Phan shoved his hand into Noah's thin pants and started jerking him off. "Hmm?"

Tobias tried very hard not to snicker. They were, after all, very pretty.

Noah tossed his head back so hard it made an audible thud on the kitchen floor. "Ow. Fuck! Phan." He was still out of breath from blowing Tobias, and it was pretty clear that Phan wasn't going to give him one bit of a break. He arched his hips into Phan's fist, which also, Tobias knew, offered Phan much more friction.

"Heh." Phan looked smug for half a minute, then his jaw relaxed and his eyes lost focus.

Tobias finally felt able to move, so he got up, made sure he was at least tucked into his pants, and got on the floor with them. "Later, we'll have more fun," he said, one hand on Phan's back, over a few cuts. "In the middle of the night. For now... I want to watch. Phan's close, Noah."

Phan pushed harder, his arm moving quicker. "Oh, God."

"Yes, sir. I see that, sir. Come on, Phan," Noah panted. "Shoot for me, beautiful."

"You first." Phan's neck was taut. Everything was taut. "Shit, shit, shit -- Noah!" His eyes closed and Tobias could feel his body shake as he climaxed.

"Very nice," Tobias said with a hum of approval. "Your turn, pet."

Tobias watched Noah reach down and wrap his fingers around Phan's, tightening Phan's grip on his cock. Noah jerked himself off, with Phan not much more help than just being gorgeous at that moment. "Sir!" Noah's eyes closed and he clenched his teeth. "Sir! Yes!" Noah came hard, his scent mixing with all the others in the room.

"You got my name mixed up," Phan panted as he curled up on top of Noah. "But that's okay. I know it's hard to remember."

Tobias snorted and kissed them both. "Silly."

"No, I didn't, I was trying to say thank you for letting Phan hump me like a horny goat." Noah groaned. "Jesus, that felt good."

Phan huffed. "Thank him after me. Or you could just kiss me."

"Right. Kisses." Noah reached up and grabbed Phan's face, kissing him hard.

Tobias slid away, rolling on the floor until he could stand without bumping into them or a chair or the table. "All right, my darlings. When you're cleaned up and the dishes are away, you can join me in the bed. I have plans for after a long nap, and I'll need you close by for them to work out."

"Which first, hon? Us or the dishes?" Noah shifted, helping Phan off of him and to his feet.

"Us." Phan went to the sink and got a clean cloth for Noah. "Just a quick wipe. I'll wash you properly in the shower before bed." He glanced at Tobias and smiled. "Thank you, sir."

"You're welcome, dear. Both of you." Tobias smiled back at him, including Noah. "You did me proud today."

Noah straightened his shoulders and smiled. "Thank you, sir. What an incredible day." He snorted as Phan went after him with a damp dishcloth. "Think you'll still be awake when we get there?"

"Oh, I can guarantee it." Tobias watched Phan do his job with a very impressive thoroughness. "Trust me." He turned and left them to their chores, smiling. A nap, boys in chains, and then midnight frolics. He'd absolutely stay awake until they were with him. After all, why waste a moment of his time when the day had been so perfect?

13

I t wasn't often that Tobias had a truly bad day. That kind of thing had vanished when he'd retired from his veterinary practice, for the most part. Long gone were the nights of too much coffee, cursing and swearing through sudden surgery that all too often failed. He no longer worked day and night for weeks during a birthing cycle, only to come home to boys who needed him. He was retired now. He played sex games for a living and filed paperwork.

So when a day blew up in his face, it was always a shock.

This time, it had started out as one of those ridiculous mornings of dropped toothpaste caps, heavy traffic, the wrong file on his desk. If it had stayed that way, one petty annoyance after another, he could have coped just fine.

But, no. Serious breaches within the club had forced emergency meetings with Bradford, and a member had been put on probation. Tobias had never had to make that choice before, and he still wasn't sure it was the correct one. The other option had been expulsion, and to be perfectly honest with himself, Tobias wanted the man exactly where Tobias could keep an eye on him.

Tobias had spent the afternoon talking to Joseph, the sub affected, knowing that his own two submissives were as in the dark about the matter as the rest of club, and right outside his office as well. After an hour or so, Tobias had gone out and sent them home. They went because they were obedient, but it was plain that neither of them were too happy about it.

Tobias wasn't, either, but he needed to concentrate and he needed to do his job. He couldn't be divided, worrying about everyone like he was.

Finally, it was supper time, and he'd made sure Joseph was all right and willing to go home. Tobias wanted his home, too, and a drink, and to just not be the one fixing everyone for a few hours.

He drove himself home, weary to the bone and vaguely lonely, definitely upset. When he stopped at the market and bought flowers for Noah, the weight on his shoulders lessened. That was what he needed. Just for a few hours. He needed Noah.

At the house, he let himself in through the kitchen instead of the front door, one hand clutching the flowers and the other loosening his tie. He felt like he'd aged five years since they'd left that morning to go to the club.

The kitchen was dark, but light spilled in from the downstairs hall. Within seconds, he heard the sound of bare feet hurrying closer, and Noah came through the kitchen door, followed closely by Phan.

"Sir?" Noah's hands were on him quickly, helping him with his tie. "We've been worried about you. Oh." Noah's fingers hesitated at Tobias' throat. "Are those for me?"

Tobias nodded and handed them over with a sigh. "I had the very worst day. Is there supper ready?"

Phan nodded, his forehead creased with a fretful look. "Yes, sir. I'll get it on the table for you."

"I didn't think there was any such thing as a bad day at the club," Noah said, sounding surprised. He took the flowers and set them on the kitchen table, and with that, the worried sub waiting on orders disappeared, and Tobias' equal partner was standing beside him. Noah pulled out a chair for Tobias, guided him into it, and kissed his temple. "You just sit. I'll get you a drink, and then we can talk about it if you want."

Tobias sighed again and watched Phan moving around the kitchen, making up a plate of something that smelled of chicken and rice. "I didn't know it could be bad there, either," he said to Noah. "But it was pretty awful. There was an incident, and I had to do a lot of damage control. Bradford was furious, and rightly so. I'm still not sure if it was my fault at the root or not." He rubbed his forehead, where a headache was looming.

"I doubt very much that it was your fault," Noah said, setting a glass with a couple of fingers of whiskey in it down on the table in front of him. "Bradford isn't one to mince words. If he felt it had anything directly to do with you, I think you'd know. If it involved the misconduct of a Dom, then it might ultimately be your responsibility to fix things, though." Noah sat at the table with him, pulling a chair close.

"I think the fixing is underway -- but I also think my testing for new members might need to be adjusted. I need to re-read the file and see where I went wrong. What I missed." Tobias sighed again and glanced up as Phan put a plate in front of him. "Thank you, Phan."

"You're welcome, sir." Phan shifted his weigh from side to side. "Is there anything I can do to help?"

Tobias smiled at him and took his hand. "Not right now. Thank you, though. Kiss me and go watch some TV or something, okay? I'll get you a little later."

After a moment's hesitation, Phan nodded, then kissed Tobias' cheek. "I'll be in my room if you need me."

Tobias nodded and let him go, reaching for his fork. "Take food with you, if you haven't eaten."

"I'm okay." Phan left the room, and a moment later Tobias heard him going up the stairs.

"Did he actually eat?" Tobias asked Noah.

Noah shook his head. "Neither of us did; we were waiting for you." He turned and looked at the now-empty doorway for a moment and then looked back at Tobias. "It's possible you didn't miss anything, you know. You can't put everything about a person on paper." Noah stood and pulled a plate for himself out of the cabinet.

"I know." Tobias picked at his supper and ate some chicken. "However, it's still my job to screen applicants. This one... I'm giving him the benefit of the doubt and letting him stay, on probation. Every time he plays for the next two months, I'm going to be in the security booth, watching. He's got eight months of being watched by me or someone else to prove himself. Which is all well and good after the fact, but maybe there was something I missed."

Tobias set his fork down and looked at the flowers on the table. "I want to stop thinking about it, really. It's been a hellish day and I'm tired and I won't actually get anywhere with this tonight."

Noah looked over his shoulder and smiled at Tobias. "Okay." There was a moment or two of silence before Noah joined him at the table with his dinner. "What would you like to talk about?" he asked, sliding smoothly into his chair. "Or not talk about at all?"

"I don't even want to think, sweetheart. I need you." It was getting easier and easier to say that kind of thing. It no longer made him want to swallow his tongue, anyway.

Noah nodded and laid a warm hand on Tobias' arm. "You've got me. I know you probably haven't eaten all day, so try to eat something, okay?"

"You, too." Tobias ate some more chicken and shook his head. "The kid was a mess, emotionally. Damn it. When there was a problem with the animals, I could leave it at the office, usually. This is stuck right between my teeth."

"I could talk to the sub if you think that would help," Noah offered easily. "Not that it's any of my business, but... well, you know." Noah rubbed his arm lightly before pulling his hand away to eat. "You can't take care of everyone, Tobias. I know you want to, but--" Noah stopped and snorted, grinning slightly. "Never mind, I forgot who I was talking to. You're not going to listen to that."

Tobias smiled ruefully. "You're right. I'm not." He pushed his plate away and looked at Noah. "The club, and both Bradford and myself personally, do not tolerate anyone ignoring safe words 'for just a moment or two' to see if he meant it. I would have preferred to have gone on thinking that such a thing was understood by everyone who pays us dues." He sighed, then went on, "But I'd like not to worry about anything for the next hour or so. I'm in your hands, Noah. I don't want to be in charge, just for a while."

Noah put his fork down. "One more sip of your drink and you're done, then." He stood, leaving their plates exactly where they were. "Come on."

Tobias smiled as he did what he was told. Noah might have left the police force, but he certainly still knew how to pull up the attitude. In a different world, Noah might have been a wonderful Dom. In this world, Tobias was glad that Noah would occasionally indulge, if only for Tobias' sake.

Quietly, Tobias followed Noah and tried very hard to leave his horrible day behind them both.

They moved wordlessly into the master bedroom, and once Tobias stepped through the door, Noah closed it behind them and locked it.

"Strip and lie on your back in the middle of the bed," Noah instructed, and though his voice was gentle, it was definitely an order.

Almost bemused, Tobias did it, courting the pleasant numbness that he could achieve by not thinking. Noah could take him there, and beyond the numb. Noah had done it before, when Tobias needed it enough to ask.

Noah turned his back and rummaged around in Tobias' armoire, coming up with a pair of leather cuffs that had a soft, padded fur lining and tossing them onto Tobias' bare stomach. "Put those on."

Tobias fingered the cuffs for a moment, trying to remember when he'd bought them. Before Noah could tell him again -- they both had far too much pride to allow that to happen -- Tobias slipped the right one on and then the left, and after a moment tightened the right a little.

"I like those on you," Noah remarked, smiling as he took his shirt off. He laid it neatly on a chair and reached for a short length of chain. Slowly he moved to the bed, sat beside Tobias, and threaded the chain through the headboard, attaching each cuff by a dog clip to the ends of the chain. "There, now," he said softly. "You're mine."

"I've always been yours," Tobias whispered. "Right from the first minute."

Noah nodded. He stroked a hand down Tobias' cheek and drew a line along Tobias' jaw with one finger. "I know."

His fingers moved lower, across Tobias' throat to the collar bone. "I'm all you need to think about right now." Tobias felt the scrape of a fingernail circling one nipple, and Noah bent and licked the other one with his tongue.

"Yes," Tobias whispered. He closed his eyes and tested the cuffs, tugging a tiny bit. "Yes, sir." He let everything be what it was, nothing more and nothing less; he knew his breathing would deepen, that he'd be able to find subspace in a few minutes. For right then, however, he would just do as he was told and keep shedding the layers of the day and who he was. He couldn't shift as quickly as Noah could; he knew better than to push for it, though.

"That's it." Noah licked a spot over Tobias' ribs and then bit lightly. Tobias felt suction against his skin and knew that Noah was drawing up a bruise. Noah's fingers moved deliberately down Tobias' body, over his hip, and down one thigh. "Pretty," Noah whispered as his hand curled around Tobias' cock.

"Thank you." Tobias gasped the words out, surprised to find he'd grown hard. He was supposed to know those things, wasn't he? He tried to be still, but one foot kept wanting to slide on the bed, and his hips wanted to lift. But Noah hadn't said he could, so he didn't.

Noah laughed softly. "Oh, my pleasure, boy."

The bed shifted as Noah climbed off it and began to remove the rest of his own clothing. There wasn't much of it; he slid his sweatpants down over his hips and tossed them aside, and then he was as naked as Tobias himself. Noah climbed back on the bed and moved over Tobias, straddling his legs. Noah's hands slid up Tobias' thighs, massaging as he went. "How do you feel?"

Tobias thought about that. "Better, but not... I'm not

there yet. Getting there, but still scattered. Does that make sense?" He wasn't sure how else to describe it.

"Yes, it does. Good boy. Close your eyes." Noah shifted and pushed Tobias' knees apart, keeping them flat on the bed, and knelt between them. "Bend your knees and open your legs wider." Tobias complied, but apparently not enough, because Noah's voice came back stronger and he rapped on Tobias' knee with his knuckles. "Wider."

Letting his knees fall open, Tobias was unable to keep a moan back. Vulnerability had always been hardest for him, and there wasn't anything more open than his current position. He opened his eyes, looking down their bodies instead of meeting Noah's gaze. Another thing that was work for him, although keeping his eyes lowered was easier than exposing the softness of his body.

"Boy. Eyes closed, I said." Noah gave Tobias' balls a slap. It wasn't hard, but it made a sharp sound and stung just enough.

Tobias bit back a curse and closed his eyes. "Sorry, sir. Too many things to sort out at the moment. I'll try harder."

"I only ask for what I know you can give," Noah chastised gently. "Do you feel safe?"

With a nod, Tobias inhaled through his nose and concentrated on exhaling slowly, looking for a calm place inside himself. "Yes, sir." He did. He was safe with Noah. He knew that in his soul.

"Why don't you tell me your words again? Tell me who you are. Tell me who you belong to." While Noah spoke, his hands roamed over Tobias' legs and hips, massaging, soothing, reminding Tobias he was there. "Tell me what you should be thinking about right now."

"Yellow and red, sir." He'd always liked his words to be

obvious and easy to remember -- partly because he used them so seldom.

"Good boy. Yellow and red. Who are you?"

"I am Tobias. At the moment -- the moment that matters -- I am your sub." He breathed again, almost scenting the air. "I belong to you, no matter what the moment is. All I need to think about is doing as you tell me and pleasing you." Tobias sank onto the bed, the cuffs tugging at his wrists.

He liked that. He liked the reminder, the feeling of his hands being bound within the context of seeking comfort. Noah was comfort. He was safe.

Tobias took another breath. "I'm here to please you, sir."

"Yes. Good boy." Tobias could hear the praise in Noah's voice. "You may open your eyes. You may make any sounds you like and you may speak, respectfully, if you want to. I'm not binding you anywhere other than your wrists, but you may not move. Understood?"

"Yes, sir." He nodded, but was slow to open his eyes, almost reluctant to add stimulation of any kind now that he'd found a little bit of calm. The room, however, was dimly lit, and after a slow moment of adjustment, Tobias was glad he'd opened them; Noah was always a joy to watch.

"Good." Moving up over Tobias again, Noah's fingers shifted, and Tobias felt the warm touch and gentle pressure around his balls. "I love being able to do anything I want to you. I love that you trust me that much. I love you." Noah tasted a nipple again, then tugged at it with his teeth.

"Oh." Tobias felt his calm fracture as a spike of desire and arousal soared through him. "I love you," he echoed. He was looking down at the top of Noah's head; he could almost have kissed him if he hadn't been told not to move. His cock lifted as the reality of being bound by orders settled in. "Yes."

Tobias felt Noah's mouth slowly exploring him, tasting his ribs, bathing his abdomen in kisses, sucking at his hip bones. Finally, Noah's hand moved from his balls and wrapped tightly around Tobias' cock. "Come whenever you want, whenever you need to, but don't expect this to stop until I want it to."

"Yes, sir." Tobias' voice was almost a croak, his throat was so tight. He moaned to let some of the tension go, and tried again. "Yes, sir. Not until you want it to stop." Tobias could feel one of his thighs tense and start to shake. "Oh, God." He wanted, and Noah was right there, so close.

"Good boy. Beautiful." Unlike Tobias, Noah sounded completely in control. Perhaps it was a skill he'd learned being a sub for so long, but there were no urgent movements, no strain in his voice, and it didn't appear he was going to allow anything to rush him.

Noah leaned to the side, letting go of Tobias' cock and reached for the bedside table drawer. Out of it, he pulled a very familiar and nearly empty tube of lube and took his time slicking his fingers first, and then his own stiff cock. Next, Noah pressed two of those slippery fingers against Tobias' hole.

"Want?" Noah whispered. "Tell me."

"I want." Tobias nodded and looked down his body to where his cock was leaking and where Noah's hand vanished from view. "Please, sir. Yes, I want. Need." There had been a time when this would never have happened; not because Tobias didn't want to have Noah in him, but because Noah had been reluctant to top, even from a submissive position. Tobias would never have imagined Noah being so comfortable taking him this way. He was immensely thankful for it, however. "Please," he said again, all but pushing against Noah's fingers.

"Good boy." Noah's fingers pushed inside him, both at once so that Tobias really felt it. They didn't do this often, and Noah knew to take his time at first, but there was decidedly a difference between taking one's time and making sure one's sub knew who was in charge. Noah had learned that lesson well. There was another lesson he'd learned well, too.

Words.

"I'm going to fuck you, boy. Long and slow until you can't stand it anymore. Until everything goes away but you and me and the things we need from each other. Until you beg me for everything you want."

"I could start begging now, if you want." Tobias held himself still, but it was a matter of will. His body wanted desperately to move, to take Noah deeper.

Noah laughed. "If you like." His fingers twisted and pushed farther inside Tobias so his knuckles pressed against Tobias' ass.

Tobias' eyes widened, and he had to force himself to breathe somewhat normally. "Yes, please. Touch me, please. I need you. I always need you, every day." He moaned when Noah's fingers moved, and his hips rocked no matter how hard he tried to be still. "More, please."

"Every day," Noah repeated. His fingers slid away and were quickly replaced by his cock. "Just because you asked so nicely." Tobias felt every inch of Noah as he pushed inside. "And because this is always so fucking good."

"Good!" Tobias arched and froze. "Sorry, sir! Oh, God, you feel good." He wanted to move, but all he could do was rattle his chain and feel Noah taking him, filling him to the point where the stretch was all that Tobias could feel. "Noah. Please. Fuck me."

"Please, fuck me, 'sir.'" Noah growled. He reached out and gave one of Tobias' nipples a warning pinch and a twist.

"Sir, yes, sir!" Tobias barked.

"Oh, I like that. Military -- make a note."

Tobias wasn't able to make a note about anything at all; all of his attention was locked on what Noah was doing to him.

Noah began to move, slowly pulling nearly all the way out and then sinking deep inside Tobias again, controlling and measuring his thrusts. His body weight was balanced on his arms, and with each stroke he would arch lower over Tobias' body. "Fuck. Tight." He took a deep breath and let it out over a long moment. There was no trembling just yet, no moaning, none of the things that Tobias had learned meant that Noah was losing control. It would come, it always did, but for now, Noah was still very much in charge.

Which meant that Tobias didn't have to be. At all. The entire point of the situation broke over Tobias, and he finally gave in to it. "Sir," he begged. "Please, sir. Use me." He wrapped his hands around the chain and pulled, straining in his cuffs. "I'm here for you to take, to use, to fuck." His hips rocked, and Tobias knew he was risking Noah's ire, but the motion had been purely instinctive; he doubted he'd have been able to stop if he'd tried. Noah's cock butted against his gland, and Tobias had to clamp down and freeze so he wouldn't start fucking himself on Noah's cock again and again. "Please," he begged again.

"Not yet." Noah meant it. The pace was painstakingly slow as Noah thrust over and over. Tobias could feel Noah's gaze on his face, feel the stare of his Dom on him, demanding, expecting, taking him out of himself. Time slid away, and it felt like forever before Noah started fucking him in earnest.

Tobias could barely beg. His whole body was tingling and his mind was focused on staying still, doing what Noah had said. He knew he could come, but he desperately wanted to hear Noah's breath quicken, to hear and feel how close Noah was before he went. He needed to know that he'd pleased Noah before he could sink into pleasure himself.

Sounds poured out of him, unbidden. Whimpers and gasps, more than one grunt as Noah slammed into him, taking his breath. He could feel the pool of pre-come on his belly growing as he leaked, and he could feel one of his wrists being rubbed raw.

It was the wrist that sent him over. One more pounding thrust, and Tobias was on the very edge of his control. "Please, sir," he whispered one more time. "I'm going to come."

"Yes," Noah replied quickly. He sounded winded and his voice was rough, and Tobias knew he was working hard to keep his composure. Hard enough that he likely wouldn't last much longer.

Noah reached up suddenly and locked fingers with Tobias', pinning him down. "Now."

What breath Tobias had was pushed out of his lungs in a rush as he tried to yell. Incoherent, speechless if not voiceless, Tobias tightened until he thought he might break, and then suddenly relaxed as he came. His body was totally out of his control, and he found he didn't even want to try; pleasure took him, and his vision swam as he spiraled up and up, every nerve firing.

He could hear Noah's voice and he felt Noah's body taking him with hard, deep thrusts, over and over through his orgasm. Their palms slipped against one another despite their tight grip. Noah's breath was coming in quick pants and low grunts, and his hips made a sharp sound against the exposed flesh of Tobias' thighs.

"Fuck! Hot. Jesus!" Noah swore, stuttering as he tried to get a deep breath, and seconds later he was coming, too, filling Tobias with heat. His hair was damp, his rhythm faltered, and his former composure seemed to leave him altogether. "Oh, God, yes!"

"Sweetheart." Tobias' eyes closed and he lay there, limp and boneless. His breath was ragged, little more than shuddering gasps, and he didn't even bother trying to move his arms. He had a feeling they'd be sore in the morning.

Noah kissed him, stealing a little more of his breath away, and he felt Noah's fingers working the buckles on the cuffs. One at a time they let go, the chain making a cheerful sound as the cuffs fell away.

"Sweetheart," Tobias whispered a second time. He willed himself to move just a little, and succeeded in wrapping his arms around Noah's torso. "Thank you."

Noah moved then, helping Tobias rearrange his legs so that Noah could lie beside him. "Really, it was my extreme pleasure." Noah laughed softly. "Holy hell, was it ever."

Tobias smiled and burrowed closer, letting Noah do the cuddling. "You do know how to make my bad days fade away."

"Shhh. Don't think about your day." Noah stroked fingers through Tobias' hair. "Just rest."

"It's a little early for actual sleep." That didn't stop Tobias from sighing and letting himself be lulled. "But I don't want to move just yet. Shower in a while, maybe."

Tobias felt Noah shake his head. "You're such a control freak, Tobias. Who says you can't fall asleep at eight o'clock? If you want to, go ahead."

"Not without at least being slightly less sticky." Tobias

laughed softly and yawned. "But maybe the shower can wait for morning."

"Give me a minute and I'll get something to sponge you off with, then." Noah didn't seem ready to make a move himself just yet. "Mmmm." Noah stretched. "That was awesome."

"I try," Tobias teased, trying to sound modest.

"You suck at being still," Noah said with a snort.

"I know," Tobias said, delighted. "And I was even trying. You're a much better sub than I am."

"I know. Good thing, because my Master is very particular." Noah kissed his forehead and then slipped away. "One nice, clean cloth coming up."

"Thank you, pet." Tobias smiled as he realized he was already slipping back into his usual mode. "Thank you." He lay comfortably warm as Noah left him, pausing to snort, and waited to be clean. Sleep would come easily, thank goodness. He'd wondered about that earlier in the day.

Once more, however, Noah had proven that occasionally stepping back from roles to merely be partners was something they needed to do. It wasn't an easy lesson for Tobias, nor was it a natural thing for him to do, but the rewards had always been there.

It was getting to be an easier step. Maybe one day it would be something he could do without getting butterflies when he bought flowers. Or perhaps not -- Tobias actually kind of liked the butterflies.

Still smiling, Tobias fell asleep, waiting for Noah to come back.

14

Noah woke early the next morning, just after the sun came up. He left Tobias asleep as he took a quick shower and then headed out into the kitchen to make coffee. He felt fabulous; loose and relaxed, clearheaded and well rested.

He measured out the coffee carefully and then dug around in the refrigerator for some eggs. He'd scramble some up, bring some to Tobias and to Phan, and get everyone off on the right foot.

He almost jumped out of his skin when Phan spoke. "Good morning," he said, his voice flat. Noah hadn't even seen him, sitting at the kitchen table.

"Jesus! You scared the hell out of me." Noah laughed and took a second to catch his breath. "I'm making some eggs. You sound like you're ready for coffee." He made his way over to Phan and leaned over him for a good morning kiss.

Phan turned his head away. "I ate, thank you."

Noah hesitated, pausing where he was for a moment before straightening up again. "O... kay." He looked Phan over. "Did you sleep?"

"Eventually." Phan looked at him and Noah doubted the truth in "eventually," given the circles under his eyes. "Once I figured out no one was actually going to come get me."

Something twisted in his gut, and Noah sighed heavily. "Yeah. Um." He leaned back against the counter and watched Phan carefully. "I'm really sorry about that. I'd meant to get Tobias to sleep and then come back out here to help clean up the kitchen and all, but we both fell asleep." He shrugged. "Really, I'm sorry."

"Whatever." Phan stood up and headed for the door to the living room and, presumably, upstairs. "Enjoy your breakfast."

"Hey." Noah jogged after him. "Hey, come back here."

"You may be boss with him sometimes, but you're not the boss of me. You want to talk to me, you can come upstairs."

Noah stood in the doorway to the kitchen and watched Phan walk purposefully toward the staircase. "Shit," he whispered, debating whether it was a better idea to follow Phan or go wake Tobias. Quietly, he followed in Phan's wake. "Okay, I'm coming."

Phan didn't even look back as he went up to his room. "I don't know why. You said you were sorry. What else is there?"

Noah shook his head, wondering what the hell he ought to say next. What else was there, indeed? "Well, if you're not accepting my apology, then there's obviously more, Phan."

"Ya think?" Phan turned at the top of the stairs and glared down at him. "Honestly, Noah. Think about this. He comes home, he needs you. I get that. What I don't get is that I'm totally forgotten after you do whatever the fuck it is you do. I can't sleep; I can't do anything but worry. I know nothing about what's wrong. He won't let me help, and then no one bothers to get me after. And you shrug a half-assed apology at me! Now do you get it?"

Noah stared at Phan. "Well, he needed me, and I didn't think past that. It isn't a half-assed apology, though; I... shit." He blinked, working through the jumble of reasons and excuses, and he couldn't figure out how to turn them into anything that Phan would understand. "He spent a lot of yesterday trying to help a sub who... had a really bad experience with one of the new Doms." He looked up at Phan again. "What do you want me to say?"

"I want you to acknowledge that it hurts, damn it! I want you to do more than shrug and pass it off as no big deal that I got dismissed and ignored. I want you to think about how you would feel if it was you." Phan turned and started walking again. "Jesus Christ, Noah."

Noah took the rest of the stairs two at a time. "Will you stop walking away from me, damn it?" When that didn't get any response whatsoever, Noah tried again. "Phan," he sighed. "Would you please stop walking away from me?" He stopped just outside Phan's bedroom door. The rules about their bedrooms were simple -- Noah wasn't allowed to enter Phan's room without permission, any more than Phan was allowed in Noah's. "I'm trying, okay?"

"Are you?" Phan stood just past the safe threshold and crossed his arms, his eyes shining. "Tell me, then. How would you feel?"

Noah crossed his arms as well and stood up tall. "I'd feel..." He tried to find the word he was looking for. "Well, I would feel like..." How would he feel if Tobias walked in the door and needed Phan instead of him? How would he feel if he had no idea what was happening behind closed doors? How would he feel if Phan was whistling while making coffee? "Fuck," Noah sighed and slouched. "I'd probably hate you a little."

Phan collapsed in on himself. His arms dropped and he turned away, reaching to his dresser to pick up a pencil. He fiddled with it, looking down at his hands, and finally mumbled, "Don't hate you. I couldn't hate you. But I'm pretty pissed, kitten."

Noah nodded. "I should have at least come out after he was asleep and told you what was going on."

"You should have fetched me to bed," Phan corrected, glancing up.

"Yeah?" Noah searched Phan's eyes. "Maybe I should have. I don't know. I'm not as good with this as I thought I was, I guess." He shifted his weight from foot to foot. "He was just such a mess and he needed so much and I didn't think of anything else."

Phan sighed. "And that's the way it's supposed to be, I guess. But... fuck, it's hard on me, Noah. I've never been forgotten in the aftermath, either. Then you just..." He waved a hand. "You blew it off like it wasn't any big deal. I sat in here for hours, waiting. Hours."

"I didn't mean to blow it off."

Phan tossed the pen onto the bed. "I know. But you did. And now I need to figure out how the hell I'm going to talk to Sir about this."

"It's my fault. He was going to get up and shower, and I told him to just rest and go to sleep. If he'd done what he wanted to, he probably would have talked to you."

"Did he need to sleep?"

"Yeah, he really did." Noah nodded, remembering how Tobias was dead asleep before he'd even made it back from the bathroom. "I'm not sure he would have been able to stand long enough for a shower."

"Then you handled that right. He's the priority." Phan shrugged and looked around his room. "But I still think it was clear I was to sleep downstairs, and I'm upset that I was flat-out forgotten. It makes me feel like I'm... something. Something less."

"You're not less, Phan. You're every bit as important. I'm just an asshole. I'm really sorry."

Phan shrugged again and sighed. "Okay. Thank you. You should go make his breakfast; he'll be awake soon, probably."

Noah felt so ashamed of himself that he couldn't even hold Phan's eyes for more than another second. "Right." He took a step back from Phan's doorway. "I'll go do that." He turned to head downstairs.

"Noah?"

"Yeah?" He stopped moving, but he didn't turn around.

"I know it wasn't intentional." Phan sounded sad and exhausted under the sincerity.

Not trusting himself to speak, Noah just nodded and then hurried down the stairs. Distraction would be good. Eggs, coffee, some time on his knees, his morning discipline. Just some time to get perspective, because right now he felt more off balance than he had in years. He couldn't remember the last time he'd let anyone down the way he had Phan. Phan had every right to be upset, every right to take him to task, and possibly Tobias, too.

Upstairs, Phan's door closed, just loudly enough that Noah heard the snick of the catch.

Noah glanced back over his shoulder at the closed door. Phan was right about another thing; Noah had no right to tell him what to do.

Downstairs in the kitchen, the coffee was ready, so Noah got the griddle hot and started beating the eggs.

15

Tobias woke up alone, which was a little out of the ordinary but not unheard of. He rolled out of bed and found some clean clothes, then wandered to the kitchen. He knew he was in dire need of a shower, but he was also in dire need of coffee. Coffee was probably easy to find, since his bed was empty, and then he'd attempt the shower.

Coffee was, in fact, the first thing that greeted him as he approached the kitchen. He could smell it all the way down the hall.

The second thing to greet him was Noah, who went to his knees as soon as Tobias entered the kitchen. "Breakfast is almost ready, sir," Noah told him, "I've made eggs."

"Thank you." Tobias absently petted Noah's hair and looked around. "Phan's not up yet?" Oh, God. Phan. Tobias' hand stilled. "Oh, dear."

"He's in his room, sir," was all Noah offered.

"Have you spoken to him?" He was almost afraid to ask.

"Yes, sir."

Tobias rolled his eyes. "And is he in need of a great deal of making up to?"

"You could say that, sir." Noah shifted slightly. "He's... very upset."

Tobias nodded. "I imagine he is. Angry or hurt? And can I please have some coffee before I try to fix this?"

"Oh! Yes, sir." Noah stood and hurried to the coffee maker. "Hurt. He only gets angry if you say something stupid."

"If I say something stupid?" Tobias felt his eyebrows lift.

"Yeah, something like 'what do you want me to say?' or... you know, shrug at him or something." Noah came over and handed Tobias a mug of steaming coffee.

"Oh. You mean if you say something stupid." Tobias took the coffee and smiled gently at him. "It'll be okay, sweetheart. I'll talk with him and apologize and find out what he needs to feel better. We'll fix it."

Noah headed back to the stove and put a spoonful of eggs and a couple of slices of bacon on a plate. He sat the plate on the kitchen table. "I'll get you a fork."

Tobias watched him, not moving. "Talk to me, pet," he said softly. "What are you feeling?"

"Just that Phan is right, and I don't know how to make it better next time. I don't know if there should be a next time. I don't know if I've just lost something or not. All I know is that he's right." Noah set a fork on the table and went to his knees again.

"He's right about what?" Tobias sipped his coffee and trod carefully. If they were both going to go to pieces, he'd have to do some fast evaluating to figure out who to ease first.

"That he felt left out. That we should have included him. That... well. You should talk to him, sir."

Tobias shook his head. "I will, trust me. Probably at length. But I need to know what you're feeling -- what his being right means to you. Also, you know as well as I do that he can't be included in things like last night -- it's in his contract at his request."

"I'm not sure he's happy to bow out, either, though." Noah sighed. "I'm not sure it's that simple for him anymore."

"Noah. Tell me how you feel." Tobias sat at the table and looked at his submissive before picking up his fork. "Not Phan. You."

Noah was quiet for a bit as if gathering his thoughts. When he finally spoke, it appeared that his words were very carefully chosen. "I understand that Phan was upset. And, truthfully, I think he had every right to be upset. But I thought I had every right to... you brought home flowers. To me, that means things are about you and me. I don't like feeling guilty about being there for you, about being us. If I were Phan, I would have been very upset about not knowing what was wrong, not being able to help, being left alone. I would have, sir. I just feel like it's an impossible balance. I feel very conflicted, and I feel like I let Phan down."

Tobias ate his breakfast and thought about that for a few minutes. "You're taking on too much," he said finally. "You absolutely do not have to consider Phan's feelings when I bring you flowers. That's up to me and me alone. Also, I understand his hurt as well -- I made a huge error last night and will have to make it up to him. You can feel badly for that part, but not for what we do."

There was another silence before Noah responded. "Apart from you, he's my best friend, sir. I don't see how I can not consider his feelings."

"Are you able to consider them but do as I want anyway?"

"I..." Noah's struggle to balance the orders of his Master and the feelings of a friend was evident. "That's my duty to you, sir. Yes, sir."

"Good." Tobias put his mug on the table and stood up. "Come with me. You can listen to me talk to Phan. This is about all three of us."

"Yes, sir." Noah fell into place behind Tobias' shoulder, but Tobias sensed that he was uneasy.

"Easy, pet. We'll talk and talk and talk and work it out. Same as always." Tobias led the way up stairs and stopped outside Phan's door. "He didn't close it in your face, did he?"

"Oh, no, sir," Noah answered quickly. After a pause he added, "But he didn't invite me in, either."

Tobias nodded. "Not ready for the kiss and make up, then. Okay." Tobias knocked politely at the door. "Phan? Are you awake?"

There was a pause, and then Phan's voice called, "Yes, sir. Coming." The door opened and Phan stepped back, his eyes down. "Good morning, sir."

"Thank you. But it's not, is it?"

Phan shook his head, and Tobias could see his lip tremble until Phan bit it. "No, sir."

Tobias, who didn't actually need permission to go into Phan's room, went in and held out his arm. "Come here, dear. Let me start to apologize."

Phan shook his head minutely but went to him, burrowing in. He also didn't say that it was okay or that Tobias didn't need to apologize.

"I'm sorry," Tobias whispered in his ear. "I'm sorry, Phan. I handled last night all wrong, and I'm so sorry you're hurt."

Phan nodded against his chest and took a deep, shuddering breath. "I'm hurt," he whispered back. "I was all alone last night. I worried."

"Mmmhmm." Tobias nodded and rubbed his hand down Phan's spine, feeling each knot of bone. "I know. I would have been very worried, too. It was unfair of me to send you off without even a word. It won't happen again."

"I know." Phan sighed and stayed where he was. "I know. Why did you forget me?"

Tobias winced. "Because I was tired and selfish and satiated. I have no excuse other than that, dear. I forgot to ask Noah to get you, even if I was too tired to come up myself. I apologize for that most of all."

Phan nodded again but didn't say anything else for a long time, long enough for Tobias to glance around the room, taking in the casual disarray of art supplies and canvases and sketch books. At least Phan was still working away at his art to express himself. Tobias was sure he didn't really want to see the painting that the previous twelve hours may have inspired. In the corner of the room by Phan's bed was a milk crate half covered with a large sheet of paper, like it was hiding something -- probably the surprise that Phan was still working on.

Assuming he hadn't wrecked it, alone in the dark around two a.m.

Tobias sighed and turned his head to look back at Noah, to see how he was doing.

Noah was still and silent and the tension in his shoulders was obvious. His eyes were riveted on the floor as if he didn't dare look anywhere else. Tobias had the feeling he was doing his best to disappear, to pretend like he wasn't there.

"Phan?" Tobias said softly, still rubbing Phan's back. "The three of us need to talk, to find a way to help you feel better. Okay?"

Phan nodded, his fingers curling into Tobias' T-shirt. "Okay, sir," he whispered.

Tobias looked around. "Here? Or would you rather come downstairs?"

"Here is okay," Phan said softly. "But it's not our space. It's mine. We should... I dunno."

Tobias nodded. Right, he was the boss. "Okay. Downstairs, come on. To the living room, and you both need to eat something."

"Yes, sir." Noah waited this time for Phan to follow Tobias before falling into line himself.

Tobias didn't waste any time getting them settled on the couch, one on either end. Toast only took a few moments, and he made sure they both ate before sitting down with them. "Okay. Let's start at the beginning. Phan, I handled things badly when I got home last night. I should have greeted you properly and made sure that you'd eaten before I asked for some time with Noah. Also, I should have allowed you to see that, while I was upset, I was physically okay, and I should have reassured you that it was just a bad day, nothing dire. You have my complete apologies, and I promise to take greater care in the future."

Phan nodded and looked at his knees. "I appreciate that, sir," he said softly. "And I'm glad you're all right, and that you're feeling better this morning."

Noah seemed to be watching Phan with some interest. He nodded gently but otherwise remained silent.

Tobias nuzzled Phan's hair for a moment. "I'm better. Thank you. I know that had to hurt, to be more or less dismissed without any idea what was going on."

Phan nodded and kept looking down. "I'm glad you have a way to feel better, though," he said softly.

"Permission to speak, sir?" Noah asked softly.

"Of course, sweetheart." Tobias nodded. "We're trying to sort everything out. Both of you are free to say what you wish."

"Sometimes in those situations, sir, you're not really in your usual mental state, so, Phan, I will try to help Sir remember to make sure you're okay before we disappear. And make sure we come get you later so you're not alone. I wouldn't want to be alone, either."

Phan nodded and leaned into Tobias. "That was the worst part. Being alone when I knew you were done and asleep. I know you do what you need... but after, when everyone is better, I should be there." He swallowed so hard Tobias could feel it. "I mean. I'm sorry. I know it's not up to me, but you said and then it didn't and I just..."

Tobias tugged him close. "Shh. You're right, I said. You should have been there, after. I'm so, so sorry. Noah is, too. It won't happen again, we promise. Shh."

Phan nodded and burrowed and Tobias could feel him shake. To Noah, he mouthed, "Exhausted?"

Noah nodded. "Didn't sleep," he mouthed back.

Tobias sighed and petted Phan until he calmed down a little. "Okay? Better? You should take a nap, dear."

Phan nodded. "Can Noah stay with me?" he asked, his voice only slightly above a whisper.

Noah's chin lifted and he looked at Phan. "Yes," Noah answered quickly, before Tobias could himself. He blushed hard, though, and dropped his eyes, likely realizing it technically wasn't his call. "I mean... if... I'm sorry, sir. It's up to you, of course."

Tobias snorted. "As if I can say no," he said dryly. "Take him to bed, Noah. Napping, petting, loving. I'll get myself to the club, and you two can come by after he's rested and fed. You're in charge of taking care of him, Noah."

Noah moved to their end of the couch. "Yes, sir. I'll take care of him, sir." He held out his arms to Phan. "Come on, hon, let's get you tucked in."

Phan disengaged and more or less attached himself to Noah. "Stay with me," he said, transferring his burrowing. "Okay? Yeah, okay."

Noah nodded. "Not going anywhere." He pulled Phan to his feet. "Thank you, sir," he said to Tobias before leading Phan away.

"No problem." Tobias watched them go and sighed. He hoped Bradford had some free time; he could see that he'd need a bit of a sounding board with his first cup of coffee at the club.

16

L ong gone were the days when Tobias' arrival at the club got him anything more than a respectful nod at the gate and a polite good morning from anyone who happened to see him. Tobias much preferred this to the scurrying of the staff and subs to spread the news of his presence; being a fixture was almost pleasant.

It was certainly a lot more peaceful, anyway.

After having a few words with Pat about Noah not being in until later, Tobias headed down the hall, avoiding the houseboys as they cleaned for the day before members arrived. He liked the houseboys -- the entire concept made him happy -- but he knew that Bradford wouldn't be anywhere near his own office while the wood was being polished. Instead, Tobias dropped his coat off in his office and headed to the dining room for a proper cup of coffee, and perhaps a proper brunch with Bradford. His eggs had long since been eaten away by the stress of the morning.

"Good morning, sir," Brian greeted him at the door. "Coffee? Master Bradford is looking over the morning paper if you'd like to join him."

Tobias squinted at the boy, trying to figure out what was different about him. Same hair cut, same carefully tailored uniform, but there was something about his face; he was practically glowing. In fact, Brian looked positively radiant this morning.

"Did you have a pleasant evening?" Tobias asked him, trying very hard not to look like he already knew the answer. He thought maybe Brian deserved all the glory he could get; he'd waited long enough for it.

"Oh, yes, sir!" Brian grinned and leaned closer to Tobias. "Very good, sir. Wonderful. Best ever." He stood there for a moment, beaming at Tobias, before he remembered himself. "Oh, but... Master Bradford is this way, sir," he said quickly, trying to hide the full extent of the blush on his cheeks. "Just right over here, sir, I'll get your coffee."

Laughing, Tobias nodded and started across the dining room. "Bring the pot, pup. Thank you."

"Yes, sir. Of course, sir," Brian chattered as he hurried away.

Tobias pulled out the chair opposite Bradford and sat, looking around for Nikki. "Good morning, Bradford."

Bradford lowered his paper as Tobias took his seat. "Well, good morning. I was wondering if you'd be coming in today. You're past your usual hour." He watched Tobias as he reached forward and picked up his coffee cup.

"There were issues at home. Where's Nikki?"

Bradford raised an eyebrow. He set his paper down and leaned back in his chair. "There were... issues at home."

Tobias raised an eyebrow right back at him, feeling waspish. "Your home, too? I know you can't mean my home, since that's exactly what I just said."

"I meant mine. There must have been something in the air yesterday. Perhaps it was a full moon."

Brian arrived with the pot of coffee and a mug for Tobias. "Oh, thank God," Bradford said with a sigh. Both men waited for Brian to fill their mugs, and then Bradford thanked him and sent him away. "So, do we want to take yesterday's events out on each other, or shall we drink our coffee and try again in a few minutes?"

Tobias drank half his cup of coffee, burning his lip in the process. "When I take things out on you, it never ends well. Tell me what happened with Nikki?"

"Long story. Why don't you start?"

"Too late, I asked you first."

Bradford scowled at Tobias, but that look was quickly replaced by something far more troubling. "Ah, well. Nikki is apparently very, very good friends with Joseph." Bradford sipped his coffee and then continued. "I suppose I ought to have been aware of the extent of their friendship, but I wasn't until last night, when Nikki came to me and, very unexpectedly, requested some modifications to his contract. We discussed in general terms the kinds of things he was talking about, and..." Bradford shook his head and appeared to be trying to keep his composure. "Well." He rubbed his forehead with his fingers.

"Well?" Tobias didn't know who Phan and Noah's closest friends were, either, other than each other. That fact was less troubling than Nikki's reaction to the situation.

"Well, you know Nikki." Bradford replied. His tone was casual, but Tobias knew him well enough to see the worry in his eyes. "He was timid as a mouse when he started with me. He hadn't had any kind of trust in his life before, and certainly no stability like he has now."

"I remember. Always polite, but very soft spoken, nervous, quick to please."

Bradford nodded and set his coffee cup down on the table in front of him. "Just so."

"So... something scared him?"

"Something terrified him. Enough that he was suddenly, irrationally, doubting me." Bradford shook his head and his voice grew harsh. "I was insulted, he was upset, and after a lengthy discussion as to why, we decided... we decided to... take a break."

Bradford ran his thumb around the edge of his coffee cup, staring into the dark liquid as if it might have something to say to him. "He's decided to go away for a couple of days, and we've agreed to talk again when he gets back." He looked up at Tobias, trying to hide his emotions, if not from Tobias, at least from the other Doms in the room. "It'll be fine."

Tobias very carefully and slowly put his coffee cup down. "I think," he said, keeping his voice low, "that we should finish this in my office." The pain in Bradford's eyes was enough to have Tobias carting him off right then, but there were eyes all around them, and stopping drama was more or less in the job description. Bradford needed support, but neither of them wanted that to happen in the dining room.

"I'd much prefer to change the subject," Bradford protested, not moving.

"Of course." Tobias nodded. "I don't doubt it. Would you, however, let me do that?"

"No. But I'd prefer to be allowed the double standard just this once."

Tobias didn't move, watching Bradford impassively.

"Oh, bloody hell," Bradford growled after a moment. He stood up, tossed his napkin into his plate, and took his mug with him. He looked down next to his chair and sighed again. "Christ. I'll get the damn pot, then, shall I?" He picked it up and gestured for Tobias to lead the way.

Tobias gave him a sympathetic look as he stood up and headed out of the dining room. "I'll have the phones switched over to the bar, too," he said, being careful not to spill his own coffee as he walked. "We'll call it a director's meeting."

"Wonderful. Can I spike my coffee?"

"Yes." Tobias opened the door to his office and scooped his coat up from where he'd tossed it over the back of a chair. "And I have the cigarettes, too." In a moment, the coat was hung up and Tobias had retrieved the bottle of whiskey from his desk, pausing long enough to redirect his phone to the bar and let Dave know that he and Bradford were not to be disturbed. "Okay. You first." He passed Bradford the bottle and tried to remember where he'd hidden his ashtray last.

Bradford set the coffee pot down on a coaster on the table and took the whiskey from Tobias. Then, without another moment's hesitation, he launched into explaining the events of the previous evening, clearly making no effort to hide his frustration at all. "Joseph was a wreck yesterday, and Nikki reacted strongly to that. He was timid enough before we... before he started working with me, and now he wants assurances I can't give him. He blames me for yesterday's incident as if I were in the damn room at the time, and he's suddenly lost his footing. He doesn't trust me the way he did before."

Bradford gestured broadly with the hand that held the whiskey bottle. "I tried to explain that it was understandable that he was upset about his friend, and he may even be right for blaming me to a certain extent, but that I've given him no reason to doubt me personally. I tried to explain that he was probably having an emotional reaction and that he might want to think about things a bit longer before we started tightening up a contract that has been working well so far."

Bradford started to pour himself some whiskey but seemed to change his mind, and set the bottle down with his mug beside it. His voice grew softer, but he didn't hide his anger. "He accused me of being unwilling to listen, unwilling to negotiate." He shrugged. "Maybe he was right, Tobias, but I'm not abusive, I never have been, and I sorely resent the very idea of extensive safeguards when I've done nothing but love him." Bradford pressed the heels of his hands to his eyes. "This is why I don't take on subs. How the fuck do you do this with two of them? I've completely lost perspective when it comes to him."

"So has he, apparently." Tobias frowned as he thought. "Oh, look. Ashtray." He brought it over and set it down, along with the cigarettes. "You're right, in a nutshell. He's having an emotional reaction to a scary thing. In short, he's having a temper tantrum."

"Thank you." Bradford snatched up the cigarettes and lit one. "But being right doesn't do me one damn bit of good right now, Tobias."

"No, I suppose not. I know not. Been there." Tobias topped off his coffee with whiskey and sat back. "On the other hand, the fact that he's able to tantrum without being terrified you'll cut him loose is a big step for him, in a way."

"Yeah. A big step." Bradford leaned forward and picked up the whiskey, this time splashing some in his coffee as well. "It's an 'I don't need you as much as you think I do' kind of step. A step away from me." He took a sip of his coffee.

"That's ridiculous, and I think you know that. It's more of a boundary-seeking step. An affirmation-seeking step."

Bradford sipped his coffee and sighed. "I know, I know. Intellectually, I know a lot of things. Physically, emotionally,

I know absolutely nothing right now except that I want him back. You know what I was thinking while I wasn't sleeping last night? I was thinking why did I let myself get so attached to him? The only other serious relationship I've ever had went to shit years ago, and I've avoided commitment quite happily since then, so why did I allow it to happen this time?" Bradford seemed to sink deeper into his chair, evidently not looking for answers to those questions.

"Do you know where he is, at least? As in, can you get messages to him?"

"I gave him a cell phone. I haven't dared use it."

Tobias sipped his coffee for a moment. "Maybe you shouldn't yet. At supper time, perhaps. He is, after all, having a tantrum. By supper, he may be at the stage where he's realizing what a brat he's being to you and seeing how he could have otherwise dealt with his legitimate fear. And you, my dear friend, aren't in that place where you're ready to talk to him yet; you're too hurt."

Bradford nodded slowly. "I am, you're right. And angry. And very nervous, besides. And if this conversation goes any further than us, I'm going to have to kill you, because, as you know, I have a reputation to uphold." He snorted and took a long drag off his cigarette.

"Who would I tell?" Tobias dismissed the banter with a shrug. Bradford was stinging, and he had to lash out at someone. "You'll have to punish him, after it's all fixed and soothed, you know. He'll expect it, too. But I'm curious as to what kind of boundaries he's really seeking, under all the fear reaction."

Bradford glanced up at Tobias. "Videotaped sessions, security on call, break away bondage gear. He's asked me to run my home the way I do the club, with someone always watching. I flatly refuse to do so. I didn't take quite that strong a stance with him because I was trying to be understanding, but there's no way in hell, Tobias." Bradford stood up and paced away from the desk. "Am I being unreasonable? Would you submit to observation in your stables?"

"Absolutely not. But that's not what I asked. His requests are unacceptable and fear-based -- what do you think he really needs? What's under his skin that needs to get out? What does he really and truly need to feel safe?"

Bradford turned around and looked at Tobias again. After a moment of thoughtful consideration, he replied, "At the root of it, I think he needs to know that what happened to Joseph isn't going to happen to him."

Tobias nodded and finally gave in to the urge -- the need -- to smoke. "Of course." He lit his cigarette and studied the burning tip as he exhaled. "And those rules in a contract aren't the real key to making him feel safe. What do you think might do that? What does Nikki need in his life that defines being safe?"

Bradford stopped pacing and moved back to his chair, sitting heavily. "Honestly, until yesterday I thought it was me." He stubbed out his cigarette in the ashtray and sipped his coffee. "So what is it about me, then? I'm firm. I'm forgiving. I believe in him. He can trust me. I'm... consistent. I don't know which of those things took the hit yesterday. Just that I let this happen to his friend? That I can't protect everyone all the time? Does he really think I should?" Looking up at Tobias, Bradford shook his head. "Do you already know the answer to this question and you're waiting for me to hit on it?"

"I don't know Nikki well enough to know the answer. I'm no more perfect than you are, as evidenced by my own home issues." Tobias took a drag off his cigarette and sighed, smoke rolling out of his mouth in a lazy curl. "He saw you as Superman. Maybe he just needs some time to remember that Superman made mistakes as well."

"Let's hope. And no Kryptonite jokes." Bradford picked up the pack of cigarettes and lit another. "So what's going on with your boys?"

Tobias winced and smoked, and the next time he exhaled, it was in a steady, tight stream. "I went home last night, signaled to Noah that he was to top me, sent Phan to his room with a promise that I'd bring him down for bed. He hadn't even eaten. And after I'd relieved my stress, I forgot about him until this morning. He was unhappy."

"Mmm. I can imagine. But that's not like you at all. Did you manage to work it out?"

"I made my most sincere apologies." Tobias shrugged. "I'll be making up for this one for a while, I think. It really threw Noah as well; there's a bit of dynamic going on there that we're feeling our way through. Right now, they're back in bed -- together -- and I hope that things won't be horrible when they come in."

"Three is a hard number, my friend. Frankly, I'd be surprised if this is the last time there's an issue. One sub is hard enough; two isn't easy to manage at all, and I think you've done an admirable job so far. I wouldn't beat yourself up too badly on this one." Bradford pushed the bottle of whiskey a little closer to Tobias. "Why don't you give them the day off? We can spend it figuring out where we went wrong yesterday and how we can make sure it doesn't happen again."

Tobias took the bottle and poured, pretty sure there was far more whiskey in his cup than coffee. "I could. Is this going to involve either of us getting flogged, though? I've already done that in the last day, and don't feel a strong need for it again."

Bradford laughed. "I really don't need the details of your sessions with Noah, Tobias, but it's nice to know the boy has your back, as it were. I consider the blows our consciences have taken in the last forty-eight hours flogging enough in any case."

"He has a nice arm," Tobias said with a shrug. "All right. A day off so you and I can discuss matters. Shall we begin with going over how we're to proceed with discipline within the club, or should we stick to our own relationships since we're already drinking?"

"Discipline within the club," Bradford repeated, the words sounding sour on his tongue. "I never thought I'd have to... Ah. Well. We're growing; it's only natural, I suppose. When my lover returns, I'll be happy to discuss with you the various ways in which I might discipline him. Assuming he returns. In the meantime, we better put the whiskey away. Keep the cigarettes out, though; we deserve one vice. Oh, and you should call for some food. Whiskey on an empty stomach is a bad idea. I've just learned this."

"Just this moment, or is this a lesson learned overnight?"

"Just this moment. I didn't dare drink last night; that would have been far too slippery a slope."

"I understand." He'd even been there a time or two. Tobias took the bottle back to his desk and put it away, then picked up the receiver of his phone. "Any food preferences?"

"I'm starving, so something filling. An omelet? Maybe some toast. More coffee." Bradford poured himself a fresh cup, this time without the whiskey.

Tobias' stomach growled. "You know," he said as he called the kitchen, "I even ate this morning." He ordered breakfast to be delivered to his office, along with juice and more coffee, then called the bar's extension. "I'm leaving the phones on forward to you," he said. "Bradford and I are having an extended closed-door meeting, so just take messages and apologize for us. We'll return calls later today and tomorrow morning -- and if there's anything particularly urgent, let Pat know. He can decide if we're needed."

He hung up and looked at Bradford. "You know, you should have an office admin, apart from Nikki. Someone to cancel meetings and handle the phones." His hand still on the receiver, Tobias flipped through his planner to see how many interviews he had to postpone; luckily, there were only two listed for the day.

"A cute little twink in a short skirt and a little operator's headset in his ear?"

"If you want. Just someone with a decent grasp of how to talk to people would be good." He called his two meetings and left apologetic messages for them, discreet but firm that he wouldn't be able to talk to them about rescheduling until later in the day. Then he called the house, hoping Phan wouldn't wake up.

The line rang a couple of times, then a click, and then Noah's voice came softly over the line. "Hello, sir."

"Hello, sweetheart. Did he fall asleep?"

"Yes, sir. And so has my arm and most of my left side." Noah was talking quietly, but he sounded cheerful enough.

Tobias smiled. "You can move him, you know."

"I could, but he's so cute and looks so happy." Noah chuckled softly into the phone. "Did you want me to wake him? What time did you need us at the club?"

Tobias watched Bradford sipping his coffee. He looked like hell, really. "Actually, you have the day off, which is why I'm calling. You and Phan stay home today, please; Bradford and I are having closed-door meetings. I should be home for supper, though."

"Mmm. All right, sir. Please take a cab home if you need to?" Noah's tone said more than his words did. He was apparently well aware by now what a bad day and a closed-door meeting could mean for Tobias and Bradford's sobriety. "Phan and I will be waiting for you."

"I'll call if I'm going to be late. Take care of Phan for me, sweetheart. I promise to spend some real time with you both as soon as I can." Tobias hung up and went to his filing cabinet. "Do we want the records for both of them, or just Mr. Adkins?"

"May as well get both, maybe there is something -- a trigger or a sensitivity -- in Joseph's file that we missed that may have made this worse. Not that having one's safe word disregarded isn't horrible enough, of course. Plus, if he's really such a friend of Nikki's, I suppose I should know something about him."

Tobias nodded and pulled both folders. With a fresh pad of paper in hand as well, he returned to his chair and passed Joseph's file to Bradford. "Do we know where Joseph is now, where he stayed last night?"

"He went home. His roommate promised me he'd check in with me this morning, but I have his number if I don't hear from them."

"Good." Tobias nodded and opened Michael Adkins' file. "I put him on probation and tight monitoring. I'll personally be watching him from security for the next two months, and he'll be under supervision for eight. If he decides not to play in that time frame to avoid being watched, he's gone. I didn't tell him that was final; we need to know more about what happens with Joseph, don't you think?"

"I agree, and I appreciate the way you're handling it. It's a strong stance, and I think that's important in terms of an example to everyone else." Bradford shifted slightly in his chair. "Listen, Tobias. I should have said this before now."

Tobias looked up.

"I really do see us both responsible here. The fact that you did Adkins' final screening does not absolve me of responsibility at all. For all we know, there was something about Joseph that I missed. This is a joint venture as I see it, and we take the falls together."

"I don't think assigning any kind of blame at this point will do anyone any good." Tobias sighed. "All we can do is learn from it and put more safeguards into effect. Maybe increase the time new members have to be screened, maybe make sure that if uncoupled new members are playing together, they use the rooms with one-way glass and know they're being watched."

Bradford nodded. "All good ideas. I'll make some notes." He reached for the cigarettes and pulled one out. "Maybe think about revising the membership rule book, too."

Tobias settled in. It was going to be a long morning, and, knowing how he and Bradford were when they put their heads together, it was likely to carry into the afternoon as well. Apart from their subs, nothing was more important to them than making sure the club remained the safe, welcoming place it had always been for its members, Doms and subs alike.

17

Tobias set his fork down and nodded to Phan, who was kneeling by the dining room door fronting Mrs. Miller's kitchen. "You can do the dishes now, boy. When you're done, meet me in the safe room."

Phan nodded and hurried to take the plate to the kitchen, clearly ready for the weekend at the farm to be underway, if Tobias would just get on with it.

Rolling his eyes and then sighing with fond exasperation, Tobias looked down at Noah. Noah had been good and had been permitted to kneel next to Tobias, had even been fed his breakfast. "I don't think that boy slept more than four hours last night," Tobias said softly to Noah. "There was a lot of chain rattling going on down there on the floor. Did he wake you?"

"He woke me once. Had I been able to get back to sleep after that while he was tossing and turning, he might have woken me again, sir," Noah replied, sounding amused more than upset. "He seems to be wound up."

"I wonder why." Tobias smirked and stood up. "Come with me. We'll see if we can't come up with something fun for him to do today. A bit of role play, I think. Any suggestions?" He walked out of the dining room with Noah at his heel and started up the stairs. "Something a little dark, maybe. Historical?"

"Hmm." Noah made a thoughtful sound, following one step behind. "Like Master and stable boy, kind of historical, sir? Wealthy landowner and lowly serf? Or do you mean like King Henry and the cute young actor who played Juliet to entertain the court kind of historical?" Noah laughed softly. "I guess that one's not so dark."

"Not dark, no. But funny." Tobias grinned as they went into the safe room. "Remind me of that one sometime. I might even make him sing for us." Seating himself in the easy chair, Tobias listened to the faint clink of dishes. "How about... well, how about pirates?" He rather liked the idea of being a captain.

Noah looked thoughtful. "I've never done pirates, sir. Done a pirate? Arrr." Noah laughed. "You look hot in boots, though."

"I know." Tobias grinned. "That's part of the draw. So, do you want be first mate or something else? Should we shanghai Phan?"

Noah grinned. "Yes, sir! First mate works for me." The glint in Noah's eye was unmistakable. "Can I tie him to the mast?"

"Sure." Tobias was feeling generous. "Okay, let's get the costumes all sorted out and then head to the stable. We can kidnap him from the ring and hustle him into one of the stalls. The black one -- there's iron manacles attached to the wall there; perfect for the brig."

Noah hurried over to the armoire in the corner of the safe room. "What did you want to wear, sir? Other than the sexy boots?"

"Leather pants, that white shirt with the wide cuffs. We have a frock coat, don't we? You can be reasonably kempt." Tobias watched Noah getting things out and stood up to change. "We'll put Phan in cotton pants and a shirt we won't mind ripping."

Noah placed a pair of Tobias' leather pants and the white shirt on the bed, then set the boots on the floor near Tobias with a thunk. They weren't pirate boots per se, but they were leather and cut high and would do nicely. For himself, he pulled out gray pants, boots, and a functional white shirt that lacked the detail of Tobias'.

"And for Phan..." Noah said out loud, searching the armoire. "Ah." He pulled out straight cut yoga pants and a white V-neck T-shirt. "How's that, sir? Do you need help dressing?"

"Just the boots -- oh, wait, Phan's coming. You just dress, sweetheart. He can help me with the boots." Tobias undressed swiftly and was just reaching for the leather pants when Phan came in. "Get the boot hooks, boy."

Phan squeaked and nodded, almost running to the wardrobe. "Yes, sir." To his credit, he didn't ask what they were doing. He just got the boot hooks and waited until Tobias had his pants on before first handing Tobias clean socks and then helping Tobias stomp into the boots.

Tobias tried not to smile as Phan watched his every move with wide eyes; he was dressed for house chores, so Tobias could tell exactly how appreciative Phan was of all the leather and the promise of a game. With a negligent gesture toward the clothes Noah had picked for Phan, Tobias told him to dress, then proceeded to ignore him. "Ready, Noah?" he asked, buttoning his own cuffs.

Noah was just stepping into his second boot. He

straightened up, smoothed himself out, and then took a position at Tobias' side. "Yes, sir. Ready."

"Wonderful. Remind me to buy a sword."

Phan whimpered.

"For show," Tobias clarified, rolling his eyes. "Come on, time and tide wait for no man." He strode out of the room, his boot heels thumping.

"Tide?" Phan whispered loudly as he fell into step beside Noah, still pulling on his shirt.

Tobias heard Noah clear his throat before speaking. "Aye. Tide. Ye heard the Captain."

Phan didn't say anything, but Tobias was reasonably sure that it was because his brain was busy leapfrogging all over the place. Maybe tying him to the mast for a while was a good idea after all, if only so he'd have some time to calm down.

They crossed the yard to the stables, and Tobias spared a glance for the bunkhouse. His yard felt like his own again, now that the construction scene had been cleaned up, and there weren't any more extra vehicles or storage containers about, and the stacks of lumber were now forming walls. Of course, the place had that damaged-landscaping-freshly-done look about it, but a few subs and a week of work would take care of that.

When they were almost at the stable, Tobias said, "Phantom, you can go right to the ring, please, and pretend to be a barkeep or something while Noah and I get things ready to set sail." He smiled, thinking that, while utterly landlocked, their ship was at least in no danger of producing motion sickness. "Noah, I'd like you to do the usual checks. Water, first aid supplies. I'll handle the lights and props."

"Yes, sir." Noah moved ahead of them a few steps and

unlocked and opened the door. Tobias and Phan had stepped inside.

"Shoo, you." Tobias swatted Phantom's ass as he went by and sent him hurrying down the center aisle to the former riding ring. Phan hadn't said anything since leaving the house, and Tobias wondered just how much he was going to have to settle Phan down.

Lighting the stall he wanted and going in to make sure that the manacles were in good working order, he kept an eye out for Noah. He could hear Noah going through the inventory and making sure that they had everything they could possibly need, muttering under his breath as he had to get another package of rolled gauze for the kit. They'd gone through quite a lot of it the day Tobias had decided to wrap Noah up like a mummy.

Finally, though, Noah came down to him with a supply of lube, a few water bottles, and an armful of washcloths.

"Do you think he's ready to forgive me?" Tobias asked, oiling the hinge on one metal cuff.

Noah nodded. "Yes, sir. I think he already has. He packed his second bag to come out to the farm -- the one he's keeping the surprise in progress in. I think he'll be very happy by suppertime, sir." He set everything aside discreetly in one corner of the stall. "Wow, we haven't been in this stall in a long time, sir."

"True. We should stockpile some ideas." Tobias stood up and let the manacle clink at the end of its chain. "One wall, ready for a prisoner. So, matey -- shall we go ashore and see if we can find some more or less willing crew for our next voyage?"

Noah grinned, obviously ready to play. Just then, he looked as eager as Phan had. "Aye, sir. Lead on."

Tobias led on, wishing he had some kind of soundtrack.

He felt a little foolish swaggering into the ring, but then he stopped dead and started to laugh.

Phan had taken his instructions to heart. There weren't any bottles kept in the ring, other than one or two bottles of lube, so Phan had taken out every dildo they had -- including the collection of glass ones that Tobias loved -- and lined them up on the big library table. A hand-lettered sign reading "Grog" was stuck on one with what looked suspiciously like bondage tape. Behind the table, Phan was polishing a dildo, looking for all the world like the country's finest perverted barkeep.

"This looks like our kind of place," Tobias said to Noah, when he could speak without laughing.

It was a few minutes before Noah responded, likely for the same reasons, though Tobias hadn't turned around to check. "I'll have... a double, please, Captain," Noah said quickly, and then coughed to cover more laughter.

"You heard the man, barkeep! A double for my mate." He had to turn around and close his eyes when Phan immediately pushed a curved, double-headed dildo at him. "Oh, God. This might have been a mistake."

"It's a double, sir," Phan said helpfully. "Service two at once."

Noah somehow pulled a straight face out of all the hysteria and leaned on the bar. He picked up the dildo and licked one of the heads, just as Tobias turned around. "Aye, that be a fair quality in a drink. Even better in a lover. Eh, Captain?"

Tobias had to try very hard to get himself together. Phan, on the other hand, was just standing there polishing a dildo and looking expectantly at him, like he was waiting for a drink order.

Tobias gave up. There wasn't any way to actually get to

where he'd been going, so he just gave up entirely and let Phan take the scene. "Aye," he said to Noah with a nod. "A strong drink, a lover, a ship. What say you, we take this fine barkeep with the quick wit? He may be of use."

"He appears to be a mite occupied at the moment, sir." Noah looked at Phan. "He may need persuading. What say you, barkeep? Looking for adventure on the high seas? Or arrrrrr ye going to give us trouble?"

Phan gave Noah a flat look. "Pirates talk funny and are kind of mean. I think I'll stay here and play with myself."

Tobias couldn't argue with the first. "We like the trouble ye be giving." He lifted his hand high and patted Noah on the back with the other one. "Grab him, me hearty -- I want him aboard my ship!"

Phan made to dive under the table, and Tobias grabbed the double dildo. "And this as well, I think. Fine booty for me booties."

Noah lunged, cop reflexes still very much intact, and caught Phan by the upper arm before Phan disappeared under the table. The next second he was across the table and hauling Phan back to his feet. He scooped up a wide, hot pink dildo and pointed it in Phan's face. "Come quiet-like, friend, or I'll be givin' ye a taste of me sword."

Phan looked at Noah's sword and blinked. "It's a little small."

Noah squinted at the dildo and shrugged. He looked at Phan and poked him in the chest with the phallus several times as he spoke. "Aye, 'tis, a bit," Pirate Noah conceded. "But it's pink! Arrrrrr. Now move it! Before the captain loses patience!"

The captain was in danger of losing far more than his patience. Tobias had no idea how Phan was managing to keep a straight face. "Bring him," he ordered, turning on his heel to stalk away. "We'll chain him up in the brig for a while, see if he learns better manners."

Behind him, Tobias heard a short scuffle, a chuckle from Noah, and then two sets of footsteps -- one booted, the other making the muted sounds of bare feet -- following him up the center aisle. Twice he heard more scuffling and the occasional giggle, but every time he looked over his shoulder, he saw nothing but a well-behaved pirate and a contrite, if somewhat devious-looking captive.

He turned into the lit stall, with its black walls and floor and the heavy manacles against one wall, and stopped, crossing his arms authoritatively. Noah pushed Phan through the doorway a little roughly, and then poked the back of one of Phan's knees with the pink dildo, making him kneel.

"He be misbehavin', sir, to be sure," Pirate Noah offered, taking a wide stance just behind Phan.

"You kidnapped me! Of course I'm misbehaving!" Phan twisted to look up Noah in mock disbelief.

"Enough!" Tobias roared, and both Phan and Noah twitched, apparently fighting the instinct to snap to attention. "Now. Kidnapped ye are, but abused ye'll not be. Well, much." Tobias put a finger under Phan's chin and lifted his face. "Almost too pretty for a life at sea."

"I could always go back to my bar?"

"I say nay, and to make sure there's no sneaking off -- and swimming the many leagues to shore in the dead of night -- ye'll be chained to my wall!" Tobias grabbed at Phan's wrists and dragged him bodily to the chains.

Phan, bless him, struggled enough to make it fun. Tobias liked to work a little bit, though it was a bit incongruous to be fitting metal cuffs, trying to pin Phan down, and also trying very hard not to laugh at the same time. "Master Noah! Lend me your expertise. The wretch is wiggly."

"Aye, Captain, with pleasure." Noah stepped up next to Phan and leaned into him, pinning him to the wall of the stall with one shoulder. "I've got the wriggling wretch now, sir."

Phan squirmed, and Tobias rolled his eyes while trying to catch one ankle. "Kiss him or something. The brat needs distracting."

"Ayyyeee, Captain," Noah drawled, turning his body so he was pinning Phan to the wall, chest to chest. "Let me have a taste, ye beauty." He hooked one hand tightly behind Phan's neck and kissed him hard. "Mmm."

Tobias looked up to watch, and smiled as Phan immediately sank into the kiss and stopped fighting. He was a little predictable, but that was all right; Tobias used what he could. Besides, it was nice to watch Noah and Phan kissing.

When Phan was attached to the wall by both arms and legs as well as by Noah, Tobias stood up and considered his options. The entire game was a treat for Phan, so they might as well get him in condition to enjoy it, without being constantly distracted by needs. Taking Phan's edge off might make things last longer for all of them.

"A sword really would come in handy." He could cut Phan's pants off. That would be -- no. That would be a bad idea. Besides, they'd picked Phan's pants because they were thin and stretchy, and like every good first aid kit, theirs had scissors. "Keep him still. It would be a shame to cut off the good bits."

"Mmmhmm," Noah mumbled around what had essentially turned into a make-out session with Phan. Noah's legs were spread wide for balance, and his boots made him quite a bit taller than Phan. He slid his free hand around to Phan's back. "Still, pretty," he added. "If ye know what's good for ye."

"I think I see your point," Phan said breathlessly. He was looking at the scissors, but they didn't seem to scare him much.

Tobias smirked and made short work of one leg, then started on the other. "He seems to like the danger," he said to Noah. "Or maybe it's merely your kisses that make him stiff."

Noah took a step back, slowly releasing his hold on Phan. "Usually works for you, Captain," he said saucily, looking Phan up and down. "Maybe it's the irons. Which is it, pretty?

"Well, in all honesty, I wasn't terribly fond of my job." Phan batted his eyelashes at them both and clinked his chains. "I'm not too sure about this part, though." He tugged one hand and his cock lifted.

Laughing, Tobias said, "Your prick seems sure enough."

"So does yours," Phan shot back, looking greedily at Tobias' midsection.

"Maybe, but that's not for you. At least, not yet. What shall we do to our captive, Noah? Torture? Taunt? Torment? Ignore?"

"I like the torment idea." He reached out and gave one of Phan's nipples a pinch through his T-shirt. "Let 'im figure out what he really wants?"

"That! I want that!"

Tobias snorted. "Do the other one. Actually, you get them hard and I'll find something to pinch them with." He went to the small cupboard in the corner and started looking in the drawers for nipple clamps.

Noah grinned widely and pushed his hands up under Phan's T-shirt. He seemed to be enjoying this dual position -

- taking his orders from Tobias but topping Phan -- and Phan, clearly, was on board with the whole thing, too.

"Like that, pretty?" Noah's hands moved under the thin white cotton. "Oh, yeah. Nice."

"You have nice hands for a pirate," Phan allowed, and Tobias saw him give Noah a warm smile.

"Our prisoner likes to flirt." Of course he did. "Here, put these on him." Tobias held out the harshest set of nipple clamps he could find, stiff alligator clamps that Tobias knew bit hard.

Noah stared at them a second and then took them. "Well, well, matey. Seems the captain has either taken quite a shine to ye," Noah held up one clamp so Phan could get a good look at it, "or has it in for ye. Still have those scissors, sir? This shirt is becoming a right nuisance."

Tobias knew better than to try to rip the shirt; he'd been hung up by a hem once before and it wasn't exactly as smooth as he'd wanted the move to be. "Aye." He held up the scissors and snipped them a couple of times for the sound. "Rags, they be." He cut the shirt up the middle and made sure to run the blunt back of the blades along Phan's chest.

"Ohhh." Phan moaned and closed his eyes for a moment, and Tobias could see him shudder.

"All right, then, that's a much better view. Aye." Noah held up the clamps and lined them up with Phan's nipples. Tobias saw him hesitate for a moment and look at the clamps before squeezing them open. Noah knew, apparently, just how painful they were going to be, and Tobias wondered for a second if his pirate mate was going to be able to follow through. But he did, if perhaps slightly out of character -- though at this point the dark kidnapping of an unwilling servant had turned into more of a raunchy nod in the direction of Penzance.

"If I didn't know you were going to love this..." Noah whispered to Phan with a quick shake of his head. Quickly, he closed both clips around Phan's nipples at once.

Phan yelled. Loudly. His eyes opened wide and his hands wrapped around the chains attached to his wrists. Tobias watched impassively, knowing that as soon as the initial pain spiked, Phan would be in his own personal heaven. Sure enough, within moments Phan's erection was swelling even harder and his eyes were fogging a little bit.

"A taste of pain," Tobias said with a tight grin. "Be glad that's all so far and I'm not of a mind to have ye walk the plank."

Phan giggled. "Plank. I don't see a plank. But I see both of you wanting and not having."

Tobias looked at Noah. "He may have a point. What do you want? A bit of plundering? Self-denial isn't in the Pirate Code."

"Aye, he has a point indeed. As do we." Noah gave the chain between Phan's nipple clamps a very light tug and listened to Phan whimper with interest. Tobias wondered exactly how much of his toppy side he'd shown Phan up to this point. "A little plundering, laddie?"

"I'm pretty sure I don't have choices here," Phan pointed out with a wink. He was breathing a lot harder, but aside from that he seemed content to have his nipples aching. "And as I'm chained to a wall, I don't think I can do a whole lot."

Tobias gave him a nasty smile. "You can do plenty." He got behind Noah and pressed close, one of his hands sliding around to massage Noah's cock through his pants. "I think he can help you with this, even if his hands are in chains. What say you?"

Noah, bless him or damn him, melted against Tobias's

chest and pushed his hips into Tobias' fingers. "Aye, sir," he answered. "Thank ye, sir."

Tobias rubbed a bit more and watched Phan watching them. "Reach. Help, or you'll suffer for your lack of effort."

Phan turned his whole body toward Noah, rattling every chain he had as he reached. "I can't."

Tobias looked and laughed as Phan strained into the two-inch gap. "You can do better than that." He helped, though, by pushing his hips into Noah's ass and shoving him forward the necessary distance.

Noah groaned. "Wait. Here." Noah reached down and yanked open the button at the top of his pants and lowered the zipper fly. Tobias was amused; his boys were so predictable.

Phan made a grab, and Tobias pulled Noah back out of his reach with a grin. "Just my mate, wretch. If you make him feel good, perhaps we won't kill you."

Phan nodded enthusiastically. "I want to keep living. Promise."

Noah leaned forward. "He seems eager to please, Captain. I say we let 'im."

"You would, wouldn't you?" Tobias sighed dramatically, ground his own prick against Noah's ass, and shifted him forward again.

"Yes. I mean, aye, Captain. Aye." Noah looked at Phan. "Come on, then, lad, don't keep a man waiting."

Phan made another enthusiastic grab, his chain clinking happily as his fingers curled around Noah's erection. "Do you like it fast or slow?" he asked, looking only at what his hand was doing. "Since I really want to live, you see."

Tobias rolled his eyes and held Noah up. He had a feeling this wasn't going to take very long.

"Fast." Tobias watched Noah reach forward and find Phan's erection as well. "You?"

Tobias and Phan spoke at the same time. "Fast."

Really, they were all predictable.

Noah nodded. "Right," he agreed, his voice tight. His fingers tightened around Phan and he started to pump, hand flying, thumb wrapped tightly over his fingers. "Won't be long, Captain, I can tell you that."

"I can tell." Tobias leaned into Noah and watched over his shoulder. "Very pretty, my pretties. Come on now, make it worth my time. I want to see what you've got; impress me and the captain will taste."

Phan gasped, his hand speeding on Noah's erection, chain making more and more noise as he frantically tried to bring Noah off without being able to use both hands or his mouth. Not that Noah seemed bothered by the lack of more stimulation.

Quite the contrary, Noah's hips were starting to move, thrusting forward into Phan's hand and then back again, where his ass bumped and rubbed against Tobias' groin. It was out of synch with the rhythm he was setting to bring Phan off, but neither of them seemed to have trouble managing the pace. The only thing Noah seemed to be having issues with was his own self-control. "Tighter, fuck," he whispered to Phan.

Tobias could only assume Phan heard him and complied; he didn't say anything, but Noah gasped. Phan's eyes were wide and getting wider, his breath coming in fast pants. Goose pimples broke out over Phan's shoulders, and his skin was suddenly shiny with sweat.

"He's almost there," Tobias whispered to Noah. "Make him come for me."

"Yes, sir," Noah panted, leaning a little closer to Phan, his voice gravelly and harsh. "Come on, barkeep. Show the captain what he wants to see. You first, then me."

Phan looked up at Noah's face, his mouth slightly open and his tongue darting out to wet his lower lip. "Oh, God," he whispered. "There. Right there -- oh!" His eyes closed and a burst of white shot from his cock, then twice more in rapid fire. "Oh, God."

"I know, hon," Tobias heard Noah say through gritted teeth. His hand slowed but didn't stop entirely yet. "Tell me when, sir!"

Tobias dipped his head and grazed Noah's shoulder with his teeth. "Now, my matey. Show me."

"Aye, sir!" Noah barely waited for the order, matching Phan's display with one of his own. The scent of his boys was thick in the stall, and they were both panting harshly. Neither of them let the other go, fondling one another gently instead as they waited for further orders. "He's a keeper," Noah said, still short of breath. "Don't you think so, Captain?"

"I'm not sure." Tobias smiled wickedly. "I haven't yet sampled him myself."

Phan whimpered as Tobias moved Noah out of his range. "Hush, wretch." Tobias stepped close to him and grabbed Phan by the hair. "You can have him back if you wish. When I'm done."

Nodding, Phan's slick hand scrabbled at Tobias' fly for a moment before Tobias batted it away. "I didn't tell you to do that." Tobias pulled Phan's head back by his hair and kissed him, hard.

The sticky hand splayed over Tobias' chest, and Phan melted into him for as long as Tobias would let him. Only a moment, though -- too much would spoil the fun. Tobias pulled away and looked at Noah with a smile. "What should we do now? Suggestions? The bottles of grog, perhaps."

Noah was busy cleaning his hand on the corner of his shirt. Following that, he removed it, tossing it into a corner of the stall. "Aye, there's an idea. I could find one he'd like the taste of," Noah suggested.

"I think he'd like the taste of anything." Tobias looked at Phan critically. "He's got the flavor of one well-used to sampling his wares."

Noah laughed. "Is that so, lad? Have ye been dippin' into yer own stock?"

Phan managed, somehow, to work up pink cheeks. Tobias was very impressed with the blush and the sidelong look he gave the pink dildo. "It would take a strange man to do that," he said.

"And are you a strange man?" Tobias stepped closer again and reached for the double dildo. "A very strange man?"

Phan's eyes widened and he froze in place, his gaze glued to the toy.

"Mmm. Noah? How about you? Are you strange?"

Noah raised an eyebrow. "Aye, Captain, but I'm not sure I'm that strange..."

"Then we're about to find out." Tobias smiled and stepped back, trying to decide on angles and what they should hold onto.

"If there's one thing I've learned about the Captain," Noah said to Phan, his fingers wiggling his trousers the rest of the way off. "It's that it's never a good idea to disappoint him." Noah leaned close to Phan. "Just a word o' caution."

"I'm pretty sure disappointing him is something I'll work to avoid. Though I'm not really sure about this idea of his.

He's not serious, right?" Phan sounded a little concerned, but the anticipation in his voice marred the act.

Tobias kept smiling as he got lube and pulled a heavy chair close to them. "Now. Me first mate. If you lean on this, does it slide along the floor?"

"Apparently he is, aye." Noah stepped away from Phan and experimented with the chair, holding the seat and putting weight on it, then turning it around and resting his arms on the back. "Seems fairly study, sir," he said in a matter-of-fact tone that was out of character for the scene, but in character for the moment. "Should do."

"And will you do..." Tobias touched Noah's back, stroking gently, "...just as I say, my pretty?"

Noah nodded. "With pleasure, as ever, sir."

Tobias felt his chest go tight at the words, and he broke what little character he had long enough to kiss Noah. "Of course you will." He turned to Phan and eyed his chains. "And you have no choice. I'm going to unchain you for a moment. Are you going to make this hard? You're facing entirely the wrong way."

"That's hardly my fault, now, is it?"

Tobias raised an eyebrow. "Hold him, Noah. And maybe spank him, too."

Noah took hold of Phan by the hips and pinned them to the wall while Tobias unlocked the manacles. Once he was free, Noah spun Phan to face the wall so fast Tobias wondered that Phan didn't get dizzy. The spin was followed by a sharp crack as Noah's hand made contact with Phan's bare ass.

"Hey!" Phan yelped, but his ass stuck out pretty damn fast, and Tobias knew he wanted another one.

"Slut," Tobias said. Then he slapped Phan's ass even harder and pointed to the manacles lying on the floor. "I'll do his ankles if you'll get his arms." Without waiting for Noah's reply, Tobias knelt and held Phan's ankle tight. "Stay still." Carefully, deliberately, he licked Phan's ass.

"Jesus!" Phan sounded utterly shocked for the first time in months.

Noah laughed loudly. "Aye, you're an easy wretch. Captain's already got you figured."

Tobias heard Noah lock the wrist restraints into place, and it sounded so easy that Phan really must have been shocked.

"Sir."

Tobias laughed. "Noah, get them all. I'm busy." He parted Phan's cheeks and licked him again, this time getting a lot more than a yelp. Phan quivered, making a sound that was close to a howl.

"As you wish, Captain." Noah sounded amused. He knelt beside Tobias and locked one leg into place, then got up and moved to Tobias' other side and maneuvered the other into place. "He likes you, Captain."

"Ohhhh, yes!" Phan was either agreeing with Noah's assessment or really, really enjoying Tobias' tongue.

Both were perfectly acceptable as far as Tobias was concerned. He gave Phan another lick and rocked to his feet, ignoring Phan's whimper. "Now, let's see." He eyed the chair and adjusted the placement, moving it a bit closer to Phan. "You need to be close, but not too close."

God, it would be a wonder if he didn't come in his pants just watching this.

"Okay, Noah. Over the chair, give me your ass." Tobias grinned, holding up the lube, and rolled his eyes as Phan tried to turn around to watch.

Noah moved smoothly and draped himself over the chair. He spread his legs in a wide stance so he was both open for Tobias as well as steady on his feet. "Like that, sir?" he asked in a teasing tone, evidently knowing full well that Tobias liked the view.

"That's just about what I was picturing, yes." Tobias shook his head and kept on grinning. He gave a little snort when he opened the lube and Phan jumped in response; it was almost Pavlovian. "Not for you. Not yet. It's my mate's turn." Fingers wet, Tobias traced around Noah's hole for a moment, knowing Phan was watching, anticipating.

"Mmm," Noah moaned gently and rolled his head back. "You have the best hands, Captain." He arched his ass up slightly, the movement so slow Tobias wasn't sure Noah knew he'd done it.

Tobias smiled and fingered Noah slowly, stretching him gently. "You want it as much as our captive, don't you? Always willing, my first mate."

"Aye, sir." Noah went up on his toes and then lowered himself again. "Aye. Might as well be captive myself."

"You've captivated me," Tobias said with a wink, pretty sure neither of them saw it and maybe Noah didn't even hear the words. He was busy moaning. With the dildo in his free hand, Tobias took a careful look at all the angles presented by two bodies and decided he'd better stay very close to them; God only knew what was going to happen. "Ready?" he asked Noah as he withdrew his fingers. "You're first. Easy now, just stay still while I get this in you."

"Aye, sir. So ready, sir."

Noah let his head fall and hang from his shoulders as Tobias worked one end of the dildo inside. "Big," Noah commented, followed by a long slow moan as Tobias seated the toy where he wanted it. "Smooth and so good." Noah stayed relaxed, even though Tobias could sense how much the boy wanted to move, wanted to feel the dildo moving inside him. He fought the desire to move with slow pants and deep breaths.

"Good boy." Tobias praised him and stroked his back. "Soon. But I need you to stay very still right now." He looked at Phan and grinned. "Eyes forward, ass back."

Chains rattled and Phan's head whipped around to face forward. "Yes, sir!"

More lube, quickly applied, and then Tobias was holding his breath without really noticing as he urged Phan's hip back, centering him and holding the dildo steady so Noah wouldn't be over-stimulated. "Okay, go slow."

Phan moaned as he eased himself back so slowly that Tobias' body almost cramped in sympathy. "Oh, God. Yes."

Tobias looked at them, joined by the toy, his hand between them, and swallowed hard. "Noah, shift forward. Phan, you too. I've got it steady, you can do as you need to. Go."

Bodies started moving. Noah started out slow, experimenting, changing the angle, taking the toy deep one time and more shallow the next, fucking himself with it exactly as he'd been instructed to -- exactly as he needed.

Phan, on the other hand, rocked at a fairly steady pace for all of a handful of strokes, then seemed to let Noah's movements guide his own; a deep moan indicated he'd found a nice place to hang out, and Tobias was tempted to take his hand off the toy, just to see what would happen.

After a couple of minutes of play, Noah groaned heavily and lifted one knee, bracing it on the seat of the chair before picking up an earnest rhythm, one that seemed to hit him in all the right places. "Oh, fuck!" he shouted, beginning to ride the smooth cock hard. He threw his head back again, his breathing becoming quick and shallow. "Fuck!"

Tobias let go and stepped back to undo his own pants.

His cock was straining, and he'd ignored it for too long; it almost hurt to touch as he watched Phan's head snap back and his body go stiff. Noah was effectively fucking them both, without knowing it, and Tobias was quickly deciding that his boys were getting a new reward for being very, very good. He'd have to keep this in mind for special occasions.

He heard Noah whine when he first let go, but the boy regained whatever resistance he needed quickly enough. "Right there. Oh, God. Yes!" He looked over his shoulder briefly, as if to gauge where Phan was or what Tobias was doing. It was hard to be sure which. "Soon..." he panted. "Really fucking soon, sir!"

"Whenever you're ready," Tobias told them both. He held his cock in a loose fist and waited, feeling tight and tense as Phan's hands wrapped around his chains and Noah's back stiffened.

"Noah," Phan cried out, completely dropping any pretense or play. "Please!"

Noah must have caught on then to just how in control he was of the situation, and Tobias saw him tense up and shove backward toward Phan. He did it once and then again, forcing sharp cries out of Phan before he went back to groping for his own orgasm, apparently hoping Phan was close enough to follow along. He grunted, and his body seemed to stretch and then collapse in on itself as Noah came, curling up as if protecting something vulnerable.

"Phan!" he shouted. "Sir!"

Tobias' breath caught as Noah came, Phan right after him. Phan didn't make a sound, just held the chains and arched his back as he shot, his eyes wide and likely unseeing.

Forcing himself to maintain control, over his own body if not the scene that had been taken from his hands almost at the moment of its conception, Tobias once more grasped the dildo. He eased Noah forward and off of it, then pulled it gently from Phan's body as well. "There," he said roughly. "Rewards for all." He set the toy aside for cleaning later and watched his subs in the aftermath.

It took a moment for either of them to move. Noah straightened up first, but only enough to turn and sit on the very edge of the chair he'd been leaning on. His skin was damp; his hair, which used to be cut too short to matter, was damp and stuck to his forehead in a couple of places. He reached forward and patted Phan on the ass, grinning broadly. "Thank you, Captain."

Phan merely mumbled something that Tobias assumed was complimentary and hung from his chains.

Making sure that Noah was capable of holding himself up, Tobias nodded and then turned to Phan. "You earned your place, boy." Covering Phan's back with his body, Tobias reached up to grasp the cuffs around Phan's wrists, his cock sliding along Phan's ass.

"Sir," Phan whispered. "You didn't."

"Yet." Tobias rubbed again, his fingers feeling their way to the hasps of the cuffs. "Never fear. I will."

Phan nodded. Then he wiggled.

"Phantom." Tobias froze.

Tobias felt Noah's hands on him a moment later, sliding up his back. "He's good, eh, Captain?"

"He's a minx." Tobias' throat was dry as dust and Phan was still shifting, still chained to the wall. Hot and slick and right there.

"He wants you," Noah whispered, stepping closer, shifting his hands to slide up under Tobias' shirt. "He's a slut is what he is, and he's yours."

Tobias closed his eyes as his erection, already harder

than he dared to think about, flexed and throbbed. "Is that true, minx? Are you a slut and are you mine?"

Phan didn't say anything, but he hardly had to. He undulated and rubbed, the lube from the toy smearing, mixing with what Tobias was leaking. The chains shifted as Phan went up on his toes, clearly trying to find the right position.

"Go ahead, take me in. If you can make it work, if you can earn it--" Tobias gasped as Phan impaled himself. Tight, silky heat surrounded Tobias' shaft, the ring of muscle squeezing all the way down Tobias' cock to its root.

Noah's fingers slipped around and pinched Tobias' nipples gently, then slid low a moment later, over his ass, squeezing through the leather. "Take him. He'll love it."

It wasn't as if Tobias really had a choice. He could move or he could die. He tried to tell Noah that, but words weren't working for him at all; instead, he grunted and moved his hips an inch, then shuddered.

He never knew if he loved his boys for getting him into such a state that he came far too fast, or hated them.

Phan was moaning under him, panting still and trying to... Tobias wasn't sure what he was trying to do, but he wouldn't keep still. He was chained to the wall, but that had no effect at all on how active he was in their lovemaking.

"Phantom," Tobias finally growled. "Keep still so I can fuck you properly."

Phan giggled a little hysterically and stopped moving. "Yes, sir. Whatever you say, sir. Sir, could you maybe just perhaps do it now? I need you."

Noah's hands roamed over Tobias' body. He could feel their warmth on his ass, his back, his shoulders, and yet the boy had the good sense to keep out of the way. Every now and then, Noah would whisper something in Tobias' ear, something just raunchy enough to make Tobias grit his teeth and thrust that much deeper.

"Phantom." Tobias closed his eyes and rested his forehead between Phan's shoulder blades, smelling sweat and sex and leather, hearing his boys and the soft sound of chains. He could feel pressure building to a level he knew wasn't sustainable, and his thighs began to shake.

"Yes," Phan said breathlessly. "I can feel you, sir. Let go, let yourself go. I'm yours, always. Yours."

"Mine!" As always, the sheer knowledge of how completely he was lord and master was so overwhelming, so fulfilling, that Tobias' inner strength turned outer. He slammed into Phan hard enough to propel them both against the wall. "All mine," he whispered, grinding his hips against Phan's ass.

"All yours." Phan nodded, his head turned to the side, against the wall.

Tobias started to come, his body jerking with each pulse. "Dearest."

Phan smiled at him, nodding. "Always yours. I promise."

Tobias knew it was true. He also knew he had to get Phan unchained, very soon, and that he was going to need help. "Sweetheart. I seem to have turned to jelly."

"Really? I didn't see that coming at all." Noah laughed softly and reached up to work on Phan's manacles. "Just stay there a minute." The chains rattled and sang out as Noah moved, and in a moment or two, both of Phan's hands were free.

Noah disappeared from view for a moment, but Tobias heard him slide the chair forward. "Sit, both of you," he said gently. "I'll get your feet, hon."

Tobias sat and held Phantom in his lap. "God, I love you."

Phan turned slightly to kiss him, his cheeks pink. "I love you, too."

"I love your sense of humor."

"Thank goodness." Phan grinned at him, and when his ankles were free, he twisted around in Tobias' lap, curling up contentedly.

"We need a bigger chair." Tobias reached for Noah and pulled him close, too. "I love you. You were beautiful."

"I love you. You're always so sweet and sappy after you come, sir," Noah teased. He kissed Tobias deeply and then Phan, too. "I'm almost glad we didn't go for Juliet, sir. After that performance, can you imagine?"

Tobias laughed weakly and then snorted at the intrigued look on Phan's face. "Maybe for your birthday, you little ingénue."

"Ingénue? Hardly that, sir." Phan's eyes glittered. "I'm much more... uh, provocative than that."

"If I want an ingénue, you'll be an ingénue."

"Good point."

Tobias smiled and kissed him again. "Help Noah clean up, dear. I think we'll have movies tonight -- musicals, so I can get more inspiration."

"Just so long as you order Phan not to sing!" Noah handed Tobias a bottle of water. "I can clean up here, sir. Why don't you let Phan draw you a bath?"

"Are you sure?" It seemed like an unfair division of labor to Tobias, but Phan was already getting up and offering Noah a kiss and a thank you.

Noah smiled at Phan and accepted the kiss. "I'm sure, sir." It was a small sacrifice to Noah, but they both knew it meant a lot to Phan. "All yours, hon."

"Thanks, Noah." Phan immediately turned and started cleaning Tobias enough so that he could dress decently to cross the yard. Not that anyone would see, but they tended to keep the nudity to a minimum out of doors, just in case a neighbor stopped by unexpectedly.

Tobias allowed it, smiling a little and not rolling his eyes. He was very capable of doing up his own pants, but Phan was in a particularly gentle and serving mood; it would hurt his feelings if he wasn't allowed to do the little things. "I'm afraid we cut up your clothes, dear. Find a blanket in one of the cupboards and that will do."

Phan nodded and left the stall, hurrying; he was walking all right, Tobias was pleased to see.

"Thank you," he said again to Noah. "We'll see you inside." He kissed Noah again, and once more. "Don't dawdle; we miss you when you're not there."

"I'll catch up. More slowly than usual, maybe, but I'll get there." Noah winked and gave his own ass a little pat. "I'm a bit sore. You two enjoy each other."

Tobias nodded and kissed him quickly before heading to the door. "One of these days, your generosity may stop astounding me. But not today." Smiling, he walked up the center aisle of the stable to meet Phan, wearing a blanket toga, at the door.

It was nice to feel balanced; it was even nicer to know that his boys felt it, too.

18

The farm was always quiet in the early morning. It was so different from their townhouse in the city, where they'd wake to the sound of garbage trucks, someone's stereo, or rush hour traffic. At the farm, there were birds, a soft wind, the occasional distant bray from one of the horses in the barn.

There were also the quiet, sleeping sounds his boys made from their pallets on the floor. Tobias knew them well -- Phan's soft purr and Noah's deeper breathing that always bordered on, but never quite became, snoring.

When the phone rang, Tobias nearly jumped out of his skin. Not only was the sound incongruous with mornings on the farm, but it was also just plain rude to call someone so soon after sunrise.

Which meant it was likely Bradford. Tobias fumbled for the receiver.

"Sorry to wake you." Bradford's voice was soft, muted as if he was trying not to be overheard.

"Not at all." Tobias' body still remembered how to wake

up quickly, the remaining legacy from too many late-night veterinary emergencies. "What's wrong?"

"Liar," Bradford replied with a snort, but his tone was gentle. "In any case, I thought I should let you know that Nikki is home. He came home late last night, and we were up most of the night talking. He's asleep now, on a chain on the floor, so I suppose that means we're going to be okay."

Tobias let out a breath and leaned back into his pillows. It had taken longer than he'd anticipated, and he'd been getting worried. "Good. I'm glad. How do you feel?"

"Well, I'm not entirely sure yet, everything is still kind of fresh. But he was embarrassed and, more than anything, he was worried that I wouldn't take him back, so as far as that goes, I feel pretty confident that we'll get our balance back. We're not touching the contract, but we may need to build back up to where we were. He's feeling pretty fragile."

"And you're not?" Tobias refused to shy away when it came to Bradford; after all, that was why the man called him.

"I am not fragile, thank you." Bradford protested. "Out of my element? Perhaps. Lacking in objectivity? Absolutely. Possibly even slightly emotional. But fragile, I am not."

"That's what fragile is, more or less." Tobias rubbed his eyes. "Plus, you're on the phone before six in the morning."

"Yes. I know." Bradford sighed. "I think what we really need, apart from a few more hours of sleep, is some time away from this club. Would you happen to be interested in entertaining visitors today?"

"Of course. You can even stay if you wish. The guest quarters are more or less ready. It might be a good thing to open the doors with something of a healing -- not to mention our closest friends."

Bradford sighed again, this time sounding less stressed

and more relieved. "Thank you. Let me see who I can get to hold down the fort while we're both away. I think as long as I keep my cell handy, things can run here without us for a day or two. I'd look out for us around lunch time, does that sound reasonable?"

Tobias nodded and heard the subtle shift of bodies on the floor. "We'll have food ready for you both, and I'll make sure a room is well prepared. And Bradford -- I'm glad he's home."

"Me, too, Tobias. Me, too." Bradford hung up on his end and Tobias set the receiver down as quietly as possible, but it was likely too late, as he heard whispers coming from the foot of the bed.

"Good morning," he said dryly. Then he stretched out and blinked at his ceiling. "We have work to do, my darlings."

Warm bodies joined him on the bed, and then in bed, under the sheets. "Work, sir?" Noah asked from one side of Tobias while Phan settled himself on the other.

"Company coming." Tobias let them burrow in; no one had to get up right away. "Bradford and Nikki are coming to visit for a few days. We need to prepare space for them, grocery shop, and stay out of their way when requested."

Noah nodded. Tobias had discussed Nikki and Bradford's situation with them briefly without too many details; just enough that they wouldn't be shocked by whatever happened next.

"Whatever we can do, sir." Noah yawned. "Do you want coffee yet?"

"I think I do." Tobias smiled as Phan wiggled a little closer. "Barn, coffee, showers... Phan, you can make the beds in the guest house and do any dusting and such that needs doing over there. Noah, you're in charge of food -- lunch for six, groceries for Nikki to keep his master fed. Phan can help with Bradford's favorite foods since he worked there long enough to know the details."

"I guess that means we have to get up, huh?" Noah stretched out long, and Tobias felt every muscle in his body go taut for a second or two.

"At some point very soon, yes."

Phan giggled. "But not yet," he murmured, hands suddenly questing. "We need to actually wake up."

Tobias couldn't help rolling his eyes. "You're up, I get it. I can feel it. Although I'll admit to a bit of surprise about it, given last night."

"It's all you, sir," Phan said seriously. "Tell him, Noah. Back me up, here."

Noah lifted his head and looked at Phan. "Phan, hon. I'm thinking it's you."

"You disappoint me." Phan sniffed and vanished under the blankets. "Look!"

"Oh, for the love of -- Phantom, out of the bed." Tobias sat up and watched a Phan-shaped lump scoot off the end of the bed and onto the floor. "Stay there, I'll unchain you in a moment. Noah, kiss me good morning."

Noah smiled. "I like that order, sir." He leaned down and kissed Tobias affectionately. "Shall I start the coffee and head out to the barn?"

"Yes, please. Phantom will make us all breakfast and then start his chores." Tobias got out of bed and unlocked both of them -- not that they couldn't do it themselves, but he was still in charge. Mostly. "Shoo, both of you. I'll be down in a few minutes."

Phan disappeared so quickly he was almost a blur. Noah hopped out of bed smartly enough but took a moment or two to dress before he headed downstairs, pulling on jeans for the barn. He didn't dawdle, though, and it wasn't long before the scent of fresh coffee was wafting up the stairs.

One of the nice things about having two boys to do the chores was that he could shower, dress, and go down to not only the barn chores done and fresh coffee made, but his breakfast well under way and the paper waiting for him in his office.

"It's good to be king," he said to himself as he sat at his desk. "Now, to make sure Bradford remains king while a prince plays with his heart..."

At precisely noon, Tobias went to his front steps and watched Bradford's car pull up the lane. For even a country date, Bradford's precision took no rest, and Tobias had known it; he'd planned the morning so everything would be done in time, and had left Noah and Phan to finish getting lunch on the table.

Bradford's driver opened the back door and Bradford stepped out, followed quickly by Nikki, who went right to his knees as the driver pulled their bags from the trunk. Bradford said nothing to Nikki, but Nikki stood and lifted the bags as Bradford headed up the steps to the front porch, where Nikki knelt again, one bag on either side. Tobias noted that Nikki looked a little thin. He'd never had much meat on him, but his angles seemed a little more pronounced than usual. He was also on his very best behavior.

Bradford just looked tired. The little lines around his eyes and mouth were more obvious, making him look older -- or perhaps just making him look his age, which was unusual enough.

"Hello, friend," Bradford said, going in for a gentleman's hug.

Tobias hugged him back. "Welcome to the farm, both of

you. I hope you can find some peace here, and space for what you need." He stepped back and led the way inside, saying, "Lunch is almost ready. Nikki, leave the bags in the hall for now; we'll show you to the suite in a while. I hope you're hungry."

Nikki didn't reply, but he did exactly as he'd been instructed, leaving the bags neatly against a wall in the front hall.

"I'm certainly ready to eat. I'd like Nikki to follow whatever orders you have for your boys." Bradford walked with Tobias toward the dining room with Nikki at his heel. "The farm is lovely this time of year."

"Thank you. Unless it's storming or March, it's generally quite nice here." Tobias smiled and sat at the dining room table, gesturing for Bradford to join him. The table was set for five, though he and Bradford had much nicer dishes than the plain stoneware for the submissives. "Would you like a drink?"

Phantom came in and set a large salad on the table. "Good afternoon, Master Bradford," he said respectfully.

"Afternoon, Phantom." Bradford looked Phan over appraisingly like he always did. Something about having had Phan under his roof for so long, Tobias assumed. "You're looking good." Bradford glanced at Tobias. "Iced tea?"

Tobias nodded at Phan, who promptly rushed off to the kitchen to fulfill the request.

"They've made chicken for lunch, and Noah did the grocery shopping for you. You're welcome to join us for supper if you wish, or you can use the kitchen in the guest house." Tobias glanced at Nikki and sighed. "I want to make sure you and Nikki do exactly what you need to do. If I can make it easier in any way, please tell me."

"We'll take you up on your dinner offer, for one,"

Bradford said easily. "Perhaps we could use one of your stalls this afternoon? Otherwise, I think Nikki will benefit from some time around your boys, and I've brought you some excellent cigars that would make good smoking on your porch tonight with a couple of fingers of scotch."

Phan set Bradford's iced tea down. "Phan, which place is for Nikki?" Bradford waited while Phan pulled out a chair and then sent Nikki to it. "Thank you."

"Of course, Master." Phan sketched a little bow and hurried off to the kitchen again, coming back with Noah and the serving dishes.

"Thank you, boys." Tobias leaned back and let them serve and seat themselves, then picked up his fork. "You're welcome to make use of the stables, of course. The barn chores have all been taken care of, but when you want Nikki to be with these two, I'm sure they wouldn't mind a hand with the rest of the cleaning in the guest house and working on the landscaping. It's amazing how construction dust can linger."

Phan made a face and nodded. He knew very well how tricky all that dust could be, and how long it took to wash up.

Bradford nodded as well. "He'll help any way he can, I'm sure."

Noah set the serving dishes he'd been carrying down on the table. "Hello, Master Bradford," he said politely.

Bradford smiled. "Hello, Noah. This looks delicious."

"Thank you, sir."

Noah crossed behind Nikki's chair and gave Nikki's shoulders a squeeze. "Good to see you, Nikki."

Noah's touch was brief, but Nikki leaned into it as if craving more. He served himself quietly and waited for Bradford to pick up a fork before he did.

Bradford took a bite or two in silence, as did everyone, before he started up conversation again. "So, Phan, how are you feeling about things? Do you like the new building? Are you ready for guests?"

Phan startled visibly and glanced toward Tobias before nodding. "Yes, sir. I am, actually. The building is really nice, and I think that Sir will be able to do some very good work here at the farm." He bit his lower lip and added, "I think I'll be much more comfortable with the majority of the domestic activity taking place across the yard and away from Elizabeth's things, out of space that was very much a personal area for all of us."

Bradford nodded silently, finishing the bite he was chewing before answering. "Wonderful. I hope you will. I know your Master has been concerned about you, I'm sure you'll continue to communicate with him on the subject in any case."

Noah studiously watched his plate and ate his lunch silently, but Nikki glanced at Phan and watched him for a moment or two.

"Yes, sir." Phan whispered the words to his plate, but he nodded. "I will, sir. Communication is important, even when it's hard."

Tobias watched him and then raised an eyebrow at Bradford. "He's not wrong. I think the next couple of days are going to be interesting, don't you?" It wasn't what he really wanted to say, but he was fairly sure that Bradford knew that. They'd known each other for an exceedingly long time.

"I do. I think we all need to slow down sometimes, right, Nikki?"

"Yes, sir." Nikki whispered.

"Good boy." Bradford took another bite of his lunch. "Mmm. Delicious."

Tobias didn't really taste the food, though he knew it must have been good; Noah had become a wonderful cook, and Phan was no slouch in the kitchen. After they'd all finished and the boys had cleared the table, Tobias waited to hear the sounds of three people washing dishes and putting the kitchen to rights.

Then he looked at Bradford. "What's first? Seeing the guest house, putting the three of them to cleaning so we can talk, or do you want to work with Nikki first? I'll follow your lead, old friend."

"Well, why don't you give me a tour of the new guest house, and then I'll work with Nikki for a while. Once he's in a good space he can rest or hang out with your boys and you and I can have a sit down. What do you think? I haven't got anything strenuous planned for Nikki today, just some quiet grounding and a reminder of who he belongs to. Just enough to leave him wanting more." Bradford grinned. "I'll talk with you later about the best approach for tomorrow... I'm interested in your opinion." Bradford stuck his head into the kitchen. "Come to the guest house when you're through, boy."

"Yes, sir," came Nikki's voice, clear as a bell.

Tobias nodded to Noah and echoed the order, then took Bradford out the back door. "The work went smoothly, for the most part," he said, gesturing to the yard and its stack of scrap wood. "The delays were cleared up by giving more money for more labor." He smiled wryly. "The only thing that happened exactly on schedule was the art and decor, because Phan had most of the paintings stored in the basement at home."

"I haven't seen much of his work," Bradford noted. "He'd given up painting by the time he was with me."

"His therapist sent him back to it. Aside from the painting of Noah I claimed, however, I've been letting him do as he wished with the canvases. Most of them, it turns out, went to the basement." Tobias walked them up the steps and into the building. "He's eclectic, thankfully, so the walls don't look like one man's emotional outpouring."

Bradford laughed. "So he's not a tortured artist? Glad to hear it." Tobias opened the door and Bradford followed him in. "Well, well. This looks like an entirely new place."

"It came together." Tobias wasn't trying to be modest, as he did like the house, but he didn't feel particularly attached to it. Likely because he wasn't meant to live in it, he assumed. "I went with a lot of tile, which is easier to keep neat than carpets, and I put cork in the dining areas; good for kneeling boys, I was informed."

Bradford laughed. "We picked the right construction company, I see." He walked through the main floor, sticking his head into one room and then the next. "It has a very comfortable feel to it, well done." He stopped short of going upstairs, though, and turned to Tobias instead. "Sorry for trotting out Phan's issues, but I think sometimes Nikki feels like he's the only sub in the world who has insecurities. I thought it might be good for him to know that even someone he idolizes, like Phantom, has his issues."

"You weren't wrong." Tobias nodded and let out a sigh. "It was probably good for Phan to articulate his feelings on the matter as well. We haven't talked about it head on; I know he's thinking about it a lot, though, and I think he's up to something in his free time. A while ago, I sent them both out to buy Noah's suits, do you remember? That was right about when Phan started having a hard time with clients and members taking over what he's calling Mrs. Miller's space."

"I remember it was a struggle to get Phan to articulate it in the first place, yes," Bradford nodded. "Are you concerned about whatever he is up to?"

"Not concerned as such." Tobias thought for a moment, wondering how best to explain his sense. "It's more like... I fear he's being creative with his personal growth the way he's creative when he finds sugar. His exuberance can be a little..."

"Overwhelming? Misguided? Ungrounded?" Bradford sighed. "Yes, I remember. Noah's no help?"

"Noah's always a help." Tobias smiled almost without realizing it. "I do know that if Phan is about to get himself in trouble Noah will step in. This doesn't feel like he's about to act out, more like he's playing at the edges of something. Processing." His smiled turned a bit sour and he pointed up the stairs. "Come on, before I say something I'll regret, like 'Yes, Bradford, I need to talk to him about it.'"

"Of course," Bradford snorted and turned around to make his way up the stairs. "Wouldn't want to say something like that, would you?" He tone was light, though, and he looked back over his shoulder and smiled at Tobias. "The good news is that you have enough dirt on me that your secrets will go to my grave with me."

"It's nice that way, isn't it?" Tobias grinned at him and followed him up to the second floor. "Who would have thought it when we were both on our knees and learning what that damn cane felt like?"

Bradford laughed. "Stop that. Now you're making me feel old."

"There are days I feel old, days I feel young, and occasionally there are days I feel like I'm a teenager, what with all the hormones floating around me in my home and working lives." Tobias rolled his eyes and showed Bradford the way to the suite he'd had prepared. "Bedroom, bedding for Nikki if he's to be on the floor, your bathroom. Also, because you're you, you get the use of the only TV we have so far."

"Nice." Bradford wandered through the space. "Really nice. We did shell out some cash, didn't we? Ah, well, it will be worth it. Almost no one is doing what we do, Tobias; what you do out here at the farm. Almost no one. So to hell with feeling old, I say we feel savvy and cutting edge instead."

"I suspect it'll all pay for itself within two years. Maybe sooner, if the longer workshops prove successful. I've been thinking about making a meeting room, too; not quite a boardroom or classroom, but definitely a place where I can talk to tops and hand out reams of study guides and such. What do you think? Too much?" He turned his head as he heard the door open on the lower level. "Mmm. We can talk about it later, I suppose. Time to heal your boy."

"You just want to hear yourself talk," Bradford teased, heading out of the room.

"There is that." Tobias chuckled as they went back down the stairs. "But that's our little secret, I'm sure." At the bottom of the stairs, they found all three boys lined up with the luggage Bradford and Nikki had brought. "Phan and Noah, please take that up to the room. Double check the supplies and things in the bathroom. I'll take our guests to the stables and unlock everything for them; you can meet us there. If all is well, we'll take ourselves out of the way for a while."

Phan nodded and picked up one of the bags. "Yes, sir."

Noah was quick to follow, echoing Phan's words and

hurrying up the stairs after him, the other bag over one shoulder.

"You'll hardly be in our way." Bradford waved a hand dismissively. "Carry on with your routine, and please don't let us disrupt anything." He followed Tobias out of the guest house and along the short path to the play barn with Nikki tight at his shoulder. "We have very low-key plans for today, but probably something more intense for tomorrow."

"The space is at your complete disposal." Tobias unlocked the main door to the stables and pulled it open. "Take a look around while I turn on the lights for you. When you know where you want to play, we can turn off everything else. If you'd like a suggestion, I find that the stall with the massage table is good for reconnecting; there's a nice spanking bench in there, too. I can find just about any restraints you'd like."

Bradford nodded and made his way down the center aisle, looking into each stall. He lingered for a moment beside the one that Tobias had suggested, moved on to have a look at the others, and then returned to the stall with the massage table. "I think I agree, Tobias. Perfect. Go inside, Nikki, and kneel." After Nikki disappeared through the door, Bradford added, "We won't be using restraints today, but have you a lead? Something leather and not too long? And if I might peruse your selection of crops and such..."

Tobias smiled and nodded. "Of course." He led Bradford to the toy boxes in the main ring and let him take a long look. It was somewhat akin to shopping, and he wasn't surprised at all when Bradford tested a few crops on the practice dummy. He left Bradford to make his choices when Phan and Noah came in, going with them to check all the first aid supplies and cleaning equipment.

"All right, then?" he asked as Bradford came back from

the ring. "You know where the emergency buzzer and everything is, and the direct line to the house."

"I do." Bradford had two crops in his hand and also a large feather. He'd closed Tobias' toy boxes carefully before heading back up the aisle. "We'll be just fine. Thank you."

"Fantastic. I'm going to take mine back to the house; I think I need to have a talk with Phan. We'll be in my office when you and Nikki are done."

"Give us a couple of hours." Bradford gave Tobias a quick nod and walked into the stall. "Nikki, my boy," Tobias heard Bradford say as Tobias turned back up the aisle to join Noah and Phan.

"Okay, my darlings. Let's go and talk." He saw Phan's lip tremble and reached for him. "It's okay, boy. Really it is. You can even cuddle with Noah, if it helps you talk to me."

Noah kept close to them as they walked back to the house. "Safe room, sir? Or did you have somewhere else in mind?"

"Safe room for now, living room if Phan wants it." He kept his arm around Phan and tried to judge his reactions. Phan was being particularly unhelpful.

They went in the house, and with Phan still being silent, Tobias took them right up the stairs. "On the bed with you two, okay? I want to see faces." If he could get them cuddled up, he might get somewhere. He dragged the chair around and sat, wishing he knew the right words to say to set Phan's mind to rest once and for all.

"Come on, hon." Noah climbed up onto the bed first and rested against the headboard. When he opened his arms, Phan only hesitated for a second before crawling right up into them. "It's okay, this is good space. Positive space. The conversations Sir and I have had in here... well. It's good, I promise. Hard, but good." Noah tucked his arms around Phan as Phan settled. "Okay?"

"Okay." Phan sighed, and Tobias watched him sink into Noah's arms. "It's not even that I don't want to talk about it, sir, I'm just not sure what to say."

"Well, let's start there." Tobias leaned back and tried to think of the whole thing like a puzzle. "You're happier with the new set-up for guests?"

"Yes, sir." Phan nodded and then looked at Noah. "It's pretty cool, right? The house and all?"

"It's very cool. There's no reason for anyone to be up at the house unless we invite them. And I happen to think the decor is first class. We hired a great artist." Noah grinned.

Phan actually blushed. It was rare enough that Tobias leaned forward to see it.

"Thanks, kitten," Phan said, then he hurried on. "Anyway, yes. That's the main thing, for me. That we don't have to have a lot of people in here if we -- you -- uh, us. We. If we don't want them."

"We," Tobias confirmed. "That's where the trouble is, huh?"

Phan sighed again and rolled his eyes. He sat up a bit, though, still touching Noah but not right on top of him. "I feel like I caused a hell of a lot of trouble and expense."

"Yep, that's you, a high-maintenance troublemaker." Noah snorted. "It's all the peanut butter you eat. And the cheese. I'm sure Sir has an appropriate punishment in mind."

Phan blinked twice and looked sheepish. "Well, it's legitimate! My neurotic behavior made a whole new thing happen!"

"Like that's never happened for anyone else, ever." Tobias rolled his eyes. "Phantom. Who loves you?"

"You do. Noah does." Phan answered immediately, though he was a little subdued.

"Right. And Bradford cares about you very much. Hell, everyone who's ever met you cares. Don't think I'm unaware that Brian's been spending time babbling at you about his current affair. People like you, dear. And if it makes you feel better to have the business end of kink happen out of this house, I'm fine with it. If I wasn't, it wouldn't have happened. Right?"

Phan nodded slowly, obviously thinking hard. "Yes, sir," he finally said. "And I'm okay with the workout room. I really am. Um. Now. I don't know if you've noticed, but I don't have an easy time with changes or saying good bye."

"Trust me, Sir noticed. I noticed. We notice a lot about you, Phan." Noah shifted so he was talking more directly to Phan. "I also noticed how hard the decision to change her room was on you, now that you mention it. It's been there a while now, so if you're bringing it up, I have a feeling you're not really so okay with it."

Phan shook his head. "No, I'm saying it because I am okay, now. I mean, a museum would be silly, and a shrine would have her tanning my hide. For real. Like, she'd use a wooden spoon on me. I really am okay with it, now. But the combination of having all those people in the house, with our things, her things, yours and mine and Sir's, and having her room gone... that was a lot. It's better now. I still miss her, but I can find her now. I couldn't, when it was all happening at once."

"I've never really lost anyone I was that close to," Noah said thoughtfully. "Actually, I've never really been that close to anyone until recently. I mean, I love my mom, but she doesn't get me at all. My dad... well, we hardly spoke anyway.

I loved Mrs. M, and I miss her, but I didn't know her like you two did."

Tobias took a deep breath. He missed her, too, some days so sharply that it was a physical ache in his chest. "Phan, when was the last time you went to see her? To visit her grave and leave flowers?"

"It's been a while," he said softly, looking at the bed cover. "It hurts."

"I know. But I think we should. You and me, together, and Noah."

Phan nodded, still looking at the bed. "Okay." He sighed and rubbed his face. "Okay. But I'll cry and be all ugly. Just so you know."

"Tears don't make you ugly, Phan," Noah said gently. He reached out and rubbed Phan's back with one hand and grinned. "But just in case you get all snotty, I'll be armed with plenty of tissues. Promise."

"Snotty is something I do all the time." Phan grinned, almost at full power. "Okay."

Tobias smiled and relaxed a bit. Phan would be okay. They all would. He got up and started toward the bed, intending to give out a hug or two, but before he could get there, Phan sat up, all but pushing Noah away.

"Um. While we're talking about her, and grief, and all this stuff..." Phan trailed off, looking distinctly uncomfortable and oddly shy. His gaze never met Tobias' eyes anyway, but he seemed to be avoiding even looking at either of them. "I have something to give you both. The... uh, the surprise. I'm all done."

Tobias stopped in place and glanced at Noah, who looked as surprised and curious as Tobias felt. "Really, dear?" Tobias allowed himself to grin but tried not to be overly enthusiastic, in case it made Phan even more uncomfortable. "That's fantastic. Where is it?" He hadn't thought that Phan had enjoyed free time since they'd arrived at the farm; he must have brought it, complete.

"It's in my bag," Phan said, his hands twisting nervously. "I can go get it if you want."

"Oh, I think we want. Don't you think, Noah?"

"Oh, yes. We definitely want. Go get it." Noah winked at Phan.

Tobias sat on the edge of the bed as Phan scurried off, half expecting that he wouldn't come back and someone -- likely Noah -- would have to go and fetch him. Phantom, however, seemed to have committed himself wholly to his mission, and he came dashing back in before Tobias could even begin to speculate with Noah.

"Okay, so here's the thing." Phan stood at the end of the bed, holding a wrinkled plastic shopping bag in front of him. "When I was first here as Sir's submissive, I spent a lot of time with Elizabeth, after I was out of recovery and had stopped being a danger to myself. When Sir was able to go back to his practice and leave me for the daytime. That's when Elizabeth taught me to cook and clean and we..." He stopped, apparently not finding the words he was looking for. "When we became close."

Tobias nodded. He remembered those days, full of worry about what was going on at home and the sweet feeling of relief when he'd get back for supper and find Phan okay and Mrs. Miller the same as ever.

Phan seemed stuck, his hands worrying the edge of the bag. "She, she taught me lots of things," he finally blurted.

"She did," Tobias said softly, with yet another nod. He started to get up, worried that Phan was going to work himself back up into a state. They'd just nicely gotten him calm. Noah, for his part, was still and listening quietly.

"Sir!" Phan held out a hand and stopped him. "You need to be with Noah. So you can share."

"All right." Tobias sat back down and moved close to Noah. "Like this?"

"Share, huh?" Noah squinted, clearly curious.

"Uh-huh." Phan took a deep breath and finally opened the bag. "It's not very good. I forgot a bunch of what she taught me, and it's a lot harder than I remember. But it's done and there's only a few holes, really, and maybe they don't matter so much?" Without looking up, and still babbling, Phan pulled a large, soft, multi-colored something out of the bag. "I remembered the knit stitch okay, but it took some tries to remember purl, and I forgot the garter stitch border to keep it from rolling and had to start over--" He was busily unfolding a blanket of many colors, his words tumbling one over another.

Tobias was speechless.

"Phan," Noah interrupted the flow of words and reached for the blanket, grinning. "Phan? Quit babbling and let us see it!"

When the blanket was finally unfolded, draped over Noah's knees and his own, Tobias found his voice. "Phan." The word came out as a croak, and he cleared his throat. "Phan," he tried again. "You made this?" It was amazing, a riot of colors and textures, bright knit squares all sewn together with a border of blue yarn. There were a few holes here and there, but on the whole the blanket was fantastic. "I didn't know you could knit."

"Elizabeth taught me," Phan said, petting a fuzzy pink square. "When you were helping horses to be born. This one's for her." He pointed at another square, soft cotton and steely gray, almost silver. "That one is for Master Bradford. The purple one beside it is Nikki."

"Where's ours?" Tobias asked immediately.

Phan's cheeks went pink. "This whole row. The blue one at the top is you. The yellow one is Noah. The orange one is me 'n Noah. The white one is you and me. The rainbow yarn is all of us."

"Rainbow, good choice." Despite the little joke, Noah's voice was full of awe. He ran his fingers over one square and then another, touching every part of it that he could reach. "Phan, it's beautiful. It's the best surprise I... so much work and thought and... it's wonderful." Noah's voice was a little rough with emotion. "It's warm, too." He smiled at Phan.

Tobias reached, gathered Phan up, and pulled him onto the bed. After a short tussle, he had Phan between himself and Noah, all three of them under the blanket. "It's beautiful," Tobias whispered. "It's better than beautiful. It's amazing. And it's so much more than just a blanket you made." It seemed important that he let Phan know that he knew that, that he was aware of the hours and hours of thinking and mourning and love that had gone into its creation. "Thank you, dear. It's a gift like no other."

Phan twisted and burrowed, somehow managing to hold tight to both of them. "It's not perfect. But it's good, right?" He nodded his head. "It's pretty and warm and I made it, so it's good."

"It is perfect. Even the imperfections are beautiful. Kind of like us, right?" Noah kissed Phan's temple. "Mrs. M would be so proud of you."

Tobias smiled and kissed the top of Phan's head. He'd been right; Phantom was going to be just fine.

19

Tobias thought that Noah's dinner had perhaps been stretching into territory that might have been a bit too complicated, but he had to admit -- as Bradford and Phan and Nikki had -- that Noah had pulled off a marvelous meal. He'd had Phan and Nikki to cut and chop and wash for him, and it seemed that he flourished with a pair of sous chefs.

Of course, a fancy meal meant a lot of dishes and a lot of washing up. Tobias and Bradford had left them to it and, armed with brandy, glasses, and cigars, had taken themselves out to the front veranda to watch night settle around them.

"Nikki seems calm," Tobias said, making himself comfortable. "I trust you found everything you needed?"

Bradford smiled and snorted softly. "Nikki is in sub heaven right now. I spent a full hour telling him how much I care about him and how special he is and validating all the things he does right, all the while teasing him with that marvelous feather. I even let him come." Bradford sipped his brandy. "The second hour took on a different tone, however."

"It usually does." Tobias laughed softly and leaned way back, putting his foot up on the rail. "Was it what you needed?"

"I think so. I gave him a chance to tell me anything that was on his mind, and all he said was how grateful he was to have been forgiven and how much he wants to make it up to me. I let him." Bradford grinned more broadly. "I feel a great deal better myself."

Tobias laugh grew more full. "Nice. Actually, very nice. I could do with that, myself."

"I have a feeling you'd get little objection from your boys," Bradford suggested, rolling his cigar between his fingers. "We could stay out of your way tomorrow if you'd like to use the stables."

"Don't be ridiculous. Or are you suddenly growing shy around me?" Tobias grinned and sipped his brandy. "It's a big place."

"Ha!" Bradford laughed. "Hardly. I was trying to be a good house guest. Emily Post would be proud."

"Emily Post would run screaming from this farm." Screaming. Hmm. "We should make them scream."

"In chorus," Bradford agreed, chomping on his cigar.

"Synchro torture." Tobias nodded. "Or synchro fucking. I could probably do that if I had another cock. Two boys is hard work sometimes."

"Oh, I feel so sorry for you." There was no hint of sympathy in Bradford's voice, naturally. "Two boys to fuck, woe is you."

"I know, it's horrible. And when they gang up on me in the mornings, it's a wonder I ever get out of bed." Tobias smirked. "Seriously, we should plan something for tomorrow. Any ideas? A full role-play scene or just toys and tools that happen to be around?"

"Hmm. I'm kind of liking the torture in tandem idea." Bradford swirled the brandy around in his glass and took a sip before continuing. "Perhaps some creative bondage and some heavy hitters? Give them something to listen to? I'd say we could see which one begs to be fucked first, but we both know who that will be."

Tobias snorted. "No bet, there. I do like this bondage and flogging idea. Need tools with sound, a lot of snap. Say, like a bull whip, or a really whippy crop. The cane."

"Nikki loves the cane, though I will say it takes it out of him. If we go for canes or bull whips, then we need to keep at least that part of it fairly concise. If we come up with some snappy cats or crops, then we've got more time to play. What appeals?"

"Longer play, lots of noise -- and if I make Phan wait and listen, things might get very interesting. We can be across the hall from each other -- or I can even keep my two from seeing each other." Tobias pondered that for a moment and smiled. "This has wonderful potential. We should tape it."

"Why, you're a pervert, Tobias."

"I think I might be, yes." Tobias turned his head and winked. "Don't tell anyone. Deviant to pervert is such a leap, and one that should only be taken behind closed doors."

After swallowing down the last of his brandy, Bradford put his cigar out. "That does it, then. If we're going to walk that perverted road tomorrow, we'd best get our rest. We're old."

"You're old. I'm the Master of two. It takes a lot out of me." Tobias stood up and stretched. "I look forward to it." Enough that he was eager to get to bed, actually.

"Fine. I'm old and you're a lunatic." Bradford followed Tobias inside, where they gathered up their boys. "Good night, Tobias. See you at breakfast," Bradford said with a wink. "Good night, boys," he added before leading Nikki back out to the guest house on one of Tobias' weighty leather leashes.

In his wake, Noah and Phan seemed to sense something was going on and were suddenly on their best behavior. The went upstairs silently, and Tobias found he was so eager to begin that he took more pleasure than usual in fastening the boys' collars and chains and ordering them to sleep on the floor.

Oh, yes. Tomorrow was going to be a good day.

———

Tobias' day started on a particularly lovely note with a two-mouthed blow job. He didn't let either of his boys get off, and after handing out their morning discipline, he had them don heavy leather cock rings.

For added measure, he put leads on their collars and made Phan carry his leash between his teeth. By the time he phoned Bradford at the guest house, both Noah and Phan were aroused, eager to please, and dying of curiosity and anticipation.

"Have you had your morning coffee yet?" Tobias asked Bradford. "We've had our breakfast, but I like to take my coffee outside in nice weather. Or we can move along, if you wish."

"I was just about to indulge." Bradford sounded equally as cheerful. "Where should we meet? Your deck or mine?"

"We'll come to you, I think." Tobias grinned and looked down at Noah kneeling at his feet. "Give us a few minutes." He hung up and poured his own coffee into a travel mug. "Okay, let's go."

They both handed him their leads, and he walked them

across the yard. Naked. They were gorgeous in the sunshine, wearing collars, leashes, and rings, and Tobias was smiling broadly as he climbed the steps to the deck. "Good morning."

"Good morning. Oh, my, don't your boys look stunning." Bradford stood as they arrived and gestured to a chair for Tobias.

Nikki was kneeling at his Master's feet, wearing a belt that likely held a plug in place and a silver cock cage that would prevent the sub from achieving an erection. He held his leash in his lap.

Bradford was dressed only in leather pants, heavy boots, and a pair of soft, black leather suspenders that crossed in the back. "Everyone sleep well?"

"I did." Tobias sat down and glanced at his boys, who immediately knelt; Phan put his lead back between his teeth. "I don't want to see marks in that leather."

Phan shook his head and then nodded.

"He's a little excited." Tobias sipped his coffee and made himself comfortable. "How was the bed? You're our first guest, you have to report on everything so we can make any changes before members start coming out."

"The bed, the house, it's all quite comfortable. Your boys even set the coffee maker for me so I woke up to fresh coffee. Very thoughtful. It's just so damned quiet out here in country; I'm not used to it. Even Nikki said he had a hard time getting back to sleep at one point because there was no white noise. Can't take the city out of the man, I guess."

"I had to soundproof my bedroom in the city," Tobias said with a laugh. "Soundproofing for various reasons is always my best investment, I think."

"So have you told them anything?" Bradford asked. It was a deliberate tease for their boys' benefit.

"Not directly, but I think they get the point. Should we tell them, do you think?" He was deliberately teasing as well, especially Phan. Noah was usually content to do as he was told and trust that he'd find out everything in due time; Phan was a curious cat, though, on about life six.

"I don't think so. They'll find out soon enough." Next to him, Nikki made a soft sound. Bradford grinned. "Something on your mind, boy?"

"No, sir."

"Very well." Bradford leaned back in his chair and sipped his coffee. "Nikki's wound up, Phan is excited... what about Noah? He looks so calm all the time. Almost too calm. I'm looking forward to seeing his feathers get ruffled."

Tobias ran his hand through Noah's hair and then tugged at it thoughtfully. "I've managed it a time or two. It's been a while, though, I must admit. Which of course means that it's overdue. What do you think, pet?"

"I'm yours, as ever, sir," Noah replied respectfully. Then, a bit more playfully, he added, "But it sounds good to me."

"It does now," Tobias said with a smile. "We'll see how you feel when we get things set up and the blows start raining down."

Phan, it was hard not to notice, wiggled, his cock bobbing.

"Yes, you, too. Maybe. Maybe you'll just have to listen." Tobias finished his coffee as Phan made a noise that was half moan, half laugh. "They think this is going to be easy, Bradford."

"Hmm." Bradford upended his coffee mug, swallowing down the last sip. He set the mug on the patio table. "They'd be wrong," he said in a steady, commanding tone. Then he looked at Tobias. "Shall we?"

"I think so, yes." Tobias abandoned his mug on the

railing and stood up, his hand held out for leashes. After a short scramble on Phan's part and an easy roll to his feet on Noah's, he curled his fingers into a fist around the straps. "Come."

He smiled smugly to himself when both leashes met with a moment of resistance as he swung his arm. The next time he swung it, his boys had sorted themselves out and there was only slack.

He didn't quite march them across the yard, but it was close. Bradford fell in alongside him, matching his stride, and the confidence between them -- the anticipation of the scenes to come -- was almost palpable, the creak and stomp of their boots the only sound until Tobias opened up the stables.

Tobias spoke pleasantly with Bradford as he let them all in, but instead of sending Noah to turn on the lights, he slapped the switches up himself and immediately took his boys down the aisle to the plain black stall. "In here, faces to the wall, arms out. Keep still while I chain you."

Phan and Noah hurried across the stall to take their places facing the wall, their leads still dangling from their collars. Bradford paused in the entry for a moment.

"I'll pick one next door, shall I? Or across the way? I don't believe there is room for both of us to swing our arms in here." That had been the plan all along, of course, but now at least the boys would know it.

"Whichever you prefer, my friend; there's chains and cuffs in all of them, so it's more a matter of aesthetic taste." He leaned into Phan, shoving him up against the wall none too gently as he bound Phan's hands. "Down low; you'll be here a while, and I don't want your arms going numb."

"Thank you, sir," Phan gasped, his face against the wall.

"You can thank me later."

"In that case, I'll be just across the hall, here." Bradford gestured to the white stall that was essentially everything the black stall was, only sterile and white. "Boy," Bradford ordered, gesturing toward the stall. "Face the wall, legs spread, arms out to the sides. Move!" Nikki sprang to his feet at Bradford's shout, and Bradford reached out and clapped Tobias on the shoulder. "Enjoy."

"Oh, I think this will be something to enjoy for a long time." Tobias let Phan go and grinned at Bradford. "Don't be too quiet, okay? There's no need."

Phan whimpered.

"I wasn't talking to you." He left Phan as was and moved to Noah. "As for you, my lovely. You're far, far too smooth these days." He stroked a hand down Noah's spine and slapped his ass, hard enough that his palm stung. "Hands on the wall, now."

"Quiet wasn't on the agenda." Bradford stepped into the white stall, and Tobias heard chains rattle and Nikki whimper.

"Yes, sir!" Noah answered, his voice sharp with the sting of Tobias' blow. He placed his hands flat on the wall, instinctively widening his stance for balance.

Bradford laughed at something Nikki must have said, and answered, "You may beg all you like, boy, but don't expect to get anything you're looking for."

"What he said," Tobias told Noah. "Although I do like the begging. But this isn't about you or Phan. Not today." Of course it was about them. It was always about them. But sometimes they needed a scene that wasn't funny or about getting off. There were dark edges to playing, and they were just as important and necessary as the other.

Plus, it made Tobias' cock hard to be rough.

He got Noah bound, the chains hanging loose in a loop

and then welded to the huge rings in the wall. "Do I need to bind your feet as well, or will you stay still?"

"I'll do my best without the chains, sir." Noah's voice was a great deal less amused than it had been back at the guest house.

"Oh, very nice, Tobias. You've white instruments to match your white room. I approve." Bradford said from across the way. "How's the cat?" His question was followed by a swooping sound as Bradford tested the tool in the air.

"Well, it's one of Phan's favorites. That should tell you something." Tobias went to the corner nearest the door and grinned out at him. "I'm sure Nikki will let you know." From the corner, Tobias picked up a crop, a whippy little braided one that he knew hurt like a son of a bitch when it came down at full strength. "After you."

"How polite," Bradford joked, and then his tone changed entirely. "Settle down, Nikki. I'll start lighter, but it'll build up quickly. Tell me when you're ready."

"Ready, sir."

Bradford swung, the first blow making a muted slapping sound, the second much the same. Nikki was quiet at first, but as the speed and intensity built, there was a whimper or a soft cry every third or fourth stroke. "That's it, boy, let me hear you."

"Yes, sir." Nikki answered quickly. "Thank you, sir!"

"Very nice," Tobias murmured. He turned back to his own boys and saw Phan trying so hard to be a good boy. He was standing still, face to the wall just like he'd been told, but long practice helped Tobias read his body language. He was listening very hard to Nikki.

Tobias thought he needed something a bit closer to listen to. "Noah. Prepare. It's a crop, and I won't go in hard, but it'll get there."

Noah tested his footing, checked his balance on the wall, and then took a deep breath. His chest and shoulders expanded and tensed, and then, as he exhaled, everything relaxed at once, from his shoulders to his toes. A familiar physical sign that Noah was grounded. "Ready, sir."

Across the hall, Bradford's steady blows continued, and Nikki moaned.

"Thank me for giving you the time to do that." Tobias struck fast across Noah's thighs. The crop was loud, the sharp snap echoing off the walls so quickly it sounded like the crop had rebounded.

Phan's ass tightened and his head dropped, but he made no sound.

"Thank you, sir!" Noah shouted, followed by a heavy exhale. He shook his head, likely chastising himself this time. "I'm sorry, sir... thank you."

"You're welcome." Tobias did it again, adding a red stripe below the first. "You've been unmarked for too long. Entirely my fault, of course." Once more his arm came down, and this time a welt rose up on Noah's ass across both cheeks.

Phan twitched each time the crop fell, and Tobias could see his hands clenching. If the boy could have willed himself to feel the crop, he would have, Tobias was sure.

Noah cried out as the crop hit his ass and moaned after, and Tobias was reminded why they did this, why they needed to, sometimes. Noah's cock was hard, his fingers curled and flattened again against the wall, and he actually stuck his ass out farther. "Thank you, sir," the boy responded, his voice low and rough. He wanted this as much as Tobias did, and that made it so much better.

Again, Tobias brought his hand down, his concentration narrowing to Noah's skin and reactions until there was a lacework of marks over his thighs and ass. Worried that he could easily push too far, Tobias finally backed off, his own breath coming in harsh pants.

There was a particularly loud crack in the other stall, and Nikki shouted "Master!" at the top of his lungs.

"Good boy," Bradford told him, and the sound of his cat went quiet.

Noah, meanwhile, was starting to babble the way he always did, telling Tobias how he felt, what the sting was like, where his ass burned. "Sir... stings like hell. Ah, God." He shifted his weight and moaned again. "Thank you, sir."

Tobias nodded to himself and moved to Phan. "All right, boy?"

Phan nodded. "Yes, sir." His voice was ragged. "Please, sir. Please."

"Please what?"

"Please touch me." Phan swayed and his chains rattled. "Please hit me. Anything."

Tobias pressed a kiss between Phan's shoulder blades. "There you go."

Phan sobbed, his hand curling around the links of his chain. "Thank you, sir."

Smiling, Tobias went to look out at Bradford, who was leaning in the doorway to the white stall drinking from a bottle of water. He looked over at Tobias and grinned.

"Did I hear Phan begging? It was lovely."

"You did." Tobias smiled, showing his teeth. "He's feeling the sting of being left without pain or attention, poor thing."

From inside the stall, one of his boys whimpered, but he wasn't sure which one it was. "Nikki is holding up?" he asked, looking past Bradford to the white stall.

"Oh, yes, very well."

Bradford let Tobias look. Nikki was standing much the way Noah was. His back and ass were red hot and marked, though the cat hadn't caused any real welts to form the way a crop would. He had his forehead pressed into the wall and his hands braced for balance. He was breathing hard, too, but silent.

"Oh, very nice. Maybe I'll do that to Phan when I get around to him." That time the whimper was definitely Phan. "Excuse me," Tobias said politely. "I need to go and gag him."

Bradford laughed and put the top back on his water bottle. "Enjoy."

"I always do." Tobias went back into the stall and grabbed a gag from the corner. "Open up, Phantom." He pushed his body against Phan's, making sure to grind his cock along Phan's ass as he gagged him from behind. "Be a good boy, and I'll use a very nice cat on you. Be exceptional, and I'll fuck you."

Phan nodded, his eyes wide as he let Tobias buckle the gag.

Smiling again, Tobias rubbed on him once more before going to examine Noah's back. "Hmm. Tender, pet?"

Noah nodded. "Yes, sir. Especially my ass, sir." Noah shifted from foot to foot. "Burns. It's good."

Tobias looked at Noah's ass. "It looks a little raw. Very pretty. I have some cream for that, later. When I'm done."

"Yes, sir." Tobias watched Noah lean in his direction, trying to get closer. "Thank you, sir."

In the next stall, Bradford hit Nikki again with what sounded like a crop this time.

"Thank you, sir! More, please!" Nikki's voice sounded softer, but every bit as needy.

"Want something, pet?" Tobias ran his finger over the untouched skin between welts and then down Noah's crack. "Nikki does. Phantom does."

Noah groaned, arching into Tobias' touch. "So hard, sir."

"Why, yes. You are." Tobias left him, picked up the cat he had waiting, and walked to Phan. "Boy," he barked. "Be ready." Without waiting for a reply or a twitch, he brought it down on Phan's back and immediately set a hard pace.

Phan howled, his head coming back and his back arching eagerly. "Yes, sir! Thank you, sir!" Relief and adoration shone on his face as he held himself open to every stroke.

Chains rattled and Nikki groaned deeply, and moments later, Bradford was making his own deep, low sounds. There was no mistaking what was happening in the white stall.

Noah's eyes were on Phan, and he wasn't unaffected by Phan's look of euphoria or Nikki and Bradford's moans. "Fuck," he whispered. "Fuck, sir."

"Soon enough. Perhaps." Tobias was a man well aware of his years and his capabilities; he also possessed enough toys to satisfy a very, very large number of men. Noah would be satisfied.

Phan's yells had not abated, and with every swipe of the cat across his back, he got louder. His skin was growing rosy, which was Tobias' intent -- but his arms and legs were beginning to shake and his head hung low. He was on the very cusp, at the top of the wall Tobias had forced him to climb.

Listening to Bradford was the final key, really. Everyone but Tobias had reached a state of intensity. The crop was thrown aside and Tobias tore open his pants, reaching for the lube. With only a swipe of it over his cock, he plunged into Phan's ass and reached around to unsnap the cock ring.

"Please, sir. Oh, God," Noah moaned. When Tobias looked over, Noah was looking away and appeared to be trying very hard to control himself.

Across the aisle, Bradford was making no such effort. "Tell me," he said, his voice tight.

"Yours, sir," Nikki answered quickly.

"Louder."

"Yours, sir!"

"That's right, boy. Mine."

"Noah." Tobias stayed where he was, buried in Phan and listening to the muffled yells around his gag. "Look at me."

"Yes, sir." Noah turned his head and looked, eyes on Tobias' chest.

"You will wait for me. I will take care of you." He circled his hips and fucked Phan slowly, holding Phan's prick in a loose fist. "Yes?"

Noah nodded. "Yes, sir," he said softly. "I will wait for you."

Tobias had to wonder if things really were just easier to do with orders, or if Noah was just that obedient.

Then he decided it didn't matter. He leaned forward and bit at Phan's shoulder, shoving in hard. "You can come whenever you want," he said, tightening his grip. "But it's the last time you'll come for ten days." The number was completely random, but it seemed to work. Phan shoved back, Tobias slammed in, and then Phan's cock flexed as he shot all over the floor.

"Yes!" Tobias' eyes closed as he fucked Phan through his orgasm. Finally, heat spreading through his body, Tobias pulled almost all the way out and used very tiny, short, and shallow thrusts to get only his sweet spot, right under the head of his cock. It was selfish fucking, but it was insanely pleasurable, and when his orgasm rushed over him, he could hear himself yelling over the ringing in his ears.

Everything in the barn went still. Apart from Phan's soft sounds and Tobias' own breathing, the barn was quiet. Even

Noah was quiet, his eyes on Phan and his body still. Moments later, Bradford appeared in the doorway of the black stall, and Nikki knelt next to him. The sub was no longer wearing his belt and plug, but the silver cock-cage was still firmly in place.

"Hope I'm not interrupting," Bradford said quietly, a grin in his voice.

"Not at all." Tobias panted for a moment, then pulled out. Without particularly cleaning up, he did up his pants and went back to Noah. "You're in time for the end." Kneeling, he took off Noah's ring and then licked one of the welts before parting Noah's ass and rimming him.

"Oh, God!" Noah shouted, and he spread his legs open even farther. "Sir! Permission to come, sir? Please, sir?"

Tobias lifted his head long enough to say, "Granted," and then he went back to tonguing Noah's ass.

Behind him, Nikki whimpered.

Noah arched and groaned, and then his breath started to come in shallow, ragged gasps. It was just a few seconds more before he shot, coming hard with a shout. "Yes! Sir! Ah, God! Thank you, sir!"

Tobias licked him again for good measure and then kissed his way up Noah's spine. "Good boy, sweetheart. Good boy." He tugged the buckles open and let Noah sink to the floor, then went to collect Phan.

Bradford looked down at Nikki. "You see, boy? That is the reward that very good boys get."

"Yes, sir. Thank you, sir."

Noah knelt, hands on his knees, still catching his breath, but he watched as Tobias let Phan out of his chains.

"Come here, dear," Tobias whispered. He almost had to carry him the few steps to Noah, but Phan made it. "There you go, snuggle for a few minutes."

Phan did as he was told, curling right up to Noah as Tobias turned to grin at Bradford. "Well. That went well."

"Oh, very well," Bradford agreed, smiling smugly. "Very well, indeed. Your boys give over so prettily."

"Nikki did well, and you were inspiring." Tobias' grin grew. "Are we done with the admiring yet? I need to tend to Noah's back, and then they need to clean up in here."

"Oh, don't be so logical." Bradford snorted. "Nikki, darling. You'll clean up our stall. Noah and Phan can show you what you need."

"Yes, sir." Nikki stood up and went to kneel beside Phan.

"Tobias, I'm going to shower. Shall I join you up at the house when I'm through?"

"Yes, absolutely." Tobias nodded and looked at his submissives. "I love it when they're like this. I'll meet you up there, Bradford." Right then, he wanted to collect a few kisses and make sure they'd both gotten what they needed. He also wanted a bit of cuddling himself; the softness after a scene was like dessert.

Bradford walked over to Nikki and gave him a kiss on the cheek. "Good boy," he said softly. "That," Bradford pointed to Nikki's cage, "will come off when you get up to the house. Be good for Master Tobias."

"Yes, sir. I promise, sir." Nikki smiled.

With that, Bradford strode from the stall and whistled his way up the aisle and out of the barn.

Tobias smiled at Nikki and motioned him over. "Come here, son. They're very affectionate at this stage." He went to Noah and Phan, slid down the wall, and opened his arms. "A few minutes before cleaning up. Careful of your back, Noah."

Phan immediately curled into Tobias' side, one hand out for Nikki, his smile still slightly unfocused and goofy.

Noah moved more slowly and was sure to stay facing Tobias so his tender skin didn't touch anyone. He sighed as he settled, not smiling like Phan was, but glassy-eyed and relaxed. He gave Nikki a light pat as Nikki took Phan's hand.

Nikki seemed caught between intruding on something and obeying an order, but he let Phan draw him in. "Thank you, sir."

"I couldn't bear to see you working while we had the luxury of this." Tobias smiled down at the three of them. "Phan, I was intending to get a bit more pain in there for you, but I couldn't resist your ass. Sorry."

Phan giggled. There was no mistaking the sound. "You're forgiven, sir." He giggled again. "Hear that, Noah? Irresistible. Told ya."

"Ah, no. Sir said your ass was irresistible," Noah joked. "Which it is. The rest of you... well." Noah laughed.

"Yeah, exactly. My ass. Which I was trying my very best to tempt you with last week." He looked mournfully at Nikki. "Noah resists out of principle, I think."

Tobias rolled his eyes.

"Phan has a thing about breaking rules, Nikki. Don't listen to him. Believe me, if Sir hadn't told us no fucking, I'd've been all over him." Noah grinned broadly. "Seriously."

Nikki's eyes grew wide. "Ohh," he said, as if learning something about Phan for the first time.

Phan sighed. "Don't listen to him. Well, yes. Listen to him. He's a good boy. I get myself in trouble rather a lot. It's a very, very good thing that Sir loves me."

Noah laughed. "Ow."

Tobias shook his head. "I do love you, brat. You make my life very... exciting." That was a kind way of putting things. "And you keep me on my toes, for sure."

"I think I've broken enough rules for now, I better listen to Noah." Nikki sighed.

Tobias waited, fully confident that Phan would pick up the ball.

"It's a smart move," Phan said with a nod. "But you pretty much have to trust your Master to mean exactly what he says. In my case, it's that he loves me, he'll protect me, and I'm safe with him no matter what. Mistakes are forgiven and made up for, rule breaking is punished and discussed, and as long as I respect him and myself, we can get through anything. The very fact that we're where we are is proof of that."

Noah looked right and then left, then shifted and looked behind him. "Wait, who said that? Some sub who's finally confident in his place? Who could that have been? That wasn't Phan... couldn't have been. Who was that?"

Phan, to Tobias' deep amusement, turned pink. "Shush, you. It only took me a few years."

Tobias smiled and slid his hand over Phan's shoulder and gave it a squeeze. "I do love you. And I'm proud of you, dear."

The pink turned red, and Phan buried his head in Tobias' chest.

"Me, too. And me, too," Noah added.

Nikki seemed to have missed most of the banter somehow and was apparently still mulling over what Phan had said. "I do trust him."

Tobias squeezed Phan's shoulder again and hoped Phan would get the point.

"Of course you do," Phan said immediately. "And you love him. Everything else flows out of that. You respect him, and you know he's ultimately got your best interests at heart."

Nikki nodded. "I'll do better."

Noah petted Nikki's knee. "We can always do better."

"But your best is all he asks for, Nikki," Tobias said softly. "If you do your best, he'll be honored and pleased."

"Yes, sir. Thank you, sir." Nikki blushed almost as red as Phan.

Tobias smiled. "All right, boys. Time to clean up. Floors, walls, each other, and all of the toys. I want every flogger used to be cleaned up. Noah, come with me and I'll spray your back first."

"Yes, sir," Noah answered easily, but standing didn't seem to be the easiest of tasks. Nikki got up readily enough despite his still-pink back, ass, and thighs, and he reached out to help Noah straighten up. "Thank you." Noah smiled at Nikki. "I think I'm okay now."

Tobias smiled at Nikki and said, "Phan, you help Nikki find the supplies." Taking Noah's hand, he led him up the aisle to the big first aid kit. "How did that go, in your opinion?" he asked softly.

"The scene, sir?" Noah asked. "I feel fabulous."

Tobias laughed. "I can see that, sweetheart. I meant with Nikki. Was that what he needed, do you think? Talking to Phan?"

Noah nodded. "Phan is... well, Nikki loves him. They were together at the club for a long while, and Nikki kind of idolizes him. I think Phan is just the right person for him to talk to. He has a way of making everything seem so simple."

"Except for in his own head, sometimes." Tobias knew that it was hardly Phantom's fault that he got tangled in his own feelings -- it was the human condition, really, and Phan had more excuse than others. "However, on that note... he seems better, too, I think."

"I think so, sir. He seems more relaxed, more... open. It's

interesting to me how important it is to him that he reassure Nikki. Maybe taking care of Nikki is helping him with his confidence a little."

"Perhaps." Tobias examined Noah's back under better light and nodded to himself. "This looks okay -- you'll have some bruises, though. I think Phan is perhaps handling his grieving a bit better."

"I like bruises," Noah replied in a low voice. "And yes, sir. I think your idea about going to the cemetery is a good one, sir. It might help him get some closure. Maybe you, too?"

Tobias sighed softly and kissed Noah's shoulder. "Maybe me, too." He spread arnica over Noah's back after making sure there was no broken skin and kissed him again. "Go clean up, pet. I'll see you back at the house."

"Yes, sir. Thank you, sir." Noah turned away and headed back down the aisle. He was moving a stiffly, but Tobias was sure his sub was enjoying the effect of the whipping as much as he himself was.

Tobias watched him go, smiling to himself. Noah wore stripes and bruises so well. Finally, though, Tobias roused himself and went up to the house. He needed a shower in the worst way, and then perhaps he and Bradford could talk about business for a while. It was time to open the new and improved farm up again.

20

Tobias looked in the mirror as he straightened his tie and wondered if he was perhaps overdressed.

"Noah," he said thoughtfully, still fussing with the knot, "did Phan actually eat breakfast this morning?" Phantom without any food in his stomach was an invitation for emotional turmoil, and going to Mrs. Miller's grave was going to be hard enough.

"He tried, sir. I'm not sure he got more than a few bites in." Noah was wearing one of the new suits that Phan had helped him pick out and looked very handsome, if a bit uncomfortable.

"I'll take a power bar with us." Tobias shook his head ruefully. "I hate to pour sugar into him, but it might get him through all of this. When you make lunch, please make sure there's enough protein to bring him back to a reasonable state. Well, reasonable for Phan." He smiled a bit and tugged at his cuffs. "You look wonderful."

"Yes, sir. And thank you, sir, I feel a bit... stiff."

"You'll get used to wearing a suit soon. I like the way you look -- do you suppose we could convince Phan to try one?"

Noah laughed. "Oh. I'm sorry, sir. Were you serious?"

"No." Tobias laughed, too, and took a kiss. "I couldn't imagine it. Keep it in mind for a scene, though; it could be fun. He did manage to find new trousers to wear today, and he said he had a shirt that wasn't made out of jersey knit. I'm not sure if he's made it all the way up to buttons, however." Oddly, Tobias couldn't at all remember what Phan had worn to the funeral.

"I guess we'll find out, sir, I hear him coming down the hall."

Tobias looked toward the door and Phan came in, his head bowed. "The car is here, sir," he said quietly. He was indeed wearing new trousers, charcoal gray and not quite jeans. He'd paired them with a cream-colored silk T-shirt, long-sleeved, seamless, and elegant-looking with his collar on display. With his hair only a little unruly, he looked absolutely subdued.

"Thank you, Phan." Tobias went to him and took his hand. "Okay?"

"Okay, sir." Phan nodded and leaned in close for a moment. "Jorge brought the flowers, too."

"All right." Tobias nodded and held out his other hand for Noah's. "Let's go, then, my loves."

Noah slipped his hand into Tobias'. Out at the car, Noah let Jorge get back in the car and held the door while Tobias and Phan got in before going around to the other side of the car and getting in so that Tobias was in the middle.

The drive was short; if they hadn't been going for an express purpose, Tobias would have suggested they ride the horses over. Thinking that, he decided to encourage Phan to do just that if he ever felt the need to just talk to her.

At the cemetery, Jorge drove down the narrow lane and stopped in the turning loop. The sun was bright and warm, and there didn't appear to be anyone else around. Tobias squeezed Phan's hand again before they got out of the car. "You don't need to actually say anything, you know."

Phan nodded. "I know. I might not. I might cry."

"I know, dear." Tobias was sure of it. "That's okay, too. I'm here, and Noah's here as well. All three of us have each other."

"I'll get the flowers." Noah opened his door and got out on his own, meeting Jorge halfway to get the flowers from the trunk. Jorge, instead, went around to open the door for Tobias and Phan. Tobias and his boys walked together, side by side, toward Elizabeth Miller's grave.

The stone was modest and understated, not unlike how she'd been. It had her name and dates, a simple statement of her marriage, and a carving of a peace dove. Tobias stood and looked at it for a long moment and said, "I miss you."

Beside him Phan sighed. "What do we do?"

"Whatever you feel like, dear. You can sit, stand, talk to her, pray... whatever it is you need to do. Both of you." He looked at the flowers Noah held and smiled. "Gardenias. Very nice."

"Of course. Her favorite." Noah knelt next to where she lay, pulled up the vase that was hidden in the gravestone, and started to arrange the flowers in it. "Every last one of the stinky things." He laughed softly. "Mrs. M, I know you love gardenias, but, well. A simple corsage is one thing. An entire bouquet is kind of overwhelming, sweetie. But here they are. That's how much I miss you."

Tobias couldn't help smiling -- Noah was right. They did stink, and she had loved them. "She couldn't have loved something nice like roses. No, gardenias that stink and peonies that need ants." He looked at Phan and sighed.

"Come here, boy." He held his arm out and Phan burrowed in. "We'll say hello together, all right?"

They crouched down, and Phan reached out one hand to touch the dove. "I miss you so much," he whispered. "You never, ever did anything but love me, and I didn't know until you were gone how much I valued that."

Noah reached out and put a hand on Phan's shoulder. "But she knew, hon. She knew. Anyway, she would never have let you thank her for something that she thought was so simple."

Phan nodded, but Tobias could feel the tremble in his shoulders. "It's okay," he whispered. "You can let it out."

Phan started to say something, but with a shake of his head, he turned into Tobias' chest instead and swallowed convulsively. "I'm okay. It's good that we had her, that we remember her. And it's good that we can come here."

"It is." Tobias swallowed himself and sighed. "She was my mother's best friend, and then like a mother to me. She was the one constant in my life, my entire life. I know how deep her heart went, Phan. She loved you and Noah like you were her own. Both of you."

"I know." Phan's whisper grew hoarse and he coughed. "She... she called me, when she was helping Noah learn your favorite recipes. To tell me he was a good fit with you. And to... to tell me that she loved me and I was always welcome in her kitchen. No matter what." And with that, he started to cry.

Noah cleared his throat. "Mrs. M," he said softly, his own voice full of emotion. "You'd be so proud of Phan. I mean, I know you pretended not to know about this stuff, but he's come so far, he's so trusting now, and... and he's been a great friend to me. And he keeps your kitchen neat. He's been known to yell at me for not putting the wooden spoons away in the right place." Noah swiped at one eye with the back of his hand, but he laughed softly, smiling. "And Tobias is everything you promised me he'd be."

Phan cried hard and Tobias held him tight, soothing the tremors and tearing up at Noah's words. He was right about all of it -- about Phan, about her pretending not to know but letting them all lead their lives and be loved for who they were, and about Phan being a bit ridiculous about the spoons. He hoped that Noah was right about him living up to the promises she'd made.

He hoped that she had been proud of him. He hoped he'd earned it.

In his arms, Phan nodded. "I hope I learned enough from her. Not about cleaning and stuff, but about being good and kind and open."

Noah finished fussing with the flowers and joined them. "I hope we all have."

"You have." Tobias nodded, sure of that, if nothing else in his life. "You are both the most caring, giving people I know. You share, you love, you devote yourselves to each other and me. You're unselfish and generous with your souls. That is why she loved you, why I love you. So, while we miss her every day, please console yourselves with knowing you were lights in her life."

Noah tucked his hand into Tobias' and gave it a squeeze. "And what about you? You know how much you meant to her, how proud she was of you, right? It showed all the time, every time she talked about you."

"I like to think that, while I may have often confused and confounded her, she wasn't displeased with how I turned out." He smiled and petted Phan as the sobs eased off, then he looked at Noah. "You're right, and I'm being disingenuous. She loved me like she loved her son, Robert, and she never pulled any punches. She was proud of me and happy with a great many of my choices."

Noah nodded. "She was." Noah sighed and straightened up. "I don't know why we waited so long to come out here together; it was a good idea. Don't you think so, Phan?"

Phan lifted a hand and wiped at his cheeks. "Uh-huh. But next time I'm wearing a proper outfit, so she doesn't get all confused at me."

Noah laughed. "Next time you can come in leather. You know, be yourself."

"Exactly." Phan nodded and sat up a bit, moving away from Tobias to hold his own weight. "And Sir can stay in his suit, like normal, and you can... actually, I like the suit on you. You should keep the look."

Tobias rolled his eyes. "See, Mrs. Miller? This is what you left me with."

"And damn lucky he is, Elizabeth," Phan said with a nod. "I'll take good care of them. I promise."

Tobias smiled to himself and nodded. "I'm sure you will."

"Already does." Noah moved again, this time to get his arms around Phan. "I love you, you know."

"You do?" Phan's eyes went wide. "Sir, did you know about this?"

"Okay, we're done." Tobias stood up and shook his head. "Phantom, behave."

Phan grinned and kissed Noah. "I love you, too. So much."

Noah laughed and struggled to his feet, still tangled up in Phan. "Bye, Mrs. M."

"See you in a while, Elizabeth." Phan kissed his fingers and pressed them to the headstone. "Ready, sir."

Tobias took their hands and nodded. "We'll be back. Until next time, Mrs. Miller. I love you." He turned and walked them back to the car, enjoying the sunshine. They'd done well, and he hoped Phan would come back as the fancy struck him. It wasn't a bad thing to remember being loved by someone who'd passed away. They could all draw strength from it, from their memories of her.

He knew he did.

21

Tobias stood in the aisle of the stable and watched quietly as first the stalls and then the ring were explored. He never minded showing off his space - - this introduction to his work was one of the things he really looked forward to on these weekends, and the Doms currently opening chests and closets and testing chains were well aware of how elaborate his set-up was.

"You are welcome to make use of the space at your discretion," Tobias said when they were all in the ring. "The schedule of the weekend allows you ample time to play if you wish. There are also areas within the guest house where you can simply relax, and if you need something specific for your submissive, I'll do my best to accommodate you. Most of the instruction time will be here, in the ring, due to space, but we'll also meet for discussion." He looked around and smiled. "Any questions so far?"

"Are we able to take, say, some of the bondage tools back to the guest house?" one of the Doms asked from a few feet away. Tobias couldn't have been more pleased that Hayden had called him and inquired about some guidance with

Brian, or about his interest in the less pain-related and more intense mental aspects of domination. "Gags, cuffs, rope... that sort of thing?"

"Absolutely." Tobias nodded. "The expectation is, of course, that they'll be cleaned and returned to the same place so Phan's inventory work isn't as stressful as it could be, but by all means -- use what intrigues you. If you see something used in instruction that you'd like to try, go right ahead. Also, if you'd like to try out the sensory deprivation equipment, I'll be more than happy to spot you."

Hayden raised an eyebrow. "That sounds interesting."

"I thought you might like the sound of that." Tobias grinned and lifted his arm to sweep around the ring. "Bradford is no stranger here, and I know that if you have questions or can't find something you need only say so. He'll have Nikki produce it, since -- as we all know -- the subs keep the order in here."

"I'm more than happy to help out," Bradford offered.

"I knew I could count on you." Tobias sat in his imposing, throne-like chair and watched Hayden and the other two Doms, Kraig and Simon, continue to explore, talking among themselves. "Bradford, who on earth is running the dining room? I don't think I've ever been in there without seeing Brian."

"Excellent question." Bradford laughed. "Unfortunately for me, Hayden has been requesting Brian more and more, and so I've had to train some new boys in his place. At the moment, there are three boys doing what Brian normally manages by himself."

"Heh." Tobias snickered. "I hope no one has let Brian know this. He'll be impossible -- or Hayden will really have to step up his game." Either way, it was going to be fun.

"Have you spent much time with Simon? He's very quiet, but a quick thinker."

"I haven't yet. I try to invite each of the new Doms to dinner at least once, and I also try to watch a couple of their sessions. I haven't had the opportunity to do either for Simon yet. He seems pleasant enough from what I can tell."

"His boy is nice -- young, though. I think that's why he's here, trying to steer them into restraint and bondage and less flogging. He told me he wants to go deeper, but that means different things for so many people." Tobias shrugged. "We'll see how it goes. Are you going to dine in the guest house with them, or are you going to pull rank and come down to the house?"

"Oh, no. I'm a student this weekend, Tobias. Nikki has been asking for some quieter work, and when you told me about this weekend, I thought it would be perfect. I think it's good for him to learn alongside other subs, and a Dom can always benefit from refresher courses." Bradford smiled. "I'll be dining with the other Doms, unless you think that would make them uncomfortable?"

"I doubt it -- not after the first few minutes, anyway." Tobias smiled at his friend. "It might help them to see you as just another Dom, really. To see that you, too, need to take time to connect with Nikki. I think it'll be a good thing." He stood up as the other three came near. "So, that's the work space. Shall we go back to the guest house? Phantom and Noah have made sure that your kitchen is stocked, Bradford's houseboys have been in to clean and make up all the rooms, and I'm sure that you're all eager to settle in for your first evening. As I said -- feel free to find whatever you think you'll need for the night. There are toys in each room as well, and leashes at the house."

Hayden had found himself a pair of cuffs that, while

made of a heavy, sturdy leather, were nonetheless lined with soft, forgiving fur. He handed them to Brian, who was kneeling with the other subs along the edge of the ring, to carry. Brian's eyes widened. "Still," Hayden admonished softly.

Tobias waited a moment while the others got themselves sorted, and then brought Noah and Phan to heel. "Come with me," he said, walking a line of ordering his own boys and inviting the guests. He hoped everyone would accept the words as they were intended, and led the way out of the barn and to the guest house. "You've all been assigned rooms, but you're free to use the common spaces whenever you feel like it. Sexual activity falls under the same rules as at the club -- get a room." He grinned and winked at Bradford.

"Really, Tobias. I fail to understand why you are looking at me," Bradford said with a laugh.

Phan giggled and turned it into a cough. "Sorry, sir."

Tobias sighed. "Two, boy."

"Yes, sir."

Nikki somehow managed not to laugh. "Good boy," Bradford said, a touch of indignant embarrassment in his voice. "Let's take our bags up, shall we?"

"Yes, sir." Nikki hopped up, grabbed the suitcases, and practically ran up the steps with them.

Bradford snorted. "Boys." He grinned. "I'll send him back down in a moment to help start supper." And with that, he excused himself.

Hayden grinned along with the others. "What's next on our agenda? We see you in the morning? Or is there something planned for this evening?"

"This evening, you get to talk amongst yourselves, settle in, eat well." Tobias smiled. "I'll leave the stables unlocked until eleven. We'll meet in the ring at nine tomorrow morning, and I expect everyone to have eaten and to be awake and ready to pay attention. Even Phantom."

Phan, two strokes up for the day, said nothing at all.

"Brian is an early riser," Hayden said with a grin. "We'll be there." He pointed to his luggage. "If you'll excuse us, then. Bring my bag, pet."

Brian was quick to move, and perhaps just a little more graceful than usual, too. He followed Hayden up the stairs easily.

Tobias shook hands with Simon, who just as silently went up with his boy, then paused with Kraig. "If you need anything, feel free to call the house or send your submissive down. We hope that everything is where it should be, but as this is the first weekend with the new set-up, I'm sure there's going to be a hitch somewhere."

Kraig nodded. "Will do. I'm very impressed so far," he said. "And thank you to your boys for stocking everything for us."

"It was their pleasure." Tobias beamed at him and headed home, his boys in tow. "See you all in the morning," he called as he left. "Noah, what are we having for dinner tonight?"

"I had planned on grilling, sir. There are steaks marinating, asparagus, and rice pilaf... and then perhaps a nice, hot cup of tea before bed."

"Oh, tea sounds nice." It had been a while since he'd had tea at bedtime.

"It sure does!" Phan said eagerly. "I'll help Noah with dinner, sir."

"Why, thank you, Phan." Noah snorted.

Tobias liked to hear that -- they were teasing and helpful and happy. The last few months had been a little bumpy, but right then, with the sun low in the sky and his boys at his side, Tobias was more than content.

He was in love and loved. He was successful, his friends were well, and his lovers were balanced and thriving. There really was no better feeling. Except, possibly...

"I think we'll have a late dinner, boys. I feel like having that tea now; no sense in waiting until tomorrow for the good parts."

Looking for more?
Soft Limits: A Deviations Novel by Jodi Payne

Chronologically a prequel,
but can be read at any point in the series.

F ans of the iconic Deviations Series will fondly recall Bradford as the beloved owner and Master of the exclusive, male-only, BDSM club that anchors the series, and also as the wise man who introduced Tobias and Noah.

Dominant Bradford's story is one defined by sudden opportunity, unimaginable heartbreak, and new-found purpose. His calling is to provide a safe and supportive environment for men in the lifestyle. Bringing Doms and subs together is his superpower, yet ironically, he feels fated to be alone himself.

In this prequel to the series, you'll discover how Bradford is first drawn to Nikki, a hungry young man living on the streets, and the unexpected ways Bradford grows and changes while helping Nikki understand a world of strange, new desires.

Deviations readers already know how Bradford and Nikki find their happy ever after. Soft Limits is a deep-dive into Bradford's story, into what makes the Dom tick, and how he ended up with ownership of the club. It also introduces Nikki, the sub that tests Bradford's patience, steals his heart, and soothes his soul.

————

Interested in learning more about Jodi's books? Want free fiction, release news, anecdotes, coffee and drink recipes...?
Join Jodi's newsletter!
What's Up with Jodi?
http://bit.ly/whatsupjodi

A NOTE FROM THE AUTHORS

Hey there!

We just wanted to take a minute to say thank you for taking the time to read Safe Words. We hope you enjoyed it. We know everyone is busy and our TBR (to be read) lists are out of control, so it means a lot to us that we ended up at the top of your pile this time.

If you have a moment, please consider dropping by the site where you purchased this book and leaving a review. All honest reviews are much appreciated.

If you're looking for more of Jodi's work, why not join her newsletter? Just go here: http://bit.ly/whatsupjodi.

And you can find Chris Owen at http://www.chrisowen.net/.

Thank you for reading!

Jodi & Chris

ABOUT JODI PAYNE

You're gonna love this guy...

JODI takes herself way too seriously and has been known to randomly break out in song. Her men are imperfect but genuine, stubborn but likable, often kinky, and frequently their own worst enemies. They are characters you can't help but fall in love with while they stumble along the path to their happily ever after. For those looking to get on her good side, Jodi's addictions include nonfat lattes, Malbec and tequila any way you pour it.

Website: jodipayne.net
Newsletter: http://bit.ly/whatsupjodi
All Jodi's Social Links: linktr.ee/jodipayne

ABOUT CHRIS OWEN

Chris lives and writes in eastern Canada. She's inspired by the day to day minutia of life, shiny things, and overheard bits of other people's conversations. Chris is a lover of cheese, curling, dogs, words, and craft beer. Her stories are usually built around totally normal people doing normal things, until everything goes sideways—that's when the fun starts. Chosen family plays a huge role in the stories Chris tells, and there is always a happy ending. Chris always has a D10 in her bag or pocket, along with a hankie. Just in case.

Website: chrisowen.net

Facebook: https://www.facebook.com/profile.php?id=100015072407034

Twitter: https://twitter.com/chris_owen

Enjoy the Deviations Books? Try a new series.

Breaking the Rules
The Triskelion Series, Book One
By Jodi Payne and BA Tortuga

https://jodipayne.net/books/breaking-the-rules/

Saul Reynolds manages a busy bicycle shop in downtown Boulder, Colorado. A recent CU graduate, he's also a Dom, and has many friends his age in the scene. Saul's an old soul, and even at twenty-five, he's had enough experience to understand his own desires. He's had plenty of lovers and he's played the role of part-time Dom, but he's never found the perfect combination of lover and sub in one man.

Troy Finch lost his lover in a rodeo accident twenty years ago, moved to Boulder, and has worked as a line cook in his friend Carter's diner ever since. He's attended many parties at Carter's home with couples in the BDSM lifestyle and feels comfortable in a submissive role, but without a Dom of his own, Troy hasn't explored what that really means to him. He has needs he doesn't entirely understand and finds his only outlet at the hands of Carter's husband, Geoff, a tattoo artist who has used Troy's skin as a canvas for as long as they've known each other, covering Troy in colorful, intricate triskelia.

Troy doesn't know what he was thinking accepting a dinner invitation from a kid half his age, but everything feels right about their evening together, including Saul's Dominant side. The rules for a twenty-five year old gay cowboy from years ago, though, are totally different than for a twenty-five year old college grad in Boulder now, and despite Saul's confidence, Troy isn't sure whether they can make it work.

Saul and Troy manage to bend a good many rules in the name of caring and compromise, but in the name of love, there are some rules they're just going to have to break.

This is a "true series" and should be read in order.

———

Interested in learning more about Jodi's books? Want free fiction, release news, anecdotes, coffee and drink recipes…?
Join Jodi's newsletter!
What's Up with Jodi?
http://bit.ly/whatsupjodi

**Readers of this series may enjoy
Used and Rare, Collected**

**Used and Rare, Collected
By Chris Owen**
https://books2read.com/b/31rywD

Dave and Archie are happy. They work in construction together, they share a couch, pizzas, beer, and usually a bed. Desmond and Wyatt are happy. They share a home, a love of books, and a lifestyle that's heavy on power exchange. When Archie sends Dave to build book shelves for his old friend Desmond, Dave is happy to oblige and doesn't even mind the initial misunderstanding about his relationship with Archie—he's even amused by it. But when things get twisty between the four of them can Dave keep it from getting kinky and still keep everyone else happy? It's difficult being the only vanilla cookie in the jar.

———

Interested in learning more about Chris's books?
Check out her website:
chrisowen.net

ALSO BY JODI PAYNE

MM and Gay Romance

A Whole Latke Love

Soft Limits: A Deviations Novel

Stable Hill

Creative Process

Linchpin

Whence He Came

With BA Tortuga

Heart of a Redneck

Land of Enchantment

Wrecked

Window Dressing

Flying Blind

Special Delivery, A Wrecked Novel - *Coming November 2020!*

The Cowboy and the Dom Trilogy

First Rodeo, Book One

Razor's Edge, Book Two

No Ghosts, Book Three

The Soldier and the Angel

The Collaborations Series

Refraction

Syncopation

ALSO BY CHRIS OWEN

MM and Gay Romance

An Agreement Among Gentlemen

Bareback

Natural Disaster

Running Away to Home

911

Cheek to Cheek

Turn the Other Cheek

Shady Ridge and the Neon Sky

Pyke's Peak

Carbon and Ash

Converge

Merge

Prove It

Used and Rare, Collected

With Jodi Payne

The Deviations Series

Submission

Domination

Discipline

Bondage

Safe Words: A Deviations Novel